LL
RIDGE

Young Person—temp. toll bridge keeper
pvt. est. Mod. wage, few resp., free
acc. toll house. Gd refs nec. Box 365.

'You'll starve,' joked Father, 'you can't boil an egg.'

'Who'll do your laundry?' cried Mother. 'I'll be worried sick, you living on your own, no neighbours, no phone, anything might happen.'

'You'll be three hours away even by car,' wailed Gill. 'How are we going to see each other?'

'What a mangy option,' scoffed the lads.

'Taking money from a few passing cars all day hardly sounds academically challenging,' objected teachers. 'If you want time out, go abroad, see life, gain some experience, don't stick yourself away in a dead-end job in the middle of nowhere.'

'I'll learn to cook, I'll do my own laundry, maybe it will be good for us to be apart for a while, I want a change from academic challenge, thank you – I want to be on my own and challenge myself and experience *my* life before I find out about other people's,' I said to scornful snickers, doubting glances, dour looks, exasperated eyebrows, huffings, puffings, and shoulders hucked against this perverse (Mother's version was pre-verse) teenager.

Also by Aidan Chambers

Breaktime
Dance on My Grave
Now I Know

THE
TOLL
BRIDGE

AIDAN CHAMBERS

RED FOX

Acknowledgements

The publishers gratefully acknowledge permission to
reprint the following: 'The Bridge' from *Franz Kafka:
The Complete Stories* by Franz Kafka. Copyright 1946,
1947, 1948, 1949, 1954, © 1958, 1971 Schocken
Books Inc. Reprinted by permission of Schocken
Books, published by Pantheon Books, a division of
Random House Inc. English translation reprinted by
permission of Martin Secker and Warburg Ltd. This
translation first published in England in 1973 by
Martin Secker & Warburg Limited, 14 Carlisle Street,
London W1V 6NN. Copyright © 1934, 1937 by
Heinr. Mercy Sohn, Prague. Copyright © 1946, 1947,
1958 by Schocken Books Inc. This translation
copyright © 1973 by Martin Secker & Warburg Ltd.

A Red Fox Book

Published by Random House Children's Books
20 Vauxhall Bridge Road, London SW1V 2SA

A division of Random House UK Ltd
London Melbourne Sydney Auckland
Johannesburg and agencies throughout the world

Copyright © Aidan Chambers 1992

1 3 5 7 9 10 8 6 4 2

First published in Great Britain by
The Bodley Head Children's Books 1992

Red Fox edition 1995

Printed and bound in Great Britain by
Cox & Wyman Ltd, Reading, Berkshire

RANDOM HOUSE UK Limited Reg. No. 954009

ISBN 0 09 950311 5

THE
TOLL
BRIDGE

FOR ADAM

Take this as a gift. The only gift I can give you that might, one day, mean anything to you.

I've visited you often. You never know me, never recognize me, always treat me as someone you're meeting for the first time.

But soon I have to go away. Perhaps I shall never see you again. And who knows, one day it might all come back to you, everything that happened in the weeks we spent together. And if it does, what will you want to know? What will you ask? What will you think of me and Gill and Tess?

And what will you do? About yourself, I mean. That's the only important question. One reason why I'm writing this is to show you how you seemed to me, to us, how we thought of you.

As I write, I remember we once argued about gifts. There is no such thing as a free gift, you said. All gifts are a payment for something. I didn't agree. A gift is only a gift if it is freely given, I said. But maybe you were right. Perhaps a gift is always an exchange for something received. Or hoped for. Perhaps this gift is a kind of repayment for the life I live now. And perhaps by giving it I hope to quieten my conscience about leaving you.

Whatever the truth is, use (y)our story any way you like. Make of it what you will.

Déjà-vu

Adam comes to me like a ghost. For a moment I think he is a ghost. And as so many times afterwards he turns his appearance into a game. He pretends to be a ghost, but only when he discovers he has made a mistake.

Searching for a place to shack up for the night, he finds the little eight-sided house by the bridge, no lights, looking empty and dead, and thinks he is in luck. He does not know I am inside; and it is Hallowe'en.

He forces the door quietly. This gives him no trouble. The lock is old and weak, and he is strong. Even though he is not tall – he's thin and lithe – he sometimes seems to possess a big man's strength, which belongs to the hidden part of him, his mystery.

He forces the lock so quietly I do not wake. I have been living in the old toll house for three months and am sleeping well, which I did not while the place was strange and I was unused to being alone.

Having broken in he sees by moonlight the door he does not know leads into the only bedroom, where I lie sleeping, and decides to try this room first. Just inside is a creaky floorboard. He steps on it. The sound wakes me with a start. I sit up, see a ghostly silhouette against the moonlit window, and scream.

At which, '*Woo-whoo!*' he flutes and flaps his arms.

I really am scared, for a moment at least. And he, it is true, is an apparition, but of a kind I know nothing about. He also, he says afterwards, is scared, his *woo-whooing* and flapping arms a reflex action. So he acts the ghost and I act spooked, each of us acting in self-defence, each having taken the other by surprise.

I fumble for the switch on my bedside lamp, a bulb stuck into an old stoneware cider bottle stood on an upturned orange box (bottle and box found in the basement that is a lavatory-cum-woodshed the day I arrived).

'Who the hell are you?' I shout, acting indignant while my fingers fail me with the switch.

'*Woo-whoo?*' he flutes again, this time more like an owl with stomach cramp than a haunting spectre.

I find the switch at last and we scrutinize each other, blinking in the raw light.

He is not exactly reassuring. Wet black hair hugging the round dome of his head. Foxy features smeared with mud, perhaps from a fall. Body draped in an ancient army combat cape, also muddy and the cause of his ghostly silhouette. Very wet and weary jeans poking beneath, and marine boots scarred from battle.

'I don't know you from Adam,' I say.

He laughs. 'Right first time.' And pulls off his cape. Beneath which he is leaner than I expect, the cape having lent a false appearance of bulk. A tatty soggy sweater, rust-red and out at his bare elbows, hangs on him like a skin ready to be shed.

And shed it he does.

'Hey, hey, hold on a sec!' I say. 'What're you doing?'

Sloughing his boots and jeans too, he says, 'How d'you mean?'

'I mean here . . . I mean stripping . . .'

Half out of bed, intending to be more forceful, I see, now he confronts me in the nude, the kind of cock boys in shower rooms honour with surreptitious glances. I stay where I am, the duvet hiding my middle.

'Frigging soaked,' he says, as if this explains everything.

'So?'

'Fell in the river.'

'What – cape and all? A wonder you didn't drown.'

'No, no. It was on the bank where I climbed out. I'm freezing.'

He turns his attention to the room, not that there's much to see. My bed – mattress on old iron bedstead. Lamp on orange box. Fireplace blocked off by sheet of cardboard. Books lining mantelpiece, river-rubbed stones for bookends. A few spare clothes hanging from a hook behind the door. Bare walls, long ago white, now a scuffed, geriatric grey.

Back to me, weighing me up, before he says, 'Any chance of a kip?'

Given the obvious idiocy of taking in, like a feral dog in the middle of the night, someone I know nothing about, except he is called Adam, has an enviable cock, and has just been careless enough to fall into the river, my second surprise of the night comes when I hear myself reply, 'Sure. Expect we can fix up something.'

❖ 2 ❖

But there was more to it than cock-and-bull. For two months I'd been living like a hermit. By desire, I mean, not accident or compulsion. Wanting to be on my own, having had enough of doing what was expected of me, of being what other people wanted me to be: Dutiful only son of ambitious parents. Conscientious student swatting to be good enough for university. One of the lads, doing boring spare-time activities so as to be sociable. Faithful boyfriend of ten months' standing (and not enough laying, if anybody ever gets enough). And the rest of the ratbag people call normal.

In fact, an actor playing roles in other people's plays. And I was fed up of performing. I didn't want to play at anything. Not son, schoolboy, friend or, come to that, lover. I just wanted To Be. And To Be on my own.

Around Christmas – God, the play-acting you have to do at Christmas! – the Great Depression set in. At first my parents put it down to anxiety about the coming exams. Teachers dismissed it as a side effect of being a year ahead of other people my age, plus tiredness – the price any over-achiever working hard enough in his final year had to pay for success. 'Keep at it,' they said, 'you can relax in the summer.'

By Easter what my father called The Glums weren't any longer patches of 'being low' now and then, but were a permanent monstrous misery. Even Gill, my girlfriend, started to complain. And she, egged on by Mother, harried me into seeing our doctor. Who tested for glandular fever, coyly referred to as 'the kissing disease' (negative), diabetes (clear), anaemia (full-blooded), and finally pronounced a chronic case of old-fashioned growing pains for which he prescribed a course of vitamin pills. One more boring routine to add to all the others.

Result: The Glums worsened, dragging with them clouds of lowering headaches that broke into sudden storming rages which usually ended in rows and me smashing anything smashable, preferably items of Mother's favourite knick-knackery.

Otherwise, when not slogging through school work, I spent hours locked in my room brooding on the more satisfying aspects of being pissed off and the likely rewards of self-slaughter. Among which was the pleasure of taking others with me, especially Gill (spite: couldn't leave her behind for others to get their gropers on) and the cheerier yahoos at school (revenge, there being nothing more infuriating when you're depressed than other people's high spirits).

One of the rows finally brought everything to a head. Exams over, nobody wanted to go on coddling this whingeing creep (except Mother of course). And Gill it was who finally flashed the storm that ended with me deciding I'd had enough. People disgusted me. I disgusted myself. I wanted out.

The way out turned up in the wanted ads. (Well, when you're depressed you try anywhere.) Next after: *Condom Testers Required – help a leading rubber company design next year's chart toppers* ... (think of all the times you'd have to do it on command, tumescent or not) was this:

Young Person temp. toll bridge keeper
pvt. est. Mod. wage, few resp., free
acc. toll house. Gd refs nec. Box 365.

'You'll starve,' joked Father, 'you can't boil an egg.'

'Who'll do your laundry?' cried Mother. 'I'll be worried sick, you living on your own, no neighbours, no phone, anything might happen.'

'You'll be three hours away even by car,' wailed Gill. 'How are we going to see each other?'

'What a mangy option,' scoffed the lads.

'Taking money from a few passing cars all day hardly sounds academically challenging,' objected teachers. 'If you want time out, go abroad, see life, gain some experience, don't stick yourself away in a dead-end job in the middle of nowhere.'

'I'll learn to cook, I'll do my own laundry, maybe it will be good for us to be apart for a while, I want a change from academic challenge, thank you – I want to be on my own and challenge myself and experience *my* life before I find out about other people's,' I said to scornful snickers, doubting glances, dour looks, exasperated eyebrows, huffings, puffings, and shoulders hucked against this perverse (Mother's version was pre-verse) teenager.

❖ 3 ❖

Tarzan's yodels woke me, followed by loud splashings from the river. My watch says six fifty, and Adam's makeshift bed – a few cushions and a blanket on the floor – is abandoned.

5

He can't be up already, can he, not after last night? And not in the river again?

I pull on my jeans and stumble to the back-door steps from where I can view the toll-house garden and the river.

Adam is clambering out of the water, glistening in the light of the morning sun filtered through a shrouding autumn mist. Shot from a TV commercial. Deodorant or Diet Pepsi.

A tree, its leaves turning paler shades of brown, droops over the water. From a riverside branch hangs a rope. I don't remember seeing it there before. Adam, unaware of me yet, runs, grabs the rope, swings wildly to and fro, flinging himself higher and higher, the motion shaking from the tree a shower of dying leaves. When he is as far out above the river as the rope can carry him, he hollers his jungle call, lets go, and plummets, neat as a needle, feet first into the water. To surface seconds later, splashing and blowing and tossing his head and swimming briskly for the bank.

This time he sees me as he climbs out, and stands beaming like a kid let loose after a bad term at school, slicking water from his face. Definitely deodorant.

I shiver and call, 'Aren't you cold?'

'It's a great game. Ever played it?'

'No,' I lie.

But why lie? I had played it – with Dad in one of his crazy moods when I was a kid.

Some memories are not for telling, I thought then, standing at the back door blearily clocking Adam and not knowing how wrong I was.

❖ 4 ❖

Adam followed me inside.

I hand him a towel while I wash. When I'm done, I go into the bedroom to finish dressing, and tidy up. I'm an obsessive tidier, inheritance from chronically tidy parents. (You can't buck all of your upbringing. Being a tidier is one of the roles I have no choice about playing because it is written in my genes. During blue periods I resent it all the more for that.)

Coming back into the living room, Adam passes me on his way to the bedroom. We avoid each other's eyes.

I set about making breakfast. Bread, honey, tea. Even now, I never bother with anything more than this, hating all the business of getting up in the morning.

6

Adam reappears, towel round his shoulders, still damp jeans and sweater in his hands. He lurks just inside the door. I can tell what he's after, and am unsettled. Having put him up for the night, do I want to encourage him by giving anything more?

All the business of giving. When we argued about it I said, as most people do, that taking from people is what makes you beholden. But Adam said, no, if people give you a present, then as far as he was concerned there were no strings. They were paying for something he'd given them, even if he didn't know what it was. But there's another side to giving that we didn't talk about because I only half sensed it then. Which is that giving to people puts you in their debt. I learned this because of Adam. Somehow, once you've given you feel obliged to give again, and to go on giving, and feel mean if you don't. A kind of reverse emotional debt.

[TESS: This is male-order talk. Women don't think about giving like that. I've noticed, as soon as you give a man something he wants to give you something back straightaway. I think it's a power thing, as if receiving a gift were some kind of threat he has to neutralize at once or else he'll be in a weak position. Seems to me that for men gifts are a kind of trade-off, which they're not for women. We give without thinking of getting anything back. We do it all the time.]

❖ 5 ❖

I begin to wonder who Adam is. And what it is about him that worries me. Nothing dangerous exactly, nothing threatening. Something betrayed by the look in his eyes and the way he stands there, silently expecting help. What unsettles me even more, I decide, is that he makes me feel violent. I want to rough him up, hit him, chuck him out, anyway be rid of him. Why, why?

'They can dry in front of the fire,' I say, 'if you get it going.'

He crosses to the hearth and dithers.

'You don't know about wood fires?'

'No.'

'I'll do it.'

Last night's ashes, under the powder of their grey deceiving surface, are still hot, quickly ignite a couple of twists of paper, the paper flames a few thin twigs which in turn soon set fire to splits of log.

Three months ago, I tell myself as the fire grows, I didn't know

7

how to do this either. And feel a kind of satisfaction I haven't felt for a year or more. A pleasure forgotten that makes me smile, and glance at Adam, who is crouching beside me now, wanting the warmth. But he gazes into the flames with a fixed unblinking stare.

'If you'd like something to eat,' I say, weakened by his lost look, 'there's bread on the table.'

He doesn't respond.

'Adam?'

Nothing. I touch him on the shoulder. He recoils. His eyes, flicking into focus, widen as though in fright at seeing me beside him. I'm sure he is going to scream, but he catches himself, and smiles, grins rather, just like last night when I switched on the light, a fox's grin, wide-mouthed, lips stretched, showing bright handsome teeth.

'There's bread on the table,' I repeat, 'if you want it.'

'Ah!' he says. 'Right.' Springs up, full of energy again, attacks the loaf and honey with a taking-it-for-granted greed that rekindles my anger, and makes me decide I don't care who he is, I don't want to know, I don't want him here disturbing my life with the switchback emotions he stirs up, I've got to get rid of him as soon as I can.

❖ 6 ❖

A car horn sounds in the road. The postman with a parcel and a letter, the parcel addressed in Mother's writing, the letter in Gill's.

As the van drives off towards the village Tess Norris comes puttering along on her Suzuki 150, L-plate flapping. Two wheels cross without paying, but she always stops for a talk. Not that she'd pay anyway. Her father is in charge of the toll bridge and of maintenance on the estate. My boss, a joiner by trade and the sort of man who can turn his hand to anything. Tess is on her way to school, her last year, English Lit., French, and Maths.

'Dad says can you manage without being relieved today? Urgent job at the hall.'

Her voice is muffled by her helmet and the putter of her engine. Her dark hazel eyes, all that's visible of her face, rouse me the more for being framed by the mask of her visor. The rest is ambiguous in old black leathers with a red flash down the sides. And biker's boots.

'I'll be OK.'

'Want anything?'

'A loaf and a jar of honey.'

8

'Already?'

I thumb at the house. 'Visitor.'

'Male or female?'

'Male.'

'Thought you were a hermit.'

'Invited himself.'

'Oh yes! I'll have a look this after.'

'Be gone by then I hope.'

She taps my parcel with a black-gloved hand. 'Weekly survival kit?'

'What else?'

'Mummy's boy!' She laughs and revs. 'See you.'

'Cheers.'

❖ 7 ❖

The hardest part, I'm finding, of telling this story – *one* of the hardest parts – is not only getting everything in, but getting everything in in the right place. Maybe this is the right place to explain about Tess.

I first met her the day after I arrived, just at the moment when I was wondering what the hell I had done. The day before, still high on adrenalin, the empty, damp bleakness of the house hadn't mattered, had even seemed just what I wanted. Satisfactory neglect. All the clutter of home left behind, all the suffocating *stuff* I'd grown up with cut away at last. Room to think. Make everything the way I wanted it, starting from scratch. From scratch with the house, from scratch with myself.

'You've not brought any bedding and such,' Bob Norris said. 'Told you at the interview that you'd need it.'

'I'll be OK for tonight.'

'I could fetch a few essentials from home to tide you over.'

'I'll be OK, thanks. You said I'd have a couple of days to settle in. I'll go out tomorrow and buy what I need.'

'Must like roughing it. But I suppose you do at your age.'

I spent a miserable night. Couldn't get the fire going, not knowing how to deal with a damp chimney or a wood fire, filled the house with choking smoke instead. Sandwiches, brought from home, tasted like cold dishcloth and gave me indigestion. An apple, to follow, only increased my hunger. All there was to drink was water because I didn't have tea or coffee or any of the everyday things you usually take for granted. By the time I hit bottom about ten o'clock, admitted defeat,

9

and walked to the village, the shops were shut of course, and at the pub door I suddenly felt such an idiotic mess I couldn't face the questions I knew the locals would ask. (The toll bridge and its fate were headline gossip I could have guessed even if Bob Norris hadn't already told me.) So I trailed back to the bridge and curled up as best I could in the only easy chair, hoping sleep would bring tomorrow quickly.

But I had reckoned without the night noises of a lonely riverside house, and without my own nervousness. Not the nervousness of fright, I wasn't scared, but the nervousness of being on my own for the first time in my life and of not knowing. Not knowing what caused the noises or why, not knowing if the skitterings across the floor were made by mice, whether the flitterings in the roof were birds roosting there that might invade my room, whether the ceaseless slurge of water passing under the bridge, sounding so much louder, more powerful, in the night, seeming to fill the house, meant the river had broken its banks and was flooding the place.

Once my mind is fixed on something I can't bear not knowing about it. So whenever a new sound caught my attention I got up to find out what caused it, which meant any warmth I'd managed to cook up, huddled in the chair, escaped, and I came back, usually little the wiser, chilled again, wearier, and narked.

In the way it often happens after a bad night, I fell asleep at last when dawn came, a smudged grey light that morning. And was woken, the next minute it seemed, the room bright with sun, by Bob Norris rattling at the door and calling my name, my mouth like a sewage farm, my body gutsick, painfully stiff, and my mind confused, not remembering where I was.

Bob laughed and teased, not taken in by the show of cheerfulness I tried to put on, and left me to pull myself together while he stood outside taking the few early morning tolls. I washed, brushed my teeth (still didn't need to shave more than twice a week), changed into fresh underclothes and shirt. But though this helped me feel physically better, the thought that already I had laundry to do and no one to do it for me and no washing machine to throw it into, finally made me face what I had brought upon myself.

All night long I'd told myself I was bound to feel strange at first, I'd soon settle down, get used to the place, make myself comfortable. But the sight of dirty clothes lying on the crushed old armchair in that bleak slummy room zapped any remaining particles of confidence and I wondered what the hell I was doing there.

Which was the moment when Tess walked in, carrying a bulging plastic bag and a blanket. Not, this first time, on the way to school, it being a Saturday, nor dressed in her biking leathers but in a loose white shirt and baggy washworn jeans and tennis shoes, a mane of lush jet-black hair framing the firm outlines of her face.

'Is it all right to come in?' she said, dumping the blanket on top of my laundry. 'Dad asked me to bring you this stuff.' She unpacked her plastic bag onto the muck-stained once-white pine table. Half-used packet of cornflakes, quarter of home-made brown loaf, jar of marmalade, bottle of milk, three eggs in a carton, quarter pound of farm butter, knife, fork, teaspoon, plate and mug, roll of paper towel. 'Should see you through till you can shop.' She looked me over as I stood gawping across the table. 'I'll give you a hand, if you like. You won't know your way around yet.'

All I could think was: Shut up, go away, I don't want any help, I'm going home, this is all a stupid mistake. What I managed to say was, 'Thanks, sure, yes, I could do with some help.'

[– What you didn't know at the time was that I was thinking: Why can't this creep look after himself? What's wrong with him? Why didn't he sort himself out yesterday? Why should I spend my Saturday morning booby-sitting him? I'd planned to play tennis but Dad asked me to help because he was worried you might be disheartened and leave. Then he'd have trouble manning the bridge again. Did he ever tell you that you were the only applicant willing to take the job?]

So there I was that first Saturday morning, cold, hungry, aching, bog-eyed, wanting only, longing, to bolt back home at whatever cost of derision, but my way out blocked by this high-energy girl standing between me and escape like a jailer (which she was, after all, as she was only there to help keep me there).

This is how my friendship with Tess began, the first true friendship of my life. My closest friendship still.

❖ 8 ❖

I don't think I believe in fate. Not if 'fate' means your future is planned, every detail, before you're born. Nor do I feel singled out, not like some people say they do, not in any special way, not destined to be anything but ordinary, muddling through life, as most people seem to.

11

But that morning with Adam, three months after first meeting Tess, as she throttled away, disappearing over the bridge, I suddenly felt I'd been here and done all this before. I know what is going to happen next, but am not able to do anything to stop it – a weird sensation of having had, sometime in the past, a glimpse into this future, of having forgotten, and only remembering now in the very second when the future becomes the present.

I hadn't experienced *déjà-vu* before. I'd heard people talk about it. But no one had said that it felt like a revelation. Suddenly the day seemed more alive, the air sharper, the light brighter, colours more colourful, objects more noticeable, more solid, more *there*. To tell the truth, as well as startled by it, I was a little frightened.

I turn towards the house, knowing I will turn in just this way. And walk inside, catching my hand on the doorknob as I pass, knowing I will catch it so but unable to prevent it. And find Adam, knowing I will, standing at the sink washing up the breakfast things, dressed in my only pair of spare jeans and my only spare sweater, sleeves pushed up above his elbows.

He will look sheepishly at me, I think as he looks sheepishly at me, and say, as he says, 'Heard you talking to somebody. Thought I'd better put sommat on in case they came in.'

At which, as suddenly as it came over me, this spooky sensation, this knowledge of the future-past invading the present, leaves me. Disappearing into my unknown future again, like Tess disappearing just now over the bridge. I feel I'm tottering on the edge of the river, and must wave my arms to keep from falling. And that I've been given a glimpse of something important, something life-changing, only for it to be swept away before I can fathom what it is or what it means.

I'm trembling a little from the excitement as well as the fright.

Which Adam notices, thinks I'm angry with him, and says, 'Was it OK, borrowing your stuff?'

Half an hour ago it wouldn't have been, but after the *déjà-vu* his cheek doesn't seem to matter because in some peculiar, inexplicable way, I know he has only done what he had to do.

I go to the fireplace and finger his clothes.

'Your own things will be dry soon.'

The warmth is calming, a comforting encouragement to do what has to be done. I plant a thick unsplit log, one that will burn slowly, on the bed of glowing cinders, and add, 'You'll be wanting to get going.'

12

'It's all right here.'

I stand and face him. He's leaning against the sink, his ice-blue eyes watching, his arms crossed over my best blue sweater.

'Look, I'm sorry, but you'll have to go, I've work to do.'

'Work? What work? I thought this was a squat.'

'No, no, it's a toll bridge, didn't you see?'

'It was dark.'

'Well . . . I collect the money.'

He thinks for a minute before saying, 'I could help. I could spell you. You could have some time off. Many hands make light work, as the Chinaman said when the electricity failed.'

He flashes his wrinkling-eyed grin but I won't give in.

'Sorry, my boss wouldn't allow it.'

'Ask him.'

'It's not just that. I want to be on my own, that's why I took the job.'

'On your own?'

'Yes.'

He shrugs, stares at his feet.

An awkward silence. The fire crackles behind me. With relief I hear a car approaching, go out, take the toll, come back inside.

Adam has gone. The back door stands open letting in a draught that is causing the chimney to backfire and fill the room with the heady incense of slow-burning wood. 'Vanished in a puff of smoke,' I say to myself.

I shut the door, glad he's gone, and only then see his clothes still hanging by the hearth.

Letters

. . . Surely, sweetheart, you've had enough by now? Aren't you fed up of looking after yourself? And aren't you lonely? You never mention any friends. It's not good for you to be stuck away in the middle of nowhere all on your own in that awful little house, which I'm sure must be damp and giving you rheumatism. Besides, it's such a waste of your young life. Your father says I mustn't nag, but, darling, what am I to do, I'm only concerned for your welfare, and hate the thought of you not getting the best out of life.

I'm sending you one of Zissler's pies this week. I'm sure you need feeding up and Zissler's are still the best. The woollen socks are from Aunty Jenny. She knitted them for you to wear when you're standing in the road taking the money, which is something I don't care to think about.

I was talking to Mrs Fletcher the other day. Her Brian only got a B and two Cs but was accepted at college quite easily – he's going to teach – so I don't think you should feel at all upset about an A and two Bs. I know you wanted As, we all wanted that for you of course but an A and two Bs when you were a year ahead of yourself anyway is respectable enough and would get you into any reasonable university. As a matter of fact, I had a talk with Mr Colbert at school today and he says if you come home in time for next term they'll be glad to have you back to do whatever you like till summer. He thought that with a bit of extra work to make up for the lost time you're quite capable of picking up a scholarship. Now you've had a break you'll feel better about things. Won't you think about it?

Gill called in on Saturday as usual. She puts on a cheerful face, but I can tell she misses you. I made her stay for supper and got out of her that you still haven't written or even phoned. Sweetheart, that's very unkind. She's devoted to you, and you've been such good friends. I told her – you don't deserve her! You don't either. If I were her I'd have gone off with someone else by now. Won't you just drop her a line? It would make all the difference.

Dad says thumbs up, whatever he means by that, and to tell you he's planted 120 daffodil bulbs where the begonias used to be, the ones that caught the strange disease and died last year, which I still think was caused by those dreadful cats from next door. And also would you like the radio he uses in the garage? Just ask and he'll post it. He says it's better than the old thing you took with you. He sends his love, of course. He's going round sniffing on the edge of a cold because he hasn't bothered to have his anti-flu shot this year, even though it did him so much good last winter, though the winter isn't here yet, but these autumn nights are quite chilly. When you talk to him on the phone next, would you encourage him to have his jab. I'm sure he listens to you more than he ever does to me.

We'll be out at the Smithsons on Sunday – it's his fiftieth birthday – so ring before 7.0. (And that's another thing – having no phone. I hate not being able to ring you and you having to use a call box.)

All my love, darling. I long to have you home again.

❖ 2 ❖

... I know she'll tell you and you'll be mad at me, but I couldn't help it. These last few months have been foul. Agony. Torture. The pain, the pain! But, honestly, I never thought I could miss anybody so much. When you went I expected withdrawal symptoms for a few days, even a week or two, but didn't think they'd go on this long. Every night I go to sleep thinking of you, every morning you're still there in my mind when I wake. During the day, when I'm doing something, I'll look up, expecting to see you, and when I don't I almost burst into tears. I have a couple of times actually, once in the middle of Gerty's French. God, the embarrassment!

I feel your skin on mine, the shape of you pressed against me, your hand on my breast, as if my body has a memory. But that only makes me feel worse because it's like loving a ghost. And then I begin to wonder if you're ill or hurt or perhaps even dead, and I can't bear it.

If only I knew what you were doing, what you're thinking and feeling. If only I knew you're missing me as much as I'm missing you. Couldn't you write? Or even just phone? I wasn't going to ask, I swore to myself I wouldn't, wouldn't make any demands. But now

I've blurted it out to your mother I might as well be honest and tell you how desperate I am, even just to hear from you.

Remember how we used to say we didn't know what 'love meant'? Didn't know if we were really 'in love' or just liked being together and screwing? Well now, if I'm not in love with you, I don't know what love can be. All the time, every minute, every day, I want to be with you, want to hear your voice, see your lovely face, caress your lovely body, wrap myself around you, put my mouth on yours, spread my fingers in your hair, feel your long hard fleshy sinewy body on mine, do *everything* with you. I want to live with you, do things for you, have you do things for me, argue with you, eat with you, read with you, dance with you, screw with you, sleep with you, die with you.

You see – I need you. Desperately. Can 'love' mean anything else?

Remember the weekend your parents were away? Our first weekend on our own together all the time. We had that silly row about condoms just because I'd bought a different kind from our usual and you didn't like it and then got the giggles when you were putting one on! Well, that weekend was the happiest two days of my whole entire life. I would give anything to have more days and more nights like them. All my days, all my nights.

This is stupid. I shouldn't be writing to you like this. Letters are hopeless. They get misunderstood. Is that why you don't write? If only we could be together even for just an hour and talk. Won't you let me visit you? Just for a weekend. Just a Saturday night.

I've taken a Saturday job in the bookshop. (Let me know of any books you want, I can get them cheap. I'll send them, though I'd rather bring them.) I'm saving my wages (for Christmas, I tell Mum) so I've money for the train, which will cut travelling time and give us as long as poss together. They're good at the shop and will let me off for one Saturday. Just seeing you would be such a relief. I won't tell your mother, *honest*. Not a word. Not to *anyone*.

I love you. I love you.

❖ 3 ❖

... No, I don't want you here. Keep away. Beware of the dog. Trespassers will be persecuted. *I do not want you here.*

I explained the best I could before I left. I can't do any better now. Not yet. When I can you'll be the first to know.

Please do not quote memories at me. I don't care about memories. I don't want to hear about them. You say letters get misunderstood.

You're right. But memories get misunderstood even worse. People do what they like with them. They make them mean what they want them to mean. I want to live only in the present. That is where I am.

Yes, I enjoyed screwing you. If you were here I'd screw you again. But that's another reason I don't want you here. It would only confuse things. And I think that was what I wanted with you the most anyway. I'm not sure I wanted anything else. I won't pretend otherwise.

Pretending has been one of my problems. I'd got into the habit of pretending. Trying to be what everybody wanted me to be.

I've made a rule for myself here. I will only be what I feel I am. I will not pretend, even if that means being disliked and saying no when people want me to say yes. I want to be honest with myself. I don't know how else to start finding out what I really *truly* am. Who I am, I mean. There is so much old garbage inside me already, so much *clutter*, even after only seventeen years. What must it be like after thirty years or fifty? Is that why so many old people go round looking like they're weighed down by two tons of compressed crap? I don't want that to happen to me. But how do you stop it?

I don't like all this talk about love. What people call love is only things they want from someone else. Like a good screw or a nice time together or even just someone to keep them from feeling lonely. As far as I can see that's what most people mean by love anyway. It isn't what they want for anybody else, it's what they want for themselves. Eating people is wrong.

I just want to be me. I take money from people crossing the bridge, I repair the house a bit, I keep the garden tidy, I read a lot, I mess about with a rowing boat on the river now and then, I listen to music, I watch telly, I think, and I look after myself. And no one pressures me. For the first time in my life I am completely responsible for myself. And not responsible for anybody else. I like that. It's what I want.

Leave it like that for now, OK?

A Yard of Ale

❖ 1 ❖

'Don't send it,' Tess said.

'Why not?'

'It's not you. Not how you really are. It's mean.'

'It's how I feel.'

'You feel mean?'

'The way she goes on about love. I don't want her here and I'm not going to lie.'

'You don't have to. All I'm saying is you should put it better. All this about persecuting trespassers – you're talking about your girlfriend, for Christ's sake! And not wanting to be reminded of the nice times you spent together, and telling her she's asking stupid questions.'

'Depends how you read it.'

'So why show it to me? You asked what I thought. That's what I think.'

We were sitting drinking coffee at the toll-house table (which, persuaded by Tess, I'd sanded down to fresh wood during the last few days and then waxed), on the Sunday morning two days after Adam and Gill's letter arrived. Sundays were free days, no tolls, a day off. It was ten thirty, and one of those bright still quiet autumn mornings when the sun's warmth recalls high summer and the sky is a hazed blue. All the leaves die in Technicolor.

Tess's Sunday morning visits began as a duty chore, sent by her father to check I was OK, and became a regular habit we both enjoyed, looked forward to, though we didn't tell each other this at the time. She always brought fruit or veg out of their garden or a slab of home-made cake, which she said, untruthfully, came from her mother, or something from the estate farm – butter or jam or eggs or cheese. Given the 'mod wage' I was trying to exist on, I'd have been pretty pinched without this help.

I coveted her acts of friendship, they made me feel better, though I tried to hide this from her. But I did try to be ready with something for her so the gift-giving wouldn't be one-sided. As I hadn't much cash, at first the presents were usually objects I'd found and 'treated'. Once a piece of wood I pulled out of the river that happened to resemble a fish, which I cleaned and painted with an eye and a mouth, and clear-varnished to give it a wet look. Once a George the Third silver shilling I dug up in the garden while clearing an overgrown corner, and buffed up bright.

[– See what I mean about men and gifts! Not that I wasn't pleased. It's one of your nicer characteristics – you can be thoughtful when you don't need to be. But I didn't want anything back. You just didn't feel comfortable receiving presents without squaring the account!]

After a couple of weeks I started writing poems for her, comic verses to begin with, as a joke. Because of her studying English Lit. We had that in common. We talked about her exam books. One week I gave her a parody of a poem by Ted Hughes she'd found difficult, a pig of a poem about pigs. After that, without thinking about it, it seemed natural to write more serious stuff. I made up the lines while collecting tolls or working on the house or mucking about on the river, and wrote them down and polished them in the evenings. It filled the time and I enjoyed it more than I expected. Soon I was writing two, even three, a week. (When I read them now they make me cringe. How could I ever have thought them worth giving anyone! Two years is an age. But it got me started, and I haven't stopped since. I discovered then that writing feels like a natural part of me: something I was born to do.)

'So why show me her letter?' Tess said, flipping it back across the table. 'You're going to be rotten to her anyway, aren't you, whatever I say?'

'No, I'm not! When I tried before, half the trouble was I didn't know what I wanted to say. So I made up the sort of thing I thought she'd want to hear.'

'Like?'

'Oh, about this place, and what I was doing. But I hated it. It

19

was all an act, nothing to do with what I really felt. Not that I was feeling anything much. Just getting through each day. You know how I've been. The Glums. I sure as hell didn't want to write letters about that to anybody, Gill least of all. She knows about it anyway.'

'You're not so depressed now though, not like when you first arrived. You looked pretty bombed then, I can tell you.'

'Couldn't have stuck it without you.'

'No, well –'

'I spent a lot of time on that letter.'

'Look, you really want to know what I think? Make up your mind whether you want Gill or not. If you do, write something more loving, because, honestly, if I was her, that letter would upset me a lot. But if you don't want her, break it off, don't keep her hanging on, hoping. It's not fair.'

She was right, I knew.

We sat in silence, me avoiding her eyes and feeling myself losing my grip and slithering back into that dark craggy pit I'd been clawing my way out of these last few weeks, even beginning to think I might have escaped. But no. Like the nightmare when you're fleeing from some murderous maniac, you turn to look behind, see nothing, he's gone, you breathe at last, and turn back relieved, and there he is, right in front of you, overwhelming, unavoidable, his axe coming straight at your head – and you wake up in the nick of time.

Depression, and I'm a first-hand expert, gets treated in two ways. Either you're told you're sick, and given pills to dull the effects by stupefying you into silence so that you stop getting on everyone's nerves, or you're told you're a malingerer, a wimp, who ought to pull yourself together and stop moaning, because there's a lot of people in the world who are worse off than you.

There is a lunatic fringe as well, a school of Holy Joes who tell you depression is a sin, a wilful wallow in self-pity which any decent Christian atheist ought not to indulge in – as if depression were a punishment for being a narcissistic wanker.

Having suffered from it for most of my seventeenth year I can only say it never seemed to me to fit any of these diagnoses. It always seemed more of an affliction, like having a hand go out of action for no good reason so you can't do all sorts of everyday things you usually do without thinking, and have to put up with this temporarily useless limb flailing about, knocking things over and thumping people, causing trouble and embarrassment. While at the same time you're being slowly

20

strangled (because your throat seizes up), and your guts churn like a sewage tank in labour (because you're worried sick about all sorts of minor problems that suddenly seem like major catastrophes), and your mind endlessly turns over the evidence of your complete failure as a human being until you've not a particle of willpower left to make yourself do anything except stare into space.

In my opinion depression is a disease caused by thinking too much about all the things you can only do well if you don't think about them at all.

'Look,' Tess said, standing up, 'it's a lovely day, there won't be many more like it this year, what are we doing sitting here? Let's take the boat upriver and I'll treat you to a drink and a sandwich at the Fisherman and Pike. I'm rich, would you believe!'

❖ 2 ❖

Tess went out to prepare the boat while I tidied up. She came back chuckling.

'There's a boy on the bridge playing Pooh-sticks.'

'What?'

'You know – dropping sticks into the river, then running to the other side of the bridge to see which one comes through first. Don't you remember? *Winnie-the-Pooh*.'

'Oh, that.'

'Dad used to play it with me when I was a kid.'

'So what's funny about a kid playing it now?'

'Well, he's not exactly a kid, he's about our age and he's by himself, and –'

'Let him. It's my day off.'

'He's having fun. I felt like joining in.'

I went to the window which gave a view along the bridge.

Adam, stood precariously on the parapet, a piece of stick in each hand which he drops with exaggerated care at the same instant, jumps down, races to the other side, leaps onto the parapet with breathtaking aplomb – and in my sweater and jeans, both the worse for his wear.

'Hey!' I shout uselessly and sprint out of the house, Tess calling after me 'What's up?' and following to the door.

Adam sees me coming and waves a greeting as to a friend he's been waiting for.

'What about my clothes?' I shout as I approach.

The affable smile fades. He jumps down. 'Eh?'

21

'You're wearing them!'

He looks at himself. 'Oh, these.'

'Why didn't you change before you left?'

He frowns.

'I need that stuff. My only spares, you see.'

'Right, sure.' He smiles suddenly, his handsome cheeky grin. 'I'll change now. That's why I'm here.'

'You'd better come in.'

Tess is waiting at the door.

Wanting to head off friendly exchanges, I say, 'This is Tess. He's Adam.'

'Adam,' Adam repeats as if prompted. 'Hi.'

'Hi,' Tess says.

'The visitor on Friday,' I say with warning emphasis.

Adam goes into the living room. Tess rolls her eyes at me in a mock swoon. I poke my tongue at her. She follows Adam. I go into the bedroom for his clothes, intending to call him in to change. But before I can, I hear Tess say, 'We're rowing upriver for a drink and a sandwich. Want to come?'

Adam says, 'I'm skint.'

'My treat.'

'Well . . . sure, thanks! I'll row if you like. Pay my way.'

'Great.'

What! I think – first my clothes, now my Sunday. What's going on here, what have I done to deserve this?

I join them.

'Adam's coming with us,' Tess says with the forced cheeriness people adopt when they know they're going against what you want and are pretending it's all right.

'Your clothes are in the bedroom,' I say, ignoring her.

'He's not going to change, is he?' Tess says. 'You know what boats are like. Ours anyway. He might as well wait till we get back.'

'Why didn't I think of that!' I say and stalk out ahead of them.

❖ 3 ❖

In the leaky old clinker-built dinghy only just big enough for the three of us, Tess has the tiller, and I'm beside her in the stern facing Adam who is rowing. Our legs interleave. Adam pulls us upstream with steady effortless strokes. His body has an animal perfection in its proportions, the neat way all its parts fit together, the easy relaxed way it moves, beautiful to watch, very sexy. Tess can't take her eyes off him, which hurts me with a double jealousy – of that animal body, and of its effect on Tess – so that I resent Adam's disturbing presence more than ever.

But being rowed in a boat on a calm river on a warm morning has a soothing effect. Soon I'm lulled, as I remember being lulled as a little boy, by the lazy motion of the boat, and begin to take pleasure in Tess's body squashed up against mine, and Adam's slow, rhythmic movements, and the in-out plashings of the oars, and the glazed autumn colours of the river bank.

I think: I ought to be glad of this, ought to be giving myself to it, not begrudging, not grinding my guts with jealous resentment.

After a while, curiosity getting the better of her, Tess asks, 'Where are you from, Adam? Not from round here.'

He shakes his head. 'Up north.'

'Thought so from your accent.' She looks at me, askance. 'Two of a kind.'

She waits. Adam takes two more strokes but he adds nothing. 'On holiday or something?'

'Something.'

'A job?'

'Anything.'

'How come?'

He takes another stroke, watching his right-hand oar rise, skim, plunge. 'They chucked me out.'

'Who?'

'Parents. Well – my dad.'

'Chucked you out?'

'Hasn't got a job himself. And I've two sisters still at school.'

'But chucking you out!'

'We didn't get on either. Kept having rows. I'm better off out of it.'

'When did this happen?'

'Couple of months ago.'

'Poor you!'

He shrugs. 'I get by.'

For some reason I don't believe a word of this but I can see Tess does. He gives her *that* smile, but his eyes have a wary look, observing the effect. A look that bothers me. For a moment someone else inhabits those eyes, not the boy with the foxy grin.

23

The pub is packed with a Sunday crowd of junior yuppies from the posh commuter end of the village vying with university undergrads from across the river for the quickest-wit-of-the-year award and pretending not to pose. We manage to order with difficulty, being obviously members of the shoddier classes if not definitely under-age untouchables.

While we wait for our sandwiches a cohort of noisier undergrads challenges a squad of yahooier yuppies to a yard-of-ale competition.

'What's that?' Adam asks.

Plastic aprons to protect the yuppies' designer informals and the undergrads' unwashables are handed across the bar while a barman decants two and a half pints of beer into a metre-long glass tube with a bulb at one end and a trumpet-flared opening at the other.

Tess tells Adam, 'They have to drink all the beer from that thing like a glass hunting horn, which is called a yard-of-ale. They have to drink it at one go without spilling any, which is pretty hard to do. The one who does it the quickest and spills the least is the winner.'

'Cruel!' Adam is fascinated.

'Don't they do it up your way?'

'Not that I've come across.'

'Round here they say it sorts out the men from the boys.'

'Or the disgusting from the gross,' I add, 'the real aim being to see who spews up first.'

A podgy yuppy, the kind of over-eager bod who'll do anything to be thought a big man by his mates, has started the match off. He's a third down and has gone too fast. The trick is to take it at a steady gentle speed, swigging rhythmically so you've plenty of breath for the worst part, which is at the end when you have to lean back far enough to raise the tube nearly upright in order to empty the last of the beer out of the bulb. By then your arms are tired, you're just about gasping, and leaning back makes it very hard to swallow.

'Easy . . . easy . . . easy!' the yuppies chant, neo-soccer. The students whoop derisively. Both have the effect of over-exciting the already over-excited dolt. He raises the yard too fast. Beer floods out of his mouth, down his front, onto the floor, and puddles round his feet. As he gulps for breath someone rescues the yard. His clothes are soaked. The reek of body-warmed beer fills the room. His supporters mockingly commiserate; the students cheer. The yard is refilled as an undergrad is prepared by his seconds who camp up the boxing image

– extracting the piss out of the whole business in general and of the yuppies in particular.

Our sandwiches arrive.

'I'm eating mine outside,' I say.

'Got to see this,' Adam says.

'Suit yourself.'

Tess says, 'I think I'll go outside too.'

'I'll come in a minute,' Adam says, not taking his eyes from the arena.

❖ 5 ❖

The tables in the garden were occupied so we sat dangling our feet over the stone-paved edge of the river bank where, in summer, holiday boats moor for visits to the pub.

'For God's sake, don't encourage him,' I said while we ate.

'Why not? I like him.'

'I told you – he wants to stay.'

'He'd be fun. No one would mind.'

'I'd mind. There's something odd about him.'

'Odd?'

'The way he looks sometimes.'

'You just don't want any competition.'

'Rubbish! Anyway, it doesn't matter what you think, the toll bridge is my place, I'll decide who stays there, thanks.'

She laughed. 'I'm going to call you Janus.'

'Who's he when he's at home?'

'The Roman god? Well, pre-Roman actually.'

'Don't know any gods, I'm glad to say.'

'You ought to know Janus, though. For one thing he's the god of bridges.'

'Terrific.'

'As well as doors and passages and archways. And he has two faces. So he can see what's coming both ways, I suppose.'

'Or going, depending on how you look at it.'

'You keep the bridge and you're also two-faced, so I'll call you Jan, son of Janus.'

'Compliments now.'

'Well, you are. In the nicest possible way of course.'

'And what way is that?'

'Take Adam.'

'You take him, you're the one who's after him.'

25

'Are you sure about that?'

'What?'

'You say he's odd but really you're jealous because he's more good-looking than you and because I fancy him.'

'I get it – it's the truth game.'

'And you're being two-faced about Gill, who you're keeping on a string while making eyes at me.'

'I like that! You don't mince words once you start.'

'I've been kind to you till now because you weren't very well.'

'But not any more?'

'I reckon you're about as normal now as you'll ever be, don't you, Jan dear?'

'Prefer my proper name, if you don't mind.'

'You call me Tess. Just because I'm big-hearted enough to fetch your groceries from Tesco's sometimes. Why shouldn't I call you Jan? What's sauce for the goose.'

'Jan's a girl's name.'

'It's both, as a matter of fact. It means John in some languages. But when I use it it means a junior Janus who looks both ways at once and can't make up his mind which way to go because he doesn't know whether he's coming or going.'

There was a roaring cheer from the pub.

'Sounds like a winner,' Tess said.

'I suppose that means we'll be graced with the presence of the adorable Adam again just when we're having such a deliriously cosy chat.'

Another prolonged roar.

Tess said, 'You know it can only be friends between us? I mean, I like you a lot. But in the sort of way sex would spoil somehow.'

'Spoil!'

'Honest . . . Janus!'

'D'you have to call me that?'

'Yes, let me, go on, I like it!' She leaned over and kissed me on the cheek.

I was supposed to smile. 'All right, have it your own way.'

'Good. I win.'

'Was it a competition?'

Another, more drunken roar.

'There's a lot of it about.'

Followed by screams and shouts and then a sudden silence.

I recited,

    'Almighty Mammon, make me rich!
    Make me rich quickly, with never a hitch
    in my fine prosperity! Kick all those in the ditch
    who hinder me, Mammon, great son of a bitch!'

'One of yours?'

'D.H. Lawrence.'

'How do you do it?'

'What?'

'Remember all that stuff.'

'Don't know. Always have. A gift, I suppose.'

'What teachers call clever, you mean.'

'Having a good memory?'

'For facts and figures and quotations and stuff like that. Not for people. Not for things that matter. No wonder they put you a year ahead. But get back to money.'

'Doesn't everything always.'

'There's nothing wrong with filthy lucre. Depends how you use it.'

'And how you get it maybe? Just think – they were like us once, that lot in there. Ordinary, normal, sane, poverty-stricken schoolkids.'

'Is that how you feel, like an et cetera schoolkid?'

'Yes and no. Yes up to the last few weeks, and no, not since The Glums started to clear. Don't know what I feel, to be honest, except empty. Haven't a clue what I want, either. Not whatever is supposed to come next though. Grown up or adult or whatever. Do you?'

She was feeding snips from her sandwiches to a family of mallards cadging on the water at our feet, who gobbled, cackled, and paddled off, as if they knew there was nothing more to be had from us.

'Don't think about it too much.'

'You're all now, you! Do you want to be, though? Adult and all that.'

'Don't you?'

'Not if it means being lumbered with some endless job and a family and a mortgage and a house to do odd jobs on every weekend or any of that sort of garbage.'

'All that responsibility is what you mean.'

'Yes, OK, all that responsibility. I don't want it, thanks. But I don't want to go on being a schoolkid, either. Had enough of that.'

'Stuck in limboland, then, aren't you? Don't know whether you're coming or going. Like I said – facing both ways again.'

The barman who'd served us came across the grass with the forced nonchalance of someone on an urgent mission who at the same time is trying not to frighten the paying customers and, crouching down between us, said, 'Weren't you with the young guy in the grotty blue sweater?'

We nodded, sensing trouble.

'Well, he's stirred up a bit of aggro in the bar.'

'What's happened?' Tess asked.

'Wanted to have a go with the yard-of-ale but the others wouldn't let him – they were having a competition, you see. Your friend insisted, and there was a bit of a row. Someone grabbed the yard, but it broke and, well – your friend cut himself. There's blood spilt and beer and not a happy reaction from the others. Could you come and help sort him out?'

'The idiot,' I said.

'Come on,' Tess said. 'We can't just leave him.'

'Yes, we can. We're not responsible.'

'We brought him.'

'So? We don't have to take him back, do we? He's a sponger. He'll just upset everything. Let him take care of himself.'

But I followed her into the pub.

❖ 6 ❖

Inside there is the kind of unnatural quiet with dark mutterings, and resentful glances, and one or two people determinedly ignoring what's going on that you only get in the aftermath of an unpleasant scene in a public place where people are supposed to be enjoying themselves.

The yuppies and undergrads have separated to either side of the disaster area, their undisguised belligerence directed at Adam, who is slumped in a chair in the middle of the deserted arena, wild-eyed and sullen. A brisk middle-aged woman, whom I take to be the landlady, is bandaging his left hand while a young barmaid mops the floor round their feet.

Tess and I edge our way through the throng, me trying to pretend we're nothing to do with this and are invisible anyhow, and take up stations on either side of the wounded public enemy.

'You all right?' Tess mutters.

'Yeah, I'm OK,' he says and suddenly turns on that surprising vulpine grin. It's as though he's a character in a play whose reactions are remotely controlled by a mischievous dramatist.

'Look,' says the landlady, 'it would be a good idea if you got him out of here.'

'Haven't had my go yet,' Adam says and stares nuke-eyed at the yard boys.

Tess says, 'We'll take you home.'

'Home?' I mutter.

'Shut up and help,' she mutters back, and, taking Adam by his good arm, says firmly, 'Come on, we're leaving.'

Irresistible Tess. Adam allows her to lead him away without another word, me following, a reluctant rearguard.

❖ 7 ❖

How easily circumstances change people, their moods, their feelings, their attitudes to themselves and the world around them. An hour earlier as we rowed upriver, relaxed, happy in the sun, I'd felt part of the landscape – at one with the world. Now, everything is reversed, Adam broodily nursing his hand, sitting where I had sat, in the stern cosied up to Tess, me tense as I row us downstream, sweating in what now seems an unfriendly sun, and feeling awkward, like an alien.

For a while I take out my simmering anger on the river, sculling through the water with as much force as I can. But soon my strength weakens; then only words will do.

I say, glaring at Adam, 'You're a pain in the arse, you know that, don't you!'

He refuses to look, his head turned away.

'Leave him alone,' Tess says. 'I'd have thought you'd be on his side, not on theirs.'

'I'm not on their side and I'm not on his, I'm on my own.'

'Selfish prig! You don't deserve any friends.'

'He's nothing but trouble.'

'And you're a jerk.'

'Oh, get stuffed!'

❖ 8 ❖

For the rest of the trip we all have lockjaw. At the bridge Tess coddles Adam into the house while I remain sitting in the boat tethered to the bank and sulk.

Quarter of an hour later Tess came out.

'I'm sorry,' she said. 'Didn't mean it.'

I won't speak.

29

'Are you really going to turn him out?'

Glowering silence.

'Seems to me people are always turning him out of somewhere. Can't he stay the night?'

'No.'

I felt a heel, which is exactly what she wanted me to feel.

'He's gone very quiet. I think he's a bit shocked. I've given him some sweet tea and made him lie down.'

'It's all an act. There's nothing the matter, really. He made a fool of himself and cut his hand, that's all.' I felt invaded, taken over. And jealous of all this pampering.

Tess said, 'Let him stay, just for tonight.'

'No.'

'Listen, I'll make us a meal. Mum'll give us some extra stuff. I'll say you've got a guest, unexpected. Which is true anyway. And I'll cadge some cans of lager off Dad. We'll have a nice time. It'll be a party. A house warming! You haven't had one yet. How about it? You'll enjoy it, honest . . . Come on, let yourself go for once, it won't hurt!'

Never able to resist Tess when she's determined, then or now, I gave in. 'All right,' I said, feigning unwilling agreement, the art of the spoilt boy (he who'd sworn he'd never pretend any more). I was on a loser, I knew. And that desire in me to be liked took over, a failing I hate but have never quite been able to shake off. 'But no passes at him while I'm around.'

'Cheek! I'll treat you both the same.'

'Great, a threesome. Now that could be fun.'

'You've got sex on the brain.'

'Not to mention other parts, and who hasn't?' I was brightening up again. Another of the virtues of Tess – something about her that dispels The Glums. One of life's natural healers, just as some people are natural destroyers.

Depression, of which a gloomy mood is a miniature version, is like being filled with iron filings all zinging about inside you, going every which way, pricking and stinging. And Tess is like the magnet that magics all the filings into a beautiful pattern, a force field, in which they act as one, harmoniously.

'I'll tell you what,' I said, 'while Prince Charming lies on my bed of his pain, let's you and me go blackberrying. Then we'll make a pud.'

'It's after Michaelmas.'

'Eh?'

'Ignorant yob. September twenty ninth. It's well known in these here parts that you shouldn't eat blackberries after Michaelmas because the Devil pees on them that night.'

'You're full of odd info today. Roman gods. Urinating devils.'

'I get it from Dad. He loves that sort of thing – country customs, folklore.'

'I'll chance it if you will. We can sweeten them with honey.'

We found a plastic bag and set off, Tess knowing the best bushes in the hedges between the bridge and the village. Blackberries big as the balls of my thumb. Not really. Long past their best, but we weren't to be put off. Doing together was what mattered.

As we picked, our fingers soon violet-red from juice and itchy-smarting from the pin-sharp thorns, Tess said, 'Why do you go on so much about responsibility?'

'I don't.'

'*Mon dieu*, you should hear yourself.'

'I don't like people expecting things of me.'

'Do they?'

'Parents. Teachers. Relatives. Don't yours?'

'Never bother to think about it. Wouldn't pay much attention anyway.'

'You're more easy-going than me. You just accept things. I envy that.'

'You are a bit heavy, that's for sure. I thought it was The Glums.'

'No, I was born that way. In most of the photos of me as a kid I'm frowning, like I'm worried to death.'

We stood back from the bushes and looked at each other. A new understanding.

'Mum calls you old-fashioned. I suppose that's what she means.'
'What?'

'That you take such a serious view of life.'

'Does it matter? To you, I mean.'

'It's how you are. I like you as you are.'

'Stodgy? Prematurely middle-aged?'

'I didn't say that! You do have your lighter side. Now and then!'

'Which is what you like.'

'If you really *must* know, Jan dear . . .'

'God, not *that* again!'

'. . . what I like most about you is your mind.'

'Not my lovely body?'

31

'No, not your lovely body. You make me think in a way nobody else has. I enjoy that, surprise surprise. And,' she added quickly, 'don't say another word about it now because you'll only go and spoil things by saying too much.'

'Can you?'

'*Sacré bleu!*' she said, but she was laughing. 'Haven't you learned *nothing* yet!'

'No,' I said.

'Oh – I dunno – how can anybody who's read so much be so – *naïve!*'

There was a sharpening of the air as the autumn sun went down. Our breath steamed. Tess's lips were purple. We started picking berries again.

'Look,' I said, 'if we're going to live off the land instead of out of your mum's freezer, what about us making cauliflower cheese for a main course? We can pinch a cauliflower out of your garden, there's about fifty more than your family will ever eat. I've plenty of cheese and milk. You just brought some butter. We'll have to cadge some flour though, I haven't any of that.'

'Haven't cooked it before.'

'I have. I'll show you. What you do is wash the cauliflower and divide it into florets. Cook in salted boiling water for ten minutes. Make a sauce by melting an ounce of butter in a pan. Blend in a couple of tablespoons of flour. Cook for about a minute, stirring all the time because it burns easily.'

'Do I want to know all this?'

'Take off the heat. Slowly stir in half a pint of milk. Put on the heat again. Keep stirring. Bring to the boil. Add about three ounces of cheese, and salt and pepper to taste. Put the cauliflower into a casserole dish, pour on the sauce, sprinkle a couple of ounces of grated cheese on top, put the casserole into the oven and bake for fifteen to twenty minutes. *Olay! Bon appétit*, et cetera.'

'Lawks a-mercy, *mon ami*, hidden talents! Where'd you learn that?'

'Haven't wasted all my time the last few weeks. What else do we housebound men have to do all day but learn to cook?'

'You've such a hard life. How about some spuds?'

'We'll bake them in the fire.'

'Great!'

On our way back from the garden, where we'd endured much teasing from the Norris tribe (father, mother, two sons, plus Tess,

32

the youngest), Tess said, 'Don't you think this is a lovely chuckle? And we wouldn't have done it if it hadn't been for Adam.'

'Careful. Proof of the pud. Might turn out like Christmas.'

'How?'

'Better in the anticipation than the event.'

'Pessimist.'

'Romantic.'

'Cynic.'

'Estragonist.'

'Eh?'

'Sewer-rat, curate, cretin, crrritic.'

'What are you on about now?'

'Samuel Beckett . . . *Waiting for Godot* . . . the play?'

'I make a point of never knowing anything other people quote at me. It lets them feel superior.'

'*Touché!* Will you have it in a basket or on a plate?'

'This is all too heady for me.'

'Must be the Devil's pee on those blackberries you ate. I expect his piddle is pretty intoxicating.'

'Intoxicating perhaps, pretty not. Glad you're feeling perky again.'

❖ 9 ❖

When we arrived back at the house Adam had gone. Again. Along with some food – all my bread, a bag of fruit Tess had brought that day, and half the cake my mother had sent in her weekly parcel.

'This is getting to be a habit,' I said.

'I suppose you're pleased,' Tess said, not hiding her disappointment.

'Yes,' I said to irritate her. 'But he'll be back. He knows when he's on to a good thing.'

Not until later, when we took our blackberry pud out into the night frost to eat by the river, did we discover that the boat had gone as well.

Letters

❖ 1 ❖

. . . but, sweetheart, there was no need to be bad-tempered. Your father says boys of your age don't like to be questioned about their doings and having their parents interfere, he says he was like that himself. Well, *he* might have been but that doesn't mean *you* have to be, does it, and I wasn't interfering but only wanting to be helpful. After all, as I have to keep reminding him, you're on your own for the first time in your life, with no one to look out for your wellbeing, and I am your mother, darling, aren't I, it's only natural, isn't it, that I should want to know how you are and how you spend your time. You've never been secretive before. And I don't think your father is right anyhow. Your Uncle Bill was always full of himself when he was your age and told us about everything he did, and Mrs Fletcher's Brian doesn't hold back either, I know because she tells me in great detail all his news when we have our Friday coffee, he seems to be doing very well at college, just as you will next year, I'm sure, and probably a lot better because you were always much cleverer than Brian Fletcher, that I do know.

I can only think you're so reserved about your doings because you aren't really happy and don't want to say so in case it upsets your father and me. I know you, when you go quiet that means trouble. I expect something's going on that doesn't suit. You were always like that. But when you were a child you were a sweet-natured good little boy who always tried to please, and I could soon make you smile again, I knew the trick, as I still could if you were here. Well, it won't be long before Christmas when you'll be home again and we can have a good old heart-to-heart. Would you like us to drive down and pick you up? Your father says the car could do with a good long run, and there's no need for you to take the bus, even if it is supposed to be express, the car would be far more comfortable, and save on expense,

34

and we'd be together for that bit longer. Your father and I do think it admirable of you to want to survive without taking money from us or depending on us at all, but things can go too far in this respect and fetching you home would give us great pleasure. So just let's take this as settled, shall we?

Gill is looking forward to seeing you then too. She was here on Sunday after you phoned as usual and told us funny but awful stories about the dreadful behaviour of customers at the bookshop. I must say I thank goodness your father and I never had to deal with members of the public in the service industries, there do seem to be some very strange people about and courtesy has gone out of the window, which I notice myself when shopping, as I said to Mrs Fletcher only last Friday after an embarrassing altercation at the cosmetics counter in Binns. Though it is bad enough for Gill it can't be any fun at all for you taking money in all weathers from people in cars, which, as I've said to your father many a time, seem to bring out the worst in people. They certainly do in him. He almost ran down a man in a Vauxhall the other day, you know how prejudiced he is against Vauxhalls. At least Gill is in the warm and dry, and working in a bookshop is quite respectable, if you have to work in a shop at all, besides being, as Mrs Fletcher remarked after we'd given Gill a wave on our way past, probably educational as well. She brought your father a very nice book on pruning roses which, as she admitted, she got cheap being an employee, but never mind, it was thoughtful of her.

Your father, being your father, said she was just trying to curry favour with him, but at least he went for his jab today. I told you he would if you had a word with him. You see how much we miss you and how much we need you. But as I say, my darling, Christmas soon, and we'll be together again . . .

❖ 2 ❖

. . . but I can't wait till then, can you? I'm desperate! Worse every day. Like thirst. I see Carole and Felicity with Daniel and Rod and can't stand it. I want you want you want you want you want you.

Besides, beloved, there's an important anniversary coming up. December 14th. One year. Twelve months. 365 days (and nights).

Remember the first time? I do, every second of it. Couldn't I come to you for our anniversary? I know it's near Christmas and you'll be home then. But we could celebrate all on our own, a whole weekend together with no one to worry about, no one to interrupt or spoil things or to have to think about at all. Just you and me. Us.

I could come down on the Friday evening. There's a train would get me to you about 9.0. And I could stay till late Monday afternoon. I could skip school that day. There wouldn't be too much fuss. Worth it however much. Three whole blissful days together. Three whole even more blissful nights together. It would be like never before, wouldn't it. Say yes. On a postcard. Just the one word. Or phone. We won't talk if you don't want to. Just say yes. That's enough. All I want. We can talk when we're together. And make love. Oh how I want to make love. I want you. Now. *This second*.

I love you love you love you.

❖ 3 ❖

. . . but I've tried to, honest. None of them was right.

It's all so complicated. How I feel, I mean, what I'm thinking. The depression isn't as bad, which is one good thing. I feel better most of the time. But sometimes it all comes flooding back. Not so often though. Like a wound healing. Some days it hurts, some days it just aches, some days, more and more often, I feel OK. Maybe depression is a kind of wound. A psychic wound, a ghostly wound that haunts you till somehow it's laid. (And not the sort of laid you mean.) Still, though, I need more time to get things sorted out in my mind.

I like it here. It's good for me. I like being on my own. That's something I've learned about myself. Actually physically enjoy it. It gives me pleasure. I don't know, maybe I'm one of those people who are best left to themselves, the sort who prefer their own company.

Not that this place is anything to write home about. Hardly even basic, in fact. Which is another reason I like it. It's stripped down to the essentials. Maybe I like it like this because I'm trying to strip myself down to my own essentials. To get to know the real me. Who is the real me? I don't know. There's so much garbage inside me already, so much *clutter*. And most of it dumped there by other people – parents, teachers, friends, neighbours, the telly, I don't know. Everybody. But not a lot of it put there by me.

Anyhow, what I'm really trying to say is please don't come here. I don't mean to be nasty or anything. But it's hard to explain. It's just – I'm not ready yet. Mother wants me home for Christmas. I suppose I'll have to. We can talk about it then.

OK? What I mean is, you said letters get misunderstood. Which is true.

And the same is true about memories. I remember our first time, of course I do. But memories don't help. They can even get in the way. It seems to me that most of the time people use their memories to make their past life seem better than it was, or happier. Or just the opposite. They only remember the worst. Either way, memories aren't real. They're a kind of fiction, if you ask me. Anyhow, people make them into what they want them to be, and then believe their life was like that. But I want to know what my life really was, really *is* now not then.

And yes, I enjoyed screwing you. You know that. But that's another of the reasons why I don't want you to come here. We'd screw all the time and I'd like it but it would only confuse things again. Confuse me anyway, about me and about you, and about me-and-you. Just when I'm beginning to sort myself out.

OK, so I'm crazy and mixed up. That's what people are saying, I expect. Well, I don't care what they're saying. I don't have to listen to them. Not here. Which is another reason why I like this place, and being on my own, and out of range of home and everybody who knows me. Or think they do! Maybe the truth is I'm not like they think I am. Maybe I'm quite different. When I find out, you'll be the first to know.

So let's leave it like that for now, yes? Till Christmas anyway.

I think about you.

He, Hi,
Hippertihop

❖ 1 ❖

'"I think about you"! Honestly!'

'But I do!'

'Not the way it means when you write it, though. You're being deceitful.'

'I'm only trying to be kind.'

'Kind! *Très drôle!* It's not kindness she wants. If you can't see that . . .'

Exasperated, Tess slapped the letter down between us.

Two Sundays after Adam disappeared for the second time, and again sitting either side of the table, but a cold, windy, grey, leaf-swirling day, this one, the river rippling with irritated gun-metal waves, and the fire blazing for the bright comfort of it as much as for warmth.

'It's better than the last one, but honestly!'

'I'm not wasting any more time on it.'

'Suit yourself.'

'All the time I was writing, my hand kept cramping like someone was gripping it hard to try and stop me.'

She laughed. 'The toll-bridge ghost.'

'Superstitious crap.'

'There's supposed to be one. Dad says he's seen her. He says she kind of floats about between this room and the bridge. She was murdered by her lover in a fit of jealous rage. He chucked her body into the river. He was never caught, but she came back to haunt him and did such a good job he went mad and drowned himself. Serve him right too.'

'You're making this up.'

'No I'm not. Dad says only men see her, and only those she likes. Perhaps she's taken a fancy to you and will turn up one night all of a quiver, wanting a bit of spooky nooky.'

'It's the only hope of getting laid around here, that's for sure.'

'Whose fault is that? You could have Gill any time. You still haven't said whether you want her or not.'

'I've told you, I don't know.'

'Janus.'

'Shut it with that, will you!'

'So you'll send this one?'

'Yes.'

Tess stood up. 'Got to go. Sorry. We've company. Mum wants some help.'

Another spoilt Sunday.

'Look at me and smile.'

I said nothing.

'Please yourself. I'll come back after tea, if they go early. They probably will. OK?'

I stood up, went to the fire, stirred a log with my foot. 'Sure.'

At the door Tess turned back. 'Nearly forgot. Dad said to tell you he'll be here tomorrow about ten thirty with Major Finn and an estate agent.'

Major Finn was the landowner and therefore my employer. I'd never seen him.

'What's this, then, a regimental inspection?'

'There's talk of selling bits of the estate. Now he's not getting a lot in tolls the major needs the money.'

'But he'd never sell the house or the bridge, would he? He can't.'

'Dunno. Dad said will you make sure to tidy up and mind your manners while they're here.'

I knuckled my forelock. 'Yes, mum,' and bowing, 'know me place, mum.'

When she'd gone I kicked the grotty armchair, then tore up my letter to Gill and chucked the pieces into the fire.

❖ 2 ❖

They turned up next morning three-quarters of an hour late, the major, once he had struggled out of the estate agent's red BMW, refusing help from Bob Norris with a growl, and supporting a geriatric hip with a swarthy stick. An aged hangover from the Second World War, like a museum exhibit on a day out. His beetroot face with hawk nose and bristly grey moustache was topped off with a fraying panama hat. A crumpled tweed shooting jacket hung from his body as if he had shrunk inside it, which in a way, I suppose, he had. His baggy heavy-duty light brown corduroy trousers were stained an unappetizing yellow at the crotch. His feet clumped in robust ox-blood brogues. A mobile fossil he might be but he still talked in words clipped sharp enough to slice across a parade ground. There was about him an assumption of authority you just knew he'd been born with. Somehow I couldn't help liking him, even though I didn't want to.

Which is more than I can say for the estate agent, a thirtyish, blue-pinstriped oleaginous creep. Podgy and suntan-brown as well as greasy, he'd just been holidaying, he had to tell us, somewhere in the Caribbean, Dominica I think he said, and kept finding opportunities to slip offhand references to the place into the chat. He sleazed around the major, whom he treated, beneath his unctuous surface, with a condescension betrayed in his eyes and in his sneering answers to the major's questions. 'No, no, sir, that sort of thing went out years ago! . . . You've rather let the property decline, not a wise tactic, major, if I may say so. You'll be well advised to give it a good going over with a paintbrush, if nothing else . . . We'll do the best we can for you, major – there's always a dumb punter around who'll buy anything, if you know how to sell it.' 'Your job, your job,' commanded the major as to a parade (he was hard of hearing as well as regimental). 'And we'll do it, sir, we'll do it, leave it to me!' mimicked Brown-and-Greasy.

I watched him, and thought of them at school, with their careers advice. 'Banking is safe. Or you might like to follow in your father's footsteps and become a solicitor, or a barrister even. There's the stock market of course, but it's very competitive, which is hardly you, is it? Accountancy might suit you, that's fairly solid, though your maths isn't up to much, but it's a nicely paid profession. Or computing, what about that? Or business management? Or you could do worse than property and estate agenting. Pays well and you could combine it with the law and do well in both areas.'

Watching him, I heard them banging on about earning power and status and career prospects and security, and knew that oleaginous prat was what they meant, what they wanted me to become, and rejected it there and then, that very moment, finally, for ever.

I don't mean there's anything intrinsically wrong with the law or accountancy or business management or even handling property. What's wrong is why Brown-and-Greasy and his kind do it. As a means to something else. To money for money's sake, and living off the fat at other people's expense, usually the people who actually produce things that make the money the B-and-G brigade are after. They're bloodsuckers. And they have the cheek to parade about as if they are the ones who matter, the ones who are superior, the ones who make the world turn. When what they really are is a drain on the rest of us. Parasites. We'd be better off without them.

An hour after they'd gone, Bob Norris returned. I was reading by the fire.

'No more easy life for you, sonny boy,' he said, in no mood for jokes. 'The major's in a huff.'

'How come?'

'That flaming agent stirred him up. I knew he'd cause trouble. The major wants the place renovated and completely repainted, inside and out. I'll bring in a builder for the renovation work but you'll have to do the painting. And a proper job, mind, not just to make it look a bit better.'

'On my own?'

'He'll do another inspection in three weeks.'

'I'll never finish by then.'

'Do the best you can. He'll probably forget. Can't remember when yesterday was most of the time.'

'What about some help?'

'Think yourself lucky you're still here. He's laying off more men. We're down to three. Three! Used to be fifteen only two years ago.'

'But if I can't get it done?'

'Don't cross your bridges . . .'

'I'm not a professional decorator, you know that.'

'You'll manage. Learn as you go. Any problems, ask. I'll keep an eye when I can.'

'And I have to take the tolls as well, remember.'

'Look, son, stop moaning. There aren't many most of the day now. Hardly worth collecting at all.'

'I'm not happy about this, Mr Norris.'

'No, well, who is. Life's like that, you'll find. Just get on with it or do the other thing. And I've no more time to waste chewing the rag with you. The builder will be in tomorrow. There'll be a van out this afternoon with the gear you'll need. Get started as soon as it's been. Do the outside first while the weather's as good as it's going to be.'

❖ 3 ❖

'He's in a really filthy mood,' Tess said two days later when she stopped off on her way from school. I was stripping down the window frames at the front. 'He's upset with what's happening. He's even talking of looking for another job. He's too young to retire, but he's probably too old to find anything else. He's worked on the estate all his life. And Grandad before him. Mum says it would kill him if he had to leave.'

'He was pretty ratty with me this afternoon, that's for sure. Not enough done, and what was done not done right. He's never been like this before. It's hopeless on my own, but he won't listen. And besides that, the bloody builder expects me to be his labourer.'

'I'll give you a hand at the weekend.'

'You've got your own job on Saturdays. You need the money. And I don't care what your dad says, I'm taking Sundays off.'

'A couple of Saturdays won't matter that much. It's hellish boring anyway.'

'It's not exactly a laugh a minute decorating this place.'

'More fun than Tesco's though. I couldn't stand it at all if it wasn't for the other girls.'

'Wouldn't mind if I was doing it for a good reason. But so they can sell the place! You know what Brown-and-Greasy said? "Make a nice little bijou residence, major, for a London weekender."'

'What's a bijou residence?'

'I didn't know either.'

'But you looked it up.'

'Something small and elegant and tasteful, and then in italics: *often ironic*.'

'Piss-taking, you mean?'

'It'd be a crime. I know it needs doing up, but not like that. I mean, there's a whole history here. I hadn't thought about it till this happened. Hundreds of years of people crossing the river, millions of them, probably, by now. Talk about ghosts! I mean, think of it, all those feet tramping across the bridge. And people living in this house watching them coming and going and taking the tolls, hundreds of thousands of pounds, and hearing the gossip and the news and keeping the bridge in good shape and watching the river and the boats going up and down, and the river flooding and even freezing sometimes, and being part of all that. So now what do they want to do? Turn it into a tarted-up Wendy house for some part-time prat with money

42

to burn who couldn't care less about what it's been, what it *stands for*. Something to be bought and sold and pulled down or chucked away or made into whatever the owner wants. This house and your dad, they're no different really. They've both been here all their lives. But that doesn't matter any more. Because what it all comes down to in the end is money and who has it and who doesn't, and how you get more of it, and if you can't or you don't want to, hard cheese, get stuffed.'

Tess was staring at me, all surprised eyes.

'Haven't seen you so worked up before.'

'No, well, haven't felt so strongly about anything for a bit.'

'Almost like you're enjoying it. I didn't think this place meant that much to you.'

'Neither did I till this week and having to stand there and watch Brown-and-Greasy poking about. It was obscene. I wanted to hit him.'

'He got on Dad's nerves as well.'

'I could see he was seething inside. But he couldn't do anything about it either.'

'Look, I've got to go. Bags of homework.'

I went with her to her bike.

'What're you going to do?' she asked through her helmet when she was ready to go.

'What can I do? What your dad tells me, that's all. I sure as hell don't want to pack up and go home.'

'Dad says it might all cool off in a week or two. The major's old, he forgets.'

'Brown-and-Greasy won't let him. Not while there's a nice fat commission in it.'

'You never know.'

'Optimist.'

'Pessimist.'

'Biker.'

'Janus.' ·

Brown-and-Greasy had arrived like a blight. 'Few responsibilities,' the ad for my job had promised. 'A cushy little number,' Bob Norris had said at my interview. Both were true until B-and-G came poking around. Then, suddenly, I could do as I liked no longer but from morning till night had to scrape at walls, and Polyfill damaged plaster, and glass-paper woodwork, and for a week act as cursed-at labourer for a sour-faced chippy ('You can't tell an awl from your arse, lad') while he replaced rotten skirting and floorboards and rehung doors and refurbished window frames, and, when he'd finished, I fetched and carried for a grumpy bricky while he repaired the living-room fireplace and chimney ('It's a wonder the frigging place hasn't burned down').

From cleaned-up neglect in which I could do as I liked, the house was transformed into a swirl of throat-clogging decorator's dust, a derangement of tools and gear, a rubbish tip of builder's waste, an echo-chamber of banging and sawing and the manic thump of Radio 1 without which apparently neither the chippy nor the bricky could function. As neither could they without mugs of coffee and cans of beer it was my job to serve up at regular intervals, like every hour, during the day.

By the Wednesday of the second week ABG (After Brown-and-Greasy) I was on my own again, left to paint the entire building inside and out, two undercoats and one gloss, ceilings and all. (Have you ever painted a ceiling? Even with non-drip it's murder.) It would take, I reckoned, four weeks' solid slog. Certainly till well after Christmas.

❖ 4 ❖

Mid afternoon, Thursday of the second week ABG. A clouded glowering day but dry, and warm enough to work outside, painting the roadside living-room window frames. There'd been very few tolls since early morning, even fewer than usual; and no movement on the river, the holiday boats being all laid up by this time of year. Even Bob Norris hadn't called.

Feeling lonely, abandoned, hard-done-by, I was brooding in the flat-headed way you get into (well I do anyway) while doing a monotonous physical job all by yourself when I spotted a movement in the house. I had to press my face close to the glass to see clearly, for the room was gloomy. The toll-bridge ghost, I thought, stupidly. But no, and yes, there he is, Adam, large as life, standing at the table, scoffing bread and chicken bits left over from my midday meal.

'Hoi!' I shout and bang on the window. He turns, sees me, waves, turns back to his – my! – food.

I rush inside, and confront him from the living-room doorway. 'What the hell d'you think you're doing?'

He flashes The Grin. 'How d'you mean?'

'Don't start that again.'

44

'What?'

I point the paintbrush I've forgotten is in my hand. 'Eating that!'

He drops the food as if he's suddenly been told it's poisoned. 'Sorry! Thought it was leftovers.'

'It is. Oh, never mind. Finish it now. What've you done with the boat?'

'Boat? What boat?'

'*The* boat. *Our* boat.'

Mouth stuffed full again, he shakes his head, frowning.

'Christ! The boat you took.'

He swallows, which somehow at that moment seems the most insulting thing he could do. 'Me? Don't know nothing about a boat. Walked here along the river from the pub. A bloke bought me a drink. Wanted me to go with him. Do him a little favour. Offered fifty quid. But I'm not that desperate.'

'But you took it.'

'Would you turn down a free drink?'

'The boat. Three weeks ago.'

'What? No, not me, sorry.'

'Course you did! When Tess and I got back, after you'd caused the trouble at the Pike, you'd gone. Disappeared. With our boat. With other stuff as well, you might remember. Including my clothes. The ones you're still wearing, I think. God, what a mess they're in. Where the hell have you been?'

He's staring at me blank-faced. Not even The Grin.

'What're you on about?'

'The boat, dammit!'

'Somebody else, mate, not me.'

'Jesus, I don't believe this!'

'Well, they could have. You don't know, do you?' He's suddenly very agitated, distressed, as if he's just woken up and doesn't like what he's found. 'You weren't here, were you? You've just said you were out. You didn't see me go, did you? So how d'you know I took the boat? Anybody could've done it. So I took some stuff. What's a bit of food? And these clothes, well . . . Anyway, I don't know nothing about no boat. All right?'

'Tell that to Tess. See if she believes you. It's her dad's boat as it happens. She'll be here in a minute.'

As suddenly as he'd turned sour he's his usual self again – or what I thought then was his usual self: laid back, smiling that annoyingly

45

handsome smile.

'You're dripping,' he says.

Jackson Pollock squiggles cover the floor at my feet, expressionist doodle of my feelings while I've been standing there.

'Shit!' I scrub up the mess with the cloth I keep ready for the purpose, not yet having learned the trick of painting without dribbling.

'Want a hand?' Adam says when I'm upright again.

My instinct is to say no, just get out of here. But his incorrigibility, what my mother calls bare-faced cheek, makes me sigh and even smile, and in that short pause it suddenly occurs to me that he might be useful. So instead of chucking him out I say, 'Why not. I'm taking any help that's going. You owe me anyway.'

'Great!' He might just have been given a present he's wanted for years. 'Where do I start?'

'Finish the window I'm working on. It'll soon be too dark to see properly. While you're doing that, I'll get some more wood for the fire. And listen —' He's taking the brush from me. Pongs like a hedge-bottom. Can't have washed for days. 'Do me a favour —'

'Sure.'

'If you decide to disappear again, leave the brush behind, will you? I can't afford to pay for a replacement.'

'I'm not going nowhere,' he says. 'Not me. It'll be nice and toasty in here tonight.'

I don't reply, didn't say, 'Who says you're staying here tonight?' or 'You've got another think coming, mate' or any of the things my guts want me to say. Instead, I smile to myself and go down to the woodstore for logs. If this mutt likes painting so much, I think to myself, then let him. The more he does the sooner the job is finished. Then I'll chuck him out and get back to normal again. Tess calls me Janus so Janus I'll be. To guard bridges maybe you have to be. To guard yourself, come to that.

But I didn't know what I'd let myself in for.

❖ 5 ❖

When you keep a bridge you develop a third ear tuned to listening for approaching vehicles. I knew the sound of Tess's bike as well as I knew her voice; heard her coming over the bridge while I was splitting logs in the woodstore. (This was the half-basement under the house formed by the bank falling steeply down from the road to the garden-river level. The loo was in there too, and brass-monkey cold it could be in winter, as well as tools and other gear and the tin bath that's used in a page or two.)

By the time I'd lugged the laden log basket up the stairs into the house, she's talking to Adam. I see them through the window. She's taken her helmet off, which she never bothers to do unless she plans to stay a while, and is flirting her hair at him, and laughing, and giving him the eye.

Adam is replying at full throttle with The Grin, The Hand Run Through the Hair, and The Pelvic Thrust. And they're performing a slow-motion ring-a-ring-a-roses; the courting dance of Homo sapiens.

I dump the logs and go out.

'Have you asked him?' I say.

She doesn't take her eyes off him. 'He didn't do it.'

'You believe him!'

Adam is preening. I'm sure The Grin has stretched round to the back of his head. The Teeth flash white semaphore in the dusk.

'I remember now.' She looks at me at last. She's fizzing. 'You were in the boat. I came out and talked to you. We decided to pick blackberries. You climbed out and off we went, but you didn't tie up. I expect it just floated away.'

'So it's my fault now!'

'No, I didn't mean that. I should have noticed.'

'Oh, thanks! Maybe you should have noticed that I'd already tied up before you came out.'

'You had?'

'Yes.'

'Oh, well, I don't remember. And what's it matter. Listen, I was just saying to Adam –' She turns, they do a Grin-Giggle-Hands-Through-Hair-Eyeballing-Pelvicthrusting exchange, and then she looks at me again. 'I'll nip home, have tea and come back about seven, OK? We can talk then.'

But does not stay for an answer.

'Good thinking,' Adam says.

'See you,' Tess says, and winks at me as she passes.

[– I know you've got to tell this story the way you remember it, but this last scene just isn't right. I wasn't the way you describe me at all. I was never that flirty. I know you'll tell all the embarrassing details when the time comes, but at this point I don't recognize myself. And if you get me wrong here, aren't you likely to get me even more wrong later when more important things are happening?

I know people remember the same events quite differently. And I know you're trying to tell what happened to Adam and Gill and me and yourself the way you saw it then, rather than the way you think about it now, but still you can't tell it *only* like that, can you? Well, yes, you can but that will give a very distorted view of us.

You're always going on about how one person's understanding of anything is only part of the truth – how no one ever really knows everything, or ever knows enough. So how are you going to get more than your own partial understanding of what went on between all four of us into your version of our story?

What I know is, in case you go on getting me as wrong as you just have, I reserve the right to tell my bit of the story in my own way at some point.]

❖ 6 ❖

As we watch Tess putter away, the stink of hedge-bottom twitches my nose.

'Look,' I say, 'you're not ponging the place out again. Before we eat you're having a bath.'

'Yes, Dad,' Adam says. 'Lead me to the water.'

There was no bathroom complete with all mod cons, only one of those galvanized tin tubs, wider at one end than the other, like a man-sized sardine can without a lid. Or a coffin, depending on your mood. You see them in old photos of working-class houses, where they're usually hanging on the wall outside the back door. *The Road to Wigan Pier* through D.H. Lawrence country. The toll-house tub was kept in the basement, had to be carried up to the living room when needed, where it had to be filled by using a length of hosepipe from the only hot tap in the place, which was at the kitchen sink.

There was an immersion heater in a tank in the roof above the sink, but as I had to pay for the electricity out of my piffling wage, I used it as little as possible. An electric kettle was enough for ordinary purposes, or, better still because it cost nothing if the fire was in, an old iron cauldron Bob Norris had given me, which I kept simmering on the hearth.

Two or three times during my pre-Adam weeks Mrs Norris took pity and persuaded me to have a bath in their house. 'I'm sure it's easier than all that palaver, and you can give yourself a good soak,' she said and, laughing, 'You must look like a man half drowned in his coffin sat in that affair.' I've always liked Mrs Norris. She has the knack of being kind without making you feel obligated or done good to.

If I hoped all the palaver of bathing would put Adam off staying more than a night I was wrong. He revels in it like a kid in his play pool. And makes about as much mess.

While I clear up the painting gear from where he's dumped it (labourer now even to my own labourer, I grumble to myself), he prepares a place in front of the fire, lugs the tub up from the basement, strips, then ponces about with the length of hosepipe, obscenely camping up a weird song which he's learned from God knows where.

> 'Old Roger is dead and gone to his grave,
> He, Hi, gone to his grave.
> They planted an apple-tree over his head.
> The apples grew ripe and ready to drop,
> He, Hi, ready to drop.
> There came an old woman of Hippertihop,
> He, Hi, Hippertihop,
> She began a-picking them up,
> He, Hi, Hippertihop.
> Old Roger up and gave her a knock,
> He, Hi, gave her a knock.
> Which made the old woman go hippertihop.
> He, Hi, Hippertihop.
> He . . . Hi . . . Hip . . . hip . . . hippertee . . . hop!'

Funny, raunchy, lightly done – I can't help watching and I can't help laughing. Even though a part of me wants to stop him – for I didn't like the way he was taking my place over, turning it into a kind of theatre for himself.

Of himself would be more accurate. What fixed me was, yes, his energy and the comedy of his randy send-up of this silly song (which I only discovered afterwards is a nursery rhyme – God, the things we stuff into children's heads!). He'd make an amazing actor, the kind who compels attention all the time, not just because of his talent, but because of his unpredictable personality, the game he plays of pretending to act a part which is actually a disguise for revealing a truth about himself.

49

Yet at the same time he's so crafty in displaying the disguise that the audience are never quite sure whether they're seeing the character who belongs in the play or the actor himself.

It was then, that evening, that I was won over by Adam. Won over *to* him I mean. Yes, sure, for a while I kept up a pretence of not wanting him around, but it was only pretence. Another pretending, this time as self-protection. From that evening on he fascinated me. As I watched him perform I felt he was ruled by some deeply hidden, risky secret. And I wanted to know what it was.

❖ 7 ❖

When he's done, and we've cleared up the mess he's made and I've cooked beans on toast, we sit either side of the table, Adam's skin still glowing.

'Look,' I say, 'there's some things we better sort out.'

'Like what?'

'Like I don't know anything about you.'

A suspicious look while he shovels beans, his fork in a fist-grip.

'Does it matter?'

'Yes, if you're staying. No promises though.'

'Cautious bugger.'

'Cautious maybe, anal screwer never. For a start, what's your name?'

'. . . Adam!'

'But Adam what?'

'Adam in the back seat. Adam in the hay. Adam on the kitchen table.'

'Groan. I meant your last name.'

'Haven't made my mind up yet.'

'Oh, come on! Stop messing about.'

'It's true. Never knew my parents. Brought up in a children's home. They made me leave when I was sixteen. So I reckon I can have whatever name I like. Nobody else cares a toss so what's the odds.'

'Well, how old are you now?'

'Seventeen. Just.'

'And what have you done since they chucked you out?'

'Odd jobs and that. But I wanted to travel a bit so I come down here. Haven't had much luck with a job though.'

I gave him a long stare.

'That's not what you said before.'

He didn't look at me. Went on shovelling beans.

'When?'

'In the boat, going to the Pike.'

'What did I say?'

'That you'd been chucked out of home by your father because you were always having rows and he was unemployed and you had two sisters still at school.'

Now The Grin. The Teeth. The Eyes. The Unblinking Gaze.

I gaze back, unblinking, unsmiling, daring him. 'Not that I believed you.'

'No? . . . Yes, well, I made it up, didn't I.'

'Why?'

'Don't want everybody knowing your personal details. Never know who you're talking to. People take advantage.'

'Have I?'

The Grin vanishes, leaving a blank-faced cold look, and suddenly occupying the eyes the other Adam, the one I'd always sensed behind The Grin – wary, troubled, a little frightened, the one who made me curious.

'Not yet,' the other Adam said.

Then The Grin banishes him again.

I say, trying to keep my own eyes steady, 'Why should I believe the orphan story?'

He shrugs, lifts his plate and, his eyes still on me, licks it clean.

'Good, that,' he says, putting the plate down.

I scowl.

He brazens it out. 'Want me to wash up?'

I don't respond.

'All right,' he says after a long pause, 'I'll tell you. But you have to promise to keep it to yourself. I don't want other people knowing. Not Tess, neither.'

'Why?'

'I just don't, that's all.'

'Depends what it is.'

'Nothing bad. I just don't want people knowing.'

'Why me, then?'

'Well, like you said, you've been OK.'

'And you want to stay.'

'Yes, well, that as well.'

'So?'

'Promise.'

'Cross my heart.'

He huffs and toys with his fork for a while, then sighs and says, 'I was adopted. When I was little. A baby. They told me when I was eight. All this stuff about how it was better for me than for other kids because they chose me. Other kids – their parents just had to take whatever they got. They were all right, my parents. The people I called my parents. They were nice and everything. But I just couldn't accept it. I hated being adopted. It felt like a disease. I wanted to know who my real parents were but they wouldn't tell me. Said they didn't know. When I was grown up, they said, I could try and find out for myself, if I still wanted to know. I hated them for that. I thought they ought to find out for me. I thought they ought to want to know for themselves. I mean, wouldn't you – wouldn't you want to know? Where you come from? Why they, why they got rid of you? Had to. Or wanted to. Or were made to. Sometimes that happens, doesn't it, young girls, they make them give their kids away. Don't they? Anyway, I kept asking, kept on and on, wanting to know, and them saying they couldn't find out, weren't *allowed* to find out. I didn't believe them. This went on till I was thirteen, fourteen, and we started having fights about it. I'd shout, call them all the names I could think of, break the place up, do anything to upset them. I was only trying to make them find out. I ran away once, tried to, but the police caught me before I got far. I hadn't planned it, just did it on the spur of the minute, so I bungled it. But that decided me. I planned the next time, every detail. Day, time, what to take, where to go, how to get there, how to cover my tracks, not leave clues, even disguised myself – dyed my hair, wore glasses, changed my clothes as soon as I was out of town. I reckoned they'd find out what clothes were missing and describe them to the police, thinking that's what I was wearing. So I'd bought some things specially and stashed them in a hut and changed into them. I saved money for months. Read about living rough. Did everything I could think of to make sure I'd get away and not be picked up again. Just wanted to vanish. And then, when they'd forgotten about me, or given up, and I could move around openly again, then I'd find out about my real parents. And when I know that, then I'll decide who I belong to. What my last name is. Who I am.'

He pushed his plate away, took a drink from his mug of coffee, wiped his mouth with the back of his other hand.

'That was six months ago. I ran out of money pretty soon. And it wasn't that easy keeping out of sight. Tried Birmingham for a bit but that was pretty foul. Tried London and that was worse. Everybody's out to get what they can from you. Some of the other kids were OK. But the guys around. Geez! Want everything, from your head to your arse. It's bad news there, I tell you. I wasn't having it, not me, might as well be dead. So I went on the tramp. Hedges are better than streets. Don't reckon much to people neither. Mostly out for what they can get, what they can do you for. In the country you can usually scrounge something. Anyhow, I survived, didn't I.'

He laughs, but humourlessly.

'Thing is, you get tired, you get really tired. You just ache for a place to stay, for somewhere you don't have to get out of in the morning, somewhere you can crawl back into at night, somewhere that's dry and warm, somewhere safe. They don't tell you about that in the survival books. Don't tell you what it's like to feel you're just a bag of rubbish, kicked around, useless, ugly, smelly, in everybody's road. Don't tell you nothing about that in books because you can't know what it's like, how bad it is, till you're there, till it's happened to you. And they don't tell you about it, I suppose, because nobody can describe hell.'

In the silence that followed I could neither speak nor move. The fire crackled in the hearth. The river surged under the bridge. Adam toyed with his mug, not looking at me. His skin shone, clean and fresh from his bath, his wet black hair hugging his round head.

His physical presence was almost overpowering. I sat looking at him and knew that this time I couldn't turn him out. Whatever his being here meant, its meaning included me. For better or worse and whether I liked it or not, there was no escape. Adam had come to stay.

Letters

. . . writing from the office, as there is news of your mother which I must give you without letting on to her. She doesn't want you to know, but in my judgement it is best that you should so that you are prepared when you come home for Christmas.

The fact is, your mother is going through a rough patch. Nothing you need be seriously worried about – she's not suffering from a life-threatening disease. The problem is more emotional and psychological. But she's going to need a great deal of support and understanding till she is out of the rough and back on the fairway again.

The best way of explaining the problem is to give you the background, which means telling you something your mother and I have kept from you, believing there was no point in your being burdened with it. However, as it is partly the cause of your mother's current difficulty, it is best that you know.

I might add that this is not an easy letter to write. Please forgive any infelicities.

You are of course our only son, but you are not our only child. Two years before you were born we had a daughter. We called her Amy. Sadly, she lived only five weeks. She died a cot death. Your mother blamed herself at the time, and has gone on blaming herself ever since, saying that if she had been more attentive we would not have suffered such a dreadful loss.

Nothing anyone has said – the doctors, close friends, or myself – has ever relieved your mother of the guilt she feels: I needn't tell you that there was absolutely no question of your mother being in the slightest neglectful. She doted on Amy, as she always has on you, and gave her all the attention anyone could expect. Cot deaths are far from rare and the cause not at all understood. It was just another of those unfair accidents of life.

54

The weeks after Amy's death were not easy for either of us, but slowly we helped each other back to something like normal, though your mother was never again the carefree lass she was when we were first married. Your mother and I were completely in love when we married. We were at our happiest in each other's company and never liked being apart. We shared the same interests and even liked the same friends – which I know you have already noticed isn't at all usual! After Amy's death it wasn't quite the same, I'm sorry to say. We remained, and still are, as devoted to each other as before. But it was as though some part of us, something of our completeness, had been taken away and it was impossible to fill the gap.

We did gain something, though, and I think this is also worth telling you while I am about it, as it is not the kind of subject you and I tend to talk about but which might be useful to you in your own life. What we gained was a different sense of the love that first brought us together. As I look back on it now, I realize that we might not have been *in love* at all but only have liked each other very much. From my experience as a lawyer I can tell you that many couples mistake liking each other for being in love. The divorce courts are full of those who discovered the difference too late.

In the months after Amy died we learned that we needed each other because we loved each other, and not the other way around. For whatever it was that helped us through those awful weeks was more than only liking each other could have made possible.

But your mother never recovered from the loss of her baby. Once we were on an even keel again, we both hoped that having another child would help heal the wound. And for a long time after you were born she did seem more like her old self. You were, as your mother has often told you, a wonderful little chap. Amy, in her short life, had been difficult. Her birth was difficult, she often cried for hours at night and was exhausting during the day. You were just the opposite. Your birth was quick and easy, you were always good-natured, quiet, a sound sleeper, and you continued like that as the years passed and you started school.

Of course your mother gave you every waking moment of her life, never leaving you alone for an instant. Even at night she wanted you beside her. I remember it was only with the greatest difficulty that I finally persuaded her to put you to bed in a room of your own. You were more than three by then, long past the age when most children sleep by themselves.

You see, the truth is that your mother invested everything in you, all of herself and her hopes for the future. We did try to have more children – I thought it would be a good idea from all points of view and your mother wanted it – but without success. And I suppose the disappointment of knowing there could be no more in the family strengthened her attachment to you.

I have to confess that I often worried about your mother being so wrapped up in you but I hesitated to say anything, for how could I know that my worries were anything but jealousy – there were times when I was very jealous of the attention she gave you. However, in your later childhood, I did try to make sure you had some time away from your mother to prepare you and her for the break when it came. Not all of my efforts were appreciated! You'll remember the Scouts was a great failure. As was my attempt to turn you into a golfing fan. But the school trips to France and Greece were useful, and you did enjoy our boating holiday on our own together when we taught ourselves to sail on the river not far from where you are now. In fact we sailed under your toll bridge more than once – well, not 'sailed' exactly, but dismasted and motored through, the arch being so low.

Your mother was aware of what I was doing. I didn't hide it from her. And one thing she never let on to you was how much she dreaded the day when you left home for good. She even found those times you and I were away very difficult to bear. She knew they were trial runs for the time when you left home permanently.

Nevertheless, she wasn't prepared for your departure this summer. She thought you would be at home for a year or two yet. And for some illogical reason, she doesn't think of being at university as leaving home. But your decision to go for the toll-bridge job took her by surprise and the way you stripped your room and stowed away all your gear – your boyhood things and your books – before you left upset her further. It seemed so definite, so final. Almost like a rejection of us and of your home.

I'm sure that is not how you meant it. And honestly, I'm not laying blame or saying what has happened since you left is in any way your fault at all. Please believe that. How hard it is to explain all this and not sound as if one *is* laying blame. (It has often struck me, as I sit in this office every day helping people sort out their problems, how bad I am at sorting out my own. Perhaps the truth is that none of us is much good at helping ourselves.)

But all that is water under the bridge, if you'll pardon the cliché.

The bare facts of the current situation are these. Soon after you left your mother began to behave oddly. At first it was nothing more worrying than sudden outbursts of tears for no apparent reason. At these times she would weep uncontrollably in the way she did in the days after Amy died, a weeping that seemed full of rage as well as sorrow. Then she began having terrifying nightmares in which she quite literally tried to climb the wall in her efforts to escape apparently nameless fears. These woke us both with the violence of her movements and the sound of her screams.

Then one day two weeks ago I was telephoned at the office by the manager of Binns. He had your mother with him. She had been apprehended shoplifting. As a result of that I discovered she had been stealing things for days previously from a number of shops. She had the stuff hidden away in your room – all baby things like talcum and clothes and toys.

Binns didn't prosecute, thank goodness. They are as familiar in their trade as I am in mine with this syndrome. Middle-aged women are sometimes afflicted with it. It goes with the menopause. I don't know whether you know anything about the female menopause. I doubt if they taught you about it at school. Though I can't think why not when you consider that my medical reference book begins its entry on the subject with the words: 'Sometimes called the change of life, the menopause is the middle-aged counterpart of adolescence, and its effects are comparable, and as natural.' No wonder a lot of middle-aged parents have trouble with their teenage children, if they are all suffering from their own versions of adolescence at the same time! Not excluding you and me and your mother. I suppose it is happening more than it used to because these days so many women don't have children until they are into their thirties.

Normally, or at least as far as I understand it, I'm not a professional expert, the menopause goes along with having hot flushes, when the woman blushes for no identifiable reason and often in a way that embarrasses her, and breaks out into very heavy sweats. This is often followed by bouts of cold shivers brought on, apparently, by a terrible nervousness, an anxiety that your mother says makes her feel breathless with panic. At these times she gets quite worked up about small things that actually don't matter, like forgetting to put the money out for the milkman or mislaying her reading glasses, and she worries about the house burning down while she's out shopping or burglars getting in when she's on her own.

Then there are other symptoms: headaches and bouts of feeling dizzy, and she sometimes finds it hard to concentrate on anything – even on TV, which is saying something. She can also be grumpy and easily offended, which, as you know, is quite uncharacteristic of her. For example, she saw me brush a cobweb out of a corner of the living room yesterday and became quite agitated, saying I was criticizing her housekeeping. Her appetite swings about as well; one day she'll vastly over-eat and another day she'll hardly eat anything at all. She says she doesn't decide these things, they simply happen.

As I say, all this is entirely normal, according to the doc, and is suffered by thousands of middle-aged women. The shoplifting isn't exactly normal, of course, but isn't unusual either, and not intentional. Your mother didn't plan it or do it for gain. The truth is the whole unhappy event seems to have nothing whatever to do with what anyone wants, least of all your mother, but is simply a matter of biology.

I say *simply*. Of course there is nothing simple about it. Knowing the background helps a little, I hope, but certainly doesn't explain anything. All I want to do in writing to you like this is to prepare you for when you come home and to ask that you try just to accept it, and help your mother by letting her behave in whatever way she feels she must, without making life worse for her or making her feel guilty or a failure because of what is happening.

It is something we should all three talk about together. Your mother and I have been learning to do this since the incident at Binns and I think it would help us all if you could talk about it too. But that must come from your mother to begin with, and at the moment she fears what your reaction will be if you know what has happened. More than anything, she fears the loss of your love and respect. That is why this letter must be only between the two of us. I'm sure in my own mind, dear lad, that you're mature enough now to cope with this kind of crisis.

If you'd like to talk, phone me at the office about five one evening, or write to me here if that suits you better, marking the envelope 'Private and Confidential'.

Your mother will give you the everyday news when you ring as usual on Sunday . . .

❖ 2 ❖

. . . that you'll let us come and pick you up. But you sounded a touch fed up, darling, I know that tone in your voice, are you sure you are all right? Are they working you too hard, I expect they are from what you said about decorating. It is such a silly business when you could be doing so much better here but I have promised your father I won't go on about it so will say no more now.

Your father also says I should tell you that I haven't been too well lately, nothing serious, don't worry, a temporary blip due to my age, which comes to us all, sweetheart, I'm afraid. I've been just a little off colour, that's all, and not feeling myself. By the time you come home I expect it will all be over and I'll be fit as a lop again. We can't expect to be on top of things all the time can we, everyone has their lows, as you know only too well, my darling, but you are getting over it, that's the great thing, so maybe the toll-bridge job hasn't been all a waste of time.

Now, my dear, you must let me know what you'd like for Christmas, or give me a hint at least, it's so silly to give unwanted gifts to someone of your advanced age, being, as your father insists on telling me every day, no longer a child, just so they'll come as a surprise. Much better give something that's wanted, so do say and I'll get it. I saw a very nice calfskin wallet that might be useful in Dressers this week when Mrs Fletcher was hunting for a Parker ballpoint for her Brian, who, by the by, has upset the applecart by announcing that he doesn't think teaching is his cup of tea after all and wants to leave college and go into computer software, which he says would pay better and have better prospects and suit him more. It seems his first taste of the classroom put him right off children, but then he never did have much patience which you certainly need with children, so perhaps it will be better for the children in the end if he does something else, though at the moment his mother doesn't agree and is very down about it.

I have always thought I would have liked teaching and even been good at it for I love children, as you know, and do have patience I think I can say without being immodest, but all I wanted at 16 was to get a job and have a lively social life and went into secretarial work instead, where anyway I met your father so some good came of it. Though this last few weeks since you left I have been thinking how nice it would have been to have a profession to take up again in my middle years. Your father suggests I should find a job of some kind anyway, as I have so much time to spare, not having you to look after, though my office skills are pretty rusty now, but I expect I could soon buff them up with a bit of effort and perhaps a refresher course. I quite fancy becoming proficient with a word processor, which these days is a requirement, and office life can be enjoyable if the place is well run and the other staff amenable. One thing for sure is that I wouldn't want to work in your father's office again, he's far too relaxed with the juniors if you ask me.

Well, we can talk about all this at Christmas and you can advise me. After all, new horizons might buck me up, don't you think . . .

A Kind of
Talisman

❖ 1 ❖

Next morning I woke regretting that I'd given in the night before.
And to such a sob story, even if it were true. In the cold grey grainy
fog of a late November dawn, when your clothes are clammy and the
house smells of tacky new paint laced with the heavy sweaty tang of
decorator's dust, then reigniting the living-room fire from the remains
of last night's cinders and getting washed in tepid water at the kitchen
sink and making breakfast are tedious enough. Having to attend to
someone else as well – the space he occupies, somehow making the place
seem smaller than it is, too small now, his coming and going, his noises
and smells, his grunts and sighs and coughs and sniffs and belches and
farts, his behaviour at the sink, splashing water onto the bench where
I'm trying to cut bread and make toast for HIM, dammit, as well as
myself – having to *think* instead of zombie your way into the day
was enough to make me wish I hadn't been such a soft touch.

To make things worse, while Adam scoffed bread and honey as
if stoking up for a winter famine, I got to reckoning the financial
cost of letting him stay. Two can live as cheaply as one? Tell it to
the birds. Two can live as cheaply as two. Or three, if one of them
eats like Adam did that morning.

I soon learned that he usually ate very little, it was just that he
liked snacky bits at times when I didn't – I'm a regular meal, no snacks
eater, due to strict training as a child. In fact, I was the problem. I'd
make plenty for two, serve him as much as myself and he'd leave half,
which I threw away, till I realized after two or three days what was
happening and gradually cut his share down. Not that Adam noticed.
And eventually I learned how much to give him in order to satisfy his
appetite with just enough left over that could safely be kept cold for
him to snack on when he wanted. I even got to the point of enjoying
this secret game. The pleasure came from the skill of judging exactly

61

how much food to make, how much to serve up at the meal and which things in the meal would do for snacks or keep till next day, when I could use them as part of another meal. He liked potatoes, for example, and he liked them done in their jackets in the fire, and he liked them mashed and fried. So I'd do more in their jackets than I knew we'd need, keep the leftovers till next day, when I'd mash them up and fry them as potato pancakes. I don't think he ever noticed that the pancakes were the old potatoes done that way. Which was another part of the game and the pleasure: his not noticing what I'd done. Of course, the weather being cold, stews were good, and keeping a stew pot of cheap scrap-ends going on the fire was easy. I simply chucked in any leftovers so that over a few days it went from being a meaty stew to being a thick vegetable soup. It was cheap and Adam could snack on it whenever he liked.

But this developed over the next few days. That first morning all I could think of was how I wouldn't have enough money to feed us both, even with the stuff Tess gave me and my mother's weekly parcel. But I was too morose to mention it. Just glowered into my tea.

And another thing niggled me.

'We'll have to get you a bed,' I say when we've finished eating.

'I'm not bothered.'

'But I am. The place looks like a dosshouse with you on the floor.'

He doesn't respond.

'And more bedclothes.'

'There's plenty.'

'No, there isn't. I was cold last night. It'll get worse as well, winter coming on.'

And that was the moment when the postman arrived, delivering Dad's letter about Mother.

❖ 2 ❖

'She'll be OK,' Adam says.

'I ought to go home.'

'Why? Your dad says don't.'

'He's just saying that so I won't feel pressured. He's always like that. Do nothing till you have to, that's his motto.'

'I like it! He's right.'

'What do you know about it?'

'OK, don't believe me, ask Tess.'

'No, no! I don't want her to know.'

'Why not? She could help.'

'No, leave it.'

'Why . . .?'

'Because I don't. I don't know why. I just don't, that's all. You said yourself, you don't want everybody knowing your personal details.'

'But Tess is supposed to be a friend.'

'Just shut up about it, will you! You say one word, and that's it, all right?'

'OK, OK, I'm not saying a word.'

'Well, just think on!'

'Calm down, will you. No sweat. I'll be tight as a duck's arse, honest. But at least talk to your dad before you go. Ring him. He says you can.'

'I'm not sure.'

'Yes, you are. Do it.'

'It's too early, he won't be at the office yet.'

'But as soon as he is.'

'There's the tolls.'

'Remember me? I'm here. I'll hold the fort. You'll not be gone for long.'

I dither.

'Told you I'd be useful, didn't I,' Adam says.

'Let's get on with it, then,' I say, clearing the table. 'Bloody painting. We'll never be done in time.'

Adam stands up, stretching in his loose-limbed animal way. 'You worry too much. Relax. Leave it to me. I like painting. You can see where you've been and it passes the time. Everything'll be OK, honest.'

'That a promise?'

'You betcha, squire.'

Suddenly I really am glad he's here. Everyone needs somebody to break the closed circle of his mind. Adam used a blunt instrument and banged his way straight in, no subtlety, no fash about wounded feelings. The quickest form of ventilation. If you can stand the blows. A month before, I couldn't have survived them.

❖ 3 ❖

Dad was adamant. Stay away. Mother would feel worse if I suddenly turned up for whatever excuse and she had to explain. Christmas was the right time. She was expecting me then, was preparing herself for it.

63

I told him about Adam. Or, at least, that I'd made friends with this out-of-work boy who was good at decorating so he was staying for a while to help me get finished.

'You'll need a bit of extra cash then,' Dad said. 'I'll send you something.' I suppose I knew he would and had subconsciously hoped he would. So didn't refuse, but felt a twinge of failure as well as guilt for exploiting him while talking about Mother's trouble.

❖ 4 ❖

Half past ten, Bob Norris appeared. We were busy clearing stuff out of the living room to get it ready for painting.

'Come outside,' he said to me while giving Adam a close inspection. 'Want a word with you.'

He took me to the middle of the bridge and leaned on the parapet, looking down at the water.

'What's this I hear about a friend staying with you? Is that him?'

'He's a good help. I need it if we're to get done in time.'

'How good a friend?'

'He's all right.'

'Known him long?'

'Long enough.'

'In other words, not long enough. You should have asked.'

'I only decided last night. There hasn't been time.'

'Look, son, you've done all right so far. Don't go and spoil it.'

I didn't reply.

'It's a position of trust, you know, yours. There's money involved.'

'We're hardly taking ten quid most days!'

'Ten quid is ten quid, and I've only your word about how much you take.'

'Are you saying I fiddle the books, Mr Norris?'

'No, no! Just the opposite. I trust you. It's this other lad. You're sure he's all right? It's not just money. There's property as well, and the bridge to keep an eye on. And with all this other business, these sackings and plans to sell, it's getting difficult, that's all. I'm having to be extra careful. There's a lot at stake.'

I recognized his tone of voice. The breathiness of anxiety. I'd heard it in my own voice only a couple of hours ago.

I said, 'I'm sorry. I didn't think. Is it OK?'

He stared down at the water and thought for a while before

saying, 'All right. But you'll have to answer if anything goes wrong. So remember, he's your responsibility.'

That word again! Another cold grey regretful realization. But I'd talked myself into it and pride wouldn't let me back out. At least I had enough wit left to say, 'While we're at it, Mr Norris, is there any chance there might be a camp bed or anything going spare somewhere? He's sleeping on the floor.'

It was the only time he smiled. 'I'll see. Might be something in the scout hut.'

'Thanks.'

His smiled faded. A few days before he'd have been joshing me now, but since B-and-G he'd become solemn, bad-tempered even.

'Sure you can manage, two of you, on your pay?'

I shrugged. 'We'll get by.'

He glanced at the toll house, his brows furrowed, lips pursed.

'Everything has its day,' he said.

'Sorry?'

He shook his head. 'Nothing. Just get on as fast as you can. The agent says there's a lot of interest. Wants to start showing the place as soon as things have settled down after New Year.'

He turned away and walked back to his van.

'There might be a sleeping bag as well,' he said as he climbed in.

❖ 5 ❖

'What did he want?' Adam asks.

'To know if I could trust you.'

'What did you say?'

'Yes.'

He smirks. 'And do you?'

'No.'

'Lied, then!'

'Yes.'

'Why?' He's serious now.

'Because I'm an idiot.'

He says nothing for a moment. Then he undoes a silver chain from round his neck and holds it out to me. 'Here, take this.'

'No. What for?'

'Because I want you to. Go on. It's worth a few quid. Real silver, nothing fake.'

'No. Why should I?'

65

'It's OK. It's mine. Didn't nick it, if that's what you're thinking.'

'I don't want it.'

'Wear it. Insurance.'

'Don't be stupid.'

'I mean it.'

'No.'

He moves towards me. I step back.

'Take it, craphead!'

'No!'

He lunges at me, grabs my shirt. I try to push him away but he pulls me to him and tries to get the chain round my neck. I knock his hand away, sending the chain flying across the room. We struggle, saying nothing, wrestling, not half-hearted, not playful, but using all our strength, meaning it. A contest. I am heavier, but he is stronger. The first time I feel his strength. It takes me by surprise. And he is so much tougher than I, harder muscled, and practised, knows what he's doing, where to hold, how to shift balance, when to move. And whereas I am tense, his body stays relaxed, supple all the time.

I feel trapped, become desperate, flay with my hands, swing and punch and strain against him and push. He easily dodges and absorbs and deflects and uses my movements to his own advantage, which makes me feel even more trapped, more a victim.

Soon I'm breathless. And Adam begins applying a painful force, a frightening violence that I don't know how to deal with except in the end by giving in, going limp, allowing him to put me down and sit astride my waist, his knees on my upper arms, like kids do in playground fights.

I stare up at his flushed face, on which a sheen of sweat has broken out, smiling, his eyes full of the pleasure of the fight.

The chain lies within reach. He leans over, causing me to cry out as his knee digs into my bicep, picks up the chain, slips it round my neck, and sits back again, regarding me now with that absent stare which turns his face into a mask.

For two, perhaps even three whole minutes we remain there, silent, unmoving, staring at each other, until able to bear it no longer I say:

'Have you done?'

The Grin then. Adam again. Pushes himself up. I too, dusting myself off. My arms ache from the bony pressure of his knees, and other bruises burn on my body.

66

A car horn tooted. I went out and took the toll. When I got back Adam was busy Polyfilling cracks round the fireplace. Neither of us said anything, not then nor later, about the silver chain. I went on wearing it simply to prevent another bout of wrestling. Or at least that's what I told myself. Every morning as we passed each other on the way to and from washing at the sink, he'd make a show of checking it was still there, and grin and nod, until this daily inspection became a routine, a ritual we would only have noticed had it not been performed.

I still wear his chain, never take it off, now as a kind of talisman, a memento, a charm against the evil comfort of forgetting. Insurance after all, though not of the sort Adam had in mind. Not that it was Adam who gave it to me, as I should have known from that mask-faced absent stare.

Toll-Bridge
Tales

❖ 1 ❖

One day we were painting the bedroom when we heard a noise like the sound of drunken children echoing up the approach road. We dropped our brushes and rushed outside, janitors ready to do a Horatius.

But there was no need of defence. Along the road came a party of about twenty Down's people. Four of them were in wheelchairs. One, a young man who was singing loudly in a strange tuneless falsetto, had no legs.

They weren't drunk on anything but happiness because they were having a trip out on a sharp, frosty, sunny December day. Five or six caretaking adults were sprinkled among them, shepherding them along and tending to the chairborne.

This patter of humanity strode, wobbled, limped, danced, skipped, hopped, rolled in well-behaved disarray towards the two of us, as we stood by habit in the middle of the road outside the toll-house door.

'Hello! Hello!' unembarrassed voices called as they approached. 'It's Timmy's birthday. Happy birthday, dear Timmy, happy birthday to you!'

Timmy was the legless young man.

'This is a toll bridge,' one of the minders said. 'It's very old.'

'As old as Timmy?'

'What's a toll bridge?'

'Dong, dong, dong.'

'You have to pay to cross.'

'Do we have to pay?'

'I haven't no money.'

'Timmy doesn't have to pay, does he, not on his birthday, do you, Timmy?'

We were surrounded, our hands taken and caressed, our arms

stroked. Faces beamed at us, some dribbling, others open, all glad to see us as if coming upon friends.

'You've been painting,' a girl said to me.

'There's a notice that tells who has to pay.'

'Where, what does it say?'

'I've no money today.'

'I like painting. I like the smell. Painting smells like you.'

'Well, it says "Four wheels twenty pence. Lorries and trucks fifty pence. Two wheels and pedestrians free."'

'What are pedestrians?'

'We are pedestrians.'

'Where are you painting? I'd help but it's Timmy's birthday and we're taking him out. He's eighteen.'

'Pedestrians are people walking.'

'Eighteen means you're grown up. I'm fifteen.'

'Four wheels pay,' Adam said, finding his voice and giving in kind. 'Two legs go free.'

'We've two legs.'

'We go free.'

'Timmy's on four wheels though.'

'So is Janice and Rachel and Jason.'

'Oh, Jason, you have to pay. Twenty pence!'

'Do I?'

'And Janice and Rachel.'

'Not Timmy though, eh, it's his birthday.'

'But he's on four wheels. We had to pay to cross the Severn and it was my birthday that day. They didn't make allowances.'

'Allowances.'

'It doesn't mean wheelchairs, does it?'

Adam said, 'No, no. I'll tell you the rule. It's like this. Four wheels pay. Two legs go free. No legs get paid.'

'Get paid!'

'Where does it say that?'

'What – you pay Timmy?'

'And Rachel and Janice and Jason,' Adam said, 'because they can't go on two legs.'

'They can sometimes.'

'But not today,' Adam said.

'Not that far.'

'There you are, Timmy,' Adam said, pulling coins out of his

pocket. 'That's your fare for crossing the bridge. And are you Rachel? OK, that's for you. And Janice. And Jason.'

There was an alarming cheer from the pedestrians.

'I needn't have legs if you don't want me to.'

'We'd better be getting on,' called one of the minders.

'We have to be getting on,' several voices ordered.

'What are you painting?'

'How much did he give you, Rachel?'

'We could come back this way and get some more.'

'What'll you spend it on?'

'I'll save it.'

'Bye.'

'You smell lovely. You could come with me if you like.'

'Come on, Sarah. The man's busy.'

'Kissy kissy.'

'Dong, dong, dong.'

Back inside, Adam grabbed his brush and slashed and slashed at the wall. Paint flew.

'Hey, steady, man, steady!' I shouted, guarding my eyes with an arm. 'What's up, what's the matter?'

He waved his brush towards the bridge and the dying sound of the Down's party. 'That's the matter! That!' A different Adam. The other Adam: the one only in the eyes before, now in this angry, violent moment all of him. 'The sodding rotten unfairness of it.'

'Being born like that?'

'Not their frigging fault. Didn't ask to be born. Life! Bloody life!'

He hurled the brush down and left the room. There was brittle silence for a few minutes before I heard him filling a glass at the sink. I got on with the painting. When he came back he was Adam again and calm.

I said, 'At least they seemed happy.'

'Happy? Yes, sure, really happy. A laugh a minute.'

'Life *is* unfair. You knew that already.'

'Just let's get on, OK?'

❖ 2 ❖

Like the early morning, when we were on our own together the evenings were a problem for a while. Reading: I liked it, Adam didn't. He could settle to nothing for very long, except TV. Obsessed

70

with old movies. Watched them tranced, sitting square to the screen only an arm's length away. Nothing distracted him, not moving about, not singing, not asking a question, not fetching logs, not washing up with a clatter, nothing except standing in front of the set, which I once did and never did again because his reaction was ugly. I thought for a second he'd flatten me.

So he was happy enough when there was an old film to watch. He'd be there sometimes well into the early hours, long after I'd gone to bed; and next morning he'd be fresh as a spring lamb. Sleep, for him, was like food – he didn't need much, would snack when he felt like it. Often we'd stop work for a drink and he'd fall asleep for ten minutes and wake up ready for work as soon as I made a move. Though I always felt that he was still aware while he was asleep of what was going on, as if he were watching through closed eyes. Like a snoozing cat.

I'm not like that at all. Seven hours a night, and I hate cat-napping during the day. Don't like old movies either, and am easily distracted no matter what I'm doing, reading especially. Reading is an essential part of my life, basic as breathing, eating, sleeping, crapping. Without it for more than a couple of days I feel my mind dying. More than just my mind. My soul dying. If soul means what my dictionary says: *the essential part or fundamental nature of everything, the seat of human personality, intellect, will and emotions.*

This was something Adam could never understand. Five or six days after he came to stay, clearing our stuff out of the bedroom, Tess helping, he said:

'What d'you want all these books for?'

'There aren't that many,' I said.

'A hundred and eight,' Tess said. 'I counted.'

'I've over a thousand at home.'

'Glad we're not painting your place,' Adam said.

'Bookworm . . .' Tess said.

'Chewing his way through paper.'

'. . . Bibliophile.'

'What d'you do with them all, once you've read them?'

I said, 'For a start, you can do more with books than you can with people, judging by the way you two carry on – or don't carry on as it happens. Here, grab these.'

'Go on then,' Adam said as I piled books into his cradled arms, 'tell us. What can you do with books you can't do with people?'

'Not another of your games, for God's sake, not while we're doing this.'

Tess said, 'Go on, tell him. I'll start you off. You can read them, which,' she added pointedly to Adam, 'is certainly more than you can do with some people.'

'You can write in them,' Adam said. 'I've seen him do it. Bloody vandal.'

'Buy them.'

'You can buy people,' Adam said.

'Sell them, then.'

'You can sell people as well. Seen it done. But why not sell these, Jan? We could have a party on the proceeds.'

'Hasn't he told you? He doesn't like parties.'

'Must be defective, poor sod.'

'It's what comes of biblioboring.'

'We should do something about that.'

'Educate him in everyday life.'

'You'll do no such thing,' I said.

'Use them to hold things up,' Tess went on, 'like wonky table legs.'

'And hold things down. But you can use people for that as well.'

'If you're lucky,' I said.

'Give them away as presents,' Tess said.

'Burn them to keep the place warm.'

'Fascist,' I said.

'Cover up nasty cracks in the wall,' Tess said pertinently.

'I'll tell you one thing,' I said. 'They don't play up the way people do.'

'Or get ill,' Tess said.

'Or puke,' Adam said.

'Or cry,' Tess said.

I said quickly, 'Or eat or drink or nick your clothes or take holidays or sleep or poop or doublecross or answer back or desert you when you need them or want to be paid or take the huff or need decorating or get The Glums or have a menopause or murder or torture or fight wars –'

'Sometimes cause them,' Tess butted in.

'– or do anything except look attractive while they wait for you to do whatever you like with them, like *read* them. OK – is that enough for now, can we get on?'

'I'm knackered after all that,' Adam said. 'I thought books were supposed to be relaxing.'

'And while we're on the subject,' I said, 'we'll have to do something about you and the telly and me and reading, unless you want to go into exile in the basement every night.'

'Why?' Tess said. 'What's the matter?'

That explained, she said, 'Easy. I've a set of headphones I used when I wanted to watch the telly at home and nobody else did. Now I've one in my room I never use them. Adam can borrow them, so he can watch while you read.'

'Brilliant,' Adam said.

'Only takes feminine lateral thinking.'

'You can go lateral for me any time.'

'I said *thinking*.'

❖ 3 ❖

One evening towards the end of the decorating there was nothing on TV that Adam wanted to watch and Tess dropped in bringing some beer she'd filched from the fridge and we were talking about sleep because when Tess arrived Adam was slumped in one of his sleep-snacks and I was reading a story about a dream, which comes into this story soon.

Adam perked up, of course, the second Tess came through the door and they joshed around, which they always did, flirting, that evening cracking suspect puns on being laid out and having a lie down and being wide to the world and heavy breathing and how thrilling a good zizz was, and when they'd got through with that Tess said they'd done something on sleep in biology the year before. They'd had to record their dreams as soon as they woke up in the morning (most of the time, of course, they hadn't dared tell the truth so they made them up) and they'd done experiments with REM (rapid eye movement – the wobbling of the eyes under the lids which happens when people are dreaming), and we nattered on about all that and the meaning of dreams and why they are so weird, till Adam suddenly said,

'What I want to know is why I wake up just about every morning with a whacking great hard on.'

'You do?' Tess said, leaning forward, agog.

'Like a broom handle.'

'Because of sexy dreams?'

'Not always. Happens quite a lot when I haven't been dreaming about anything.'

'Or not that you remember when you wake up.'

'Me too,' I said, no less than the truth, but rather so as not to be left out. 'Didn't they tell you anything about that in biol?'

'Grief, no! They only talk about sex in Human Relations and they didn't say anything about early morning erections then, only about Aids and not having babies.'

'What about your brothers,' I said, 'don't you know about it from them?'

'We're not the kind of family where the men lie around with their dingers on show, if that's what you mean. And you know my mum, she's pretty open but she wouldn't go much on talking about erections.'

'Well, all I know is I wake up stiff as a bat,' Adam said.

'Ready for a good innings,' I said.

'A big score, you're telling me.'

'Boys!' Tess said with mock scorn. 'Sex mad.'

'Unlike girls,' Adam said, 'who aren't, eh? They don't have nothing like that, I suppose.'

'What, like early morning blooming of the nips or clutching of the clit, that kind of thing?'

'Very elegantly put,' I said.

'To be honest, yes.'

'You do?' Adam said, himself agog now. 'There you are, then, it isn't just us.'

'Another of the uncontrollable pleasures of growing up, you mean. Like acne.'

'I enjoy it more than acne,' Adam said. 'All you can do with acne is pick it.'

'Easier to get rid of as well,' I said.

'Oo – you don't, do you!' Tess said, this time demonstrating shocked innocence. 'Not that I know what you're talking about, of course.' And we all laughed.

'But here, listen,' Adam said. 'I've been having a funny dream lately.'

'Funny ha-ha or funny disgusting?' Tess asked.

'Funny how it makes me sweat. I'm coming along this road, not walking or running or in a car or anything, just sort of floating along, and there's a bridge up ahead, not this bridge, just a bridge, a flat straight bridge, and as I come nearer I get more and more scared, I'm not sure why, because there's something dangerous on the other side I think, that's how it feels anyway, and I go slower and slower and all I can see is the bridge, nothing neither side, which is just a

74

blur, and there's nobody with me, I'm all alone, I feel lonely, and when I reach the bridge where the road becomes the bridge, there's a yellow line painted across the road and I stop just before it and I can't make myself go no further, just can't move at all, can't make myself cross the bridge, I'm stuck because of whatever it is I'm scared of, and I can't turn round and go back because there's something behind that I'm trying to get away from, I'm right stuck, and near freaking out, I'm breathing hard, and sweating, and ... well ... and, well, that's the end of it really, that's it, I'm stuck and I'm alone and I'm scared of something and I can't cross the bridge.'

He'd even broken out in a sweat as he spoke. Tess and I said nothing, seeing how disturbed he was and not knowing what to say. The Ancient Mariner. It was as if the whole evening had been working up to this point, when Adam would tell his dream.

He fell silent, his eyes grasping us, expecting, wanting us to say something that would release him from his nightmare.

'That's it,' he said after a while. 'That's all.'

Taking a deep breath, Tess said, 'I wonder what it is on the other side that scares you?'

I said, 'Maybe it's nothing to do with what's on the other side.'

'What then?'

'Dunno. Doesn't have to be something on the other side, though, does it? Could be the bridge itself he's afraid of. Or what he's running away from. Or the yellow line. What does that mean?'

Tess said, 'Does it have to mean anything? You're always trying to find a meaning in everything. Sometimes things don't mean anything, you know, they don't *have to*, do they? They might just be *there*.'

Adam watching us like a spectator at a tennis match, closely assessing every stroke.

I said, 'I don't believe that. Everything means something. Everything is there for a reason. Nothing just happens.'

'You're an appalling intellectual, you know that, don't you.'

'Why do people use "intellectual" as an insult? What's so bad about thinking? I enjoy thinking.'

'All right, don't let's go into that now. What we're talking about is Adam's dream,' Tess said. 'Dreams have their own kind of logic, don't they. They're not like ... I don't know ... like this happens, then that happens as a result, and then the next thing happens, and so on. They're weird. Everything is jumbled. Things don't seem to connect.'

'Exactly. They have their own logic. And all logic has a meaning. So things do connect. What you have to do is puzzle out the logic by finding some sort of pattern to it, don't you. Then the meaning becomes clear. Like poetry. Some poetry doesn't seem to make any sense when you first read it, so you just keep on reading it and rereading it while you puzzle out what the logic is, the ideas, the images, the words, all the rest of it, till you find the pattern – how everything connects in a way you hadn't noticed at first. I mean, that's one of the things that's so interesting about poetry, isn't it, you know that.'

'*Sacré dieu!*'

'I'm only trying to explain how I think about dreams, that's all. Look, I'll give you an example.'

'He's off, Adam, here he goes.'

'No, listen,' Adam said, 'I want to know.'

I went on, 'As it happens, I was just reading a story about a bridge. I'm interested in bridges at the moment, not surprisingly.' I fetched the book. 'It's a story called "The Bridge". It's by Franz Kafka.'

'The guy who wrote the one about the boy who wakes up and he's turned into a beetle?' Tess said.

'The very same,' I said, finding the place.

'Well then it's bound to be weird.'

'Want to hear it or not? It's very short, won't strain your powers of concentration.'

'Cheek!'

'Sure,' Adam said.

'OK, here goes:'

I was stiff and cold, I was a bridge, I lay over an abyss; my toes buried deep on one side, my hands on the other, I had fastened my teeth in crumbling clay. The tails of my coat fluttered at my sides. Far below brawled the icy trout stream. No tourist strayed to this impassable height, the bridge was not yet marked on the maps. Thus I lay and waited; I had to wait; without falling no bridge, once erected, can cease to be a bridge. One day towards evening, whether it was the first, whether it was the thousandth, I cannot tell – my thoughts were always in confusion, and always, always moving in a circle – towards evening in summer, the roar of the stream grown deeper, I heard the footsteps of a man! Towards me, towards me. Stretch yourself, bridge, make yourself ready, beam without rail, hold up the one who is entrusted to you. If his steps are uncertain steady them unobtrusively, but if he staggers then make yourself known and like a mountain god hurl him to the bank. He came, he tapped me with the iron spike of his stick, then with it he lifted my coat-tails and folded them upon me; he plunged his spike into my bushy hair, and for a good while he let it rest there, no doubt as he gazed far round him into the distance. But then – I was just following him in thought over mountain and valley – he leapt with both feet on to the middle of my body. I shuddered with wild pain, quite uncomprehending. Who was it? A child? A gymnast? A daredevil? A suicide? A tempter? A destroyer? And I turned over to look at him. A bridge turns over! And before I fully turned I was already falling, I fell, and in a moment I was ripped apart and impaled on the sharp stones that had always gazed up at me so peacefully out of the rushing waters.

Silence. The fire burned our faces.

Adam stirred, flexing himself as he did sometimes after a film he'd specially liked.

'Great!'

'You liked it?' Tess said, surprised.

'Is that all of it?'

I nodded.

'Let's have a look.'

Tess and I watched as, like a boy with a new toy, Adam pawed the open page and pored over the words, too.

'I'll have a read of this later on.' He looked up, smiling. 'I'm too slow for it now with you two watching.'

'But what does it mean?' Tess said.

He shrugged.

'But you like it?'

'Sure. You can kind of feel what it means.'

'There you are,' I said to Tess, 'he's a natural. He really knows how to read. Don't struggle with it. Just let it happen. Right? And don't snort at me. What do *you* think it means?'

'Oh no, you're not getting out of it that easy!' she said, laughing. 'I know you. You'll get me to say something stupid off the top of my head, having just heard the thing for the first time, and then you'll come up with something clever, because you've read it half a dozen times and been thinking about it for days! You're like Bishop at school, he does that, and it's not fair. It's easy to be clever about something when you've had plenty of time to work it out and the other person hasn't.'

'I've only read it once, just before you arrived, and I haven't a clue what it means.'

'Then why did you read it to us? Not just because we were talking about dreams and Adam told us his. That's too simple for you.'

'I really do want to know what you think. I'm not playing games, honest.'

'All right, I'll believe you though there's many who wouldn't. All I can say is that it seems to me to be a typical male fantasy about sex and failure.'

Adam said, 'How d'you work that out?'

'Let's have a look.'

Now it was Tess who pored over the pages. Adam watched as you watch someone who knows how to do something and hope by watching to learn the trick.

'I mean,' Tess said after a while, 'all this about being stiff and lying over an abyss! He even uses the word "erected". You don't erect bridges, do you? You build them, surely? Then there's the river. That's always got to do with sex, hasn't it. Water, flowing, channels. The image of the female. *And* it's a trout stream! We all know what fishes swimming in a river are supposed to mean.'

'What?' Adam asked, not batting an eye.

Tess shot a glance at me. Did he really not know?

'Well . . .' she said, 'penises, sperm, the male in the female . . . And then there's this dark stranger with the stick – I suppose you'll say that's another penis – which he plunges into the man's hair and then jumps onto the middle of his body. And after that the storyteller falls and smashes onto stones in the river and is ripped apart. All that is sex, and the failure is that he's supposed to be a bridge but he can't bear the first person who comes along without cracking up. So he's a failed bridge. Sex and failure.'

'So all you think it means is he can't get it up?' I said.

'But the figure who comes along is a man,' Adam said.

'Yes, well, I'd rather not go into *that*, thank you,' Tess said, making her mock-shock face. 'The whole thing seems pretty dubious to me. Unless the figure is his father, which would be bad enough. Which reminds me – it's time I left you two to it.'

'Now *there's* an Oedipal connection,' I said, laughing.

'Left us to what?' Adam said, beginning the banter of departure that matched the banter of arrival.

'Whatever you do when I'm not here.'

'Nothing near as exciting as we could do if you stayed.'

'This place is becoming a den of vice,' Tess said, making for the door. 'In your minds, anyway. Night all. May flights of angels sing you to your rest.'

When she had gone, the sound of her bike echoing down the road, Adam picked up the book again and sat reading for long minutes. After a while he started humming (was he conscious of doing so or not?) a tune I couldn't at first remember; then it came back: '. . . like a bridge over troubled waters I will lay me down . . .'

When at last he looked up, his expression serious, his eyes the other Adam's eyes, he said, as if making the meaning plain, 'It's the stones, the stones in the rushing water.'

I nodded, pretending I understood. But I didn't.

[– You and me, being so so clever, did we sense that talking about bridges and what *bridges* might mean wasn't a good idea that night? It's funny, but I can't remember. I can remember the evening and saying the things you say we said – or most of them; I don't remember any of those twittish puns! I do remember what we did and what we said and I even remember how I felt, but I don't remember what I *thought*.

But I'm off the point, which is that it didn't seem to occur to us that Adam's dream was about a bridge and Kafka's story was about a bridge and that there we all were sitting by a bridge, and that bridges are always about connecting two separated things, about joining things together that can't meet otherwise, and about crossing from one side to the other. In either direction. That bridges are borders and boundaries. And are walls with holes in them. That things (rivers, roads, cars, boats) and people go through and under them as well as on and over. That they are places where people meet, where they hide, where they go to look down on what goes under. From where they fish, play Pooh-sticks, and sometimes have to pay to cross. And even throw themselves off.

We hadn't found wonderful Calvino then, more's the pity, or we might have also known about Marco Polo in *Invisible Cities*, and you might have read that to us, which would have made a lot of difference to the way we thought about Adam's dream. I'm thinking of this bit:

Marco Polo describes a bridge, stone by stone.

'But which is the stone that supports the bridge?' Kublai Khan asks.

'The bridge is not supported by one stone or another,' Marco answers, 'but by the line of the arch that they form.'

Kublai Khan remains silent, reflecting. Then he adds: 'Why do you speak of the stones? It is only the arch that matters to me.'

Polo answers: 'Without stones there is no arch.'

I think the thing we didn't really understand was what Polo says to Kublai Khan. We didn't understand yet that, yes, we are each individual stones, but that together we can make an arch. We hadn't made that connection. We hadn't bridged that gap.

By the way, you really were painfully jealous of Adam and me, weren't you! Perhaps you were so jealous that even now you find it hard to admit? Or is writing it a kind of confession? Come to that, isn't this whole story a kind of confession? Or do I read it like that because I'm a lapsed Catholic from a family of lapsed Catholics? That's what you'll say, I suppose, never having been anything yourself but a lapsed atheist.]

❖ 4 ❖

One day a raven came to the bridge, perching on the peak of the toll-house roof, and returned day after day. Adam took a fancy to it.

The raven would stand on the roof and peer around with its reptilian eyes, spying for food I expect, as it was winter.

They are so impressively big are ravens, bigger bodied than a carrion crow, and armed with a long heavy beak set off by shaggy throat feathers that give them an evil predatory appearance. You can see why they get such a bad press. But Adam admired our visitor and would stand in the road and speak to it. Not the billing-and-cooing of sentimental animal lovers, as if animals were human babies of low intelligence, but in something that sounded like a foreign language, with its own rhythm and music and vocabulary. I can't capture it in writing, it would look like gobbledegook. He didn't speak loudly, either. There was the raven up on the roof, and there was Adam down on the road, and he would look up at the raven and mutter his animalian no louder than he would speak to someone standing right in front of him. You wouldn't have thought the bird could hear. But it would turn to face him and stretch its cruel head down and fix him with its cold eyes and twist and cock its head as if listening hard to every nuance.

Adam did this for four or five days in a row whenever he heard the raven's coarse deep-throated croaking from the roof. I began to wonder if it was actually calling for him. He would go out and talk for two or three minutes and then come back inside. Nothing else.

But on the sixth or seventh day he was there so long that I went to the window to see what was happening. He was standing in the middle of the road as usual, but this time holding his right arm up, gently beckoning with his fingers and murmuring his animalian so quietly I could hardly hear him from inside. He's never, I thought, at once feeling fearful, he's never trying to tice it down!

But that is exactly what he did do. I'd only been watching for a few seconds when the raven swooped shockingly into view, the great black metre-wide fans of its wings throbbing the air, powering the bird round Adam's head, once, twice, three times, while it let out a high-pitched metallic cry as it circled, Adam standing statuesquely still, until it came gliding in, claws extended, and clutched Adam's wrist, where it settled, after a dodgy wobble back and forth till they both found the right balance. Then the two of them stood still, gazing into each other's unblinking eyes.

By now I had broken into a cold sweat. And the sight of that scimitar beak only a fist away from Adam's eyes completely unnerved me. My knees buckled and I sat down on the windowsill, grasping the edge to keep me from falling. But I couldn't stop looking.

Adam waited for a while that seemed an age, murmuring murmuring, the tension so great I desperately wanted to pee.

The pair of them remained there, the one talking, the other listening, for endless minutes. Then Adam began to move slowly, slowly, careful step by careful step, first in a wide circle, then in a straight line up the middle of the road onto the bridge for a few metres before turning and coming back again. All the time he talked his quiet animal talk. And all the time the raven stared at him, only occasionally looking away with a sharp twist of its head as if to assess the view.

When they were near the house again, where I hoped he would launch the bird into the air and be done with his circus act, Adam paused for a moment. But then set off again, slowly, slowly, this time towards the front door.

Dear God, I thought, he's never going to bring it in!

But he did. Step by step, and pausing every two or three steps, allowing the raven to take in what was happening, and talking his lingo all the time, calmly, lightly, soothingly, gradually edging his

81

way through the door, and on into the living room, right past me, where I sat pressed against the window utterly speechless, every muscle paralysed though I could hear my heart thumping in terror and feel an effusion of sweat soaking my clothes.

At last, reaching the centre of the room Adam gently turned so that he faced me and the door, and stopped, the bird twisting its head and stabbing its beak nervously in this direction and that, and Adam's monologue the only sound.

Could he have got away with it? Might he have kept the bird quiet until he had taken it outside again? We never found out because a car arrived just then. I was so spelled that I wasn't aware of it coming. The first I heard was the noise of an engine outside the house. There was a moment when we all – Adam, the raven, myself – cocked our ears in its direction, Adam like me thinking, What now?, and the raven gathering itself for flight.

At which second the car's horn blew and the raven took off, seeming in one spread of its wings to fill the room. Instinctively, I threw myself onto the floor and lay there, curled up as tightly as I could and shielding my head with my arms while the bird blundered and buffeted around the room, squawking loud angry croaking cries and banging into walls and ceiling light and furniture, such a confined space being far too small for it to achieve proper flight. Adam ducked and dodged as it flayed about his head, its wings raising a draught that swirled up clouds of dust and caused the chimney to backfire, sending wood smoke billowing into the room. In seconds the place looked and smelt like a dungeon in the bowels of hell during an attack from an avenging angel.

In the middle of this confusion the car must have driven off, at any rate it wasn't there a few minutes later when everything was under control again. Probably the driver took fright at the noise, which must have sounded like ritual murder, and decided he was better off out of it.

After beating about for I don't know how long, time being now a commodity I'd completely lost sense of, the raven careered headfirst into a wall, fell onto the back of the armchair, clutched at it wildly, dug its claws into the upholstery, and found itself perched there, ruffled, agitated, defensive (that cruel beak stab-stab-stabbing) and the room suddenly silent again.

Slowly the swirls of dust and smoke settled to a haze. And as if to mark the time a lone black feather floated lazily down from the ceiling, coming finally to rest at Adam's feet.

He by now was hunkered half under the table watching with a satisfied smirk as if this were the very scene he had hoped to create.

From my exposed position flat on the floor I muttered, 'What the hell do we do now?'

'Hush,' Adam said. 'Keep still.'

And he started talking his beastspiel again. I thought, This time it won't work. But it did. Slowly, oh so slowly! His patience was impeccable. I remember thinking, How can he be so calm and patient at a time like this when normally he's such an unpredictable volatile fidget? Which only goes to show how little I understood Adam or myself or human nature in general.

With delicate care he approached the nervous bird, coaxed it after repeated attempts onto his arm, and then half-step by half-step eased his way across the room and through the living-room door and at long last through the outside door and into the road, where for a moment he stood still, the pair of them again like a sculpture, 'Boy with Bird', before he raised his arm, and the raven launched itself cleanly into the air and flapped off, soaring into the sky, repeating as it went its deep-throated cry in farewell.

Once the bird was out of sight the tension broke. The relief was almost as unbearable.

I stormed outside yelling, 'What in hell's teeth d'you think you're playing at! You must be crazy! You could have lost an eye! That was just about the stupidest thing I've ever seen anybody do! You're mad! Never do anything like that again, d'you hear! Never!! *Jesus!!!*'

Adam grinned at me as I frothed.

'And don't stand there grinning!' I blathered on.

'It was fun.'

'Fun! You call that fun!'

'Sure. Gave you a thrill as well.'

'Me!'

'You loved every minute.'

'I did not!'

'Yes, you did. Look at you, you're shaking with excitement.'

'I'm shaking from anger, you great steaming ape, that's why I'm shaking.'

He raised his hand to run it through his hair, that irritating tic whenever he was excited. It was then that I saw blood soaking through the arm of his sweater.

'What's this?' I said, catching hold of his hand.

'Nothing.' He tried to tug his hand away, but half-heartedly.

I eased the sweater back. Blood was oozing from torn flesh just above his wrist.

'Christ, its claws must have dug into you! Thank God it missed the vein. We'd better see to that.'

He allowed me to lead him to the sink where I cleaned the wound and dressed it as best I could with strips of cloth torn from a T-shirt. Doing that calmed me, maybe for the same reason that the raven calmed Adam.

'Why the hell did you do that?' I said quietly as I worked.

'Just to see if I could.'

'Well, I hope that's all the proof you want.'

'Till I think of something better.'

'Not while I'm around, if you don't mind. The beak on that bird! You could easily have lost an eye. One peck – And look at your arm. It's a mess.'

'Worth it though,' he said.

❖ 5 ❖

'Hey!' Tess called out.

We turned from our work. Her camera clicked.

'Not again!' I said. 'How many more?'

She was taking photos for an optional course on photography at school. She'd chosen the toll bridge as a topic, photographing it regularly for six months. At the beginning she thought it would just make an interesting subject, a study of stones and water and people and the effect on them of weather and the changing seasons. She called the finished portfolio 'Tolling the Bridge'.

Adam enjoyed being snapped enormously, camping up the poses if he got the chance, which Tess liked for a while, but when she'd had enough of it, would creep up on us and take us unawares. Early on, she persuaded Adam to perform his Tarzan act for her (not that he needed much persuading of course), which she shot in black and white from various angles – on and under the bridge, from the garden, from the back-door steps, from the river (she had to get into the water for these shots and nearly died of the cold), even from above in the tree itself. It took three sessions during which I was required to act as general runabout and slave to the pair of them. Of course I pretended to be sniffy about this at the time but I have to admit the resulting pictures are my favourites, beautifully capturing the sense of movement and energy. (The school made Tess cut the sequence out of the portfolio before putting it on show with the work of the rest of the group because Adam was in the nude and Tess refused to crop away or cover with airbrushed shadows the full frontal naughty bits. Another example of how prissy puritanism still rides shotgun in certain sectors of the British social system. [– Compare and contrast in two hundred words the 'page three' popsies in the tabloid dailies and then write three hundred words in their defence, imagining yourself to be one of the dishy dolls.])

❖ 6 ❖

One drizzly morning a Range Rover stopped at the door. I went out to take the toll but already the driver, a young guy, incipient version of B-and-G, dressed in a cheap grey junior businessman suit and sporting one of those fluffy moustaches that grow on the faces of insecure post-adolescents who want you to think they're older than they are, was hauling out of the back a large notice on a pole. FOR SALE, the notice said, and the usual details of agent's name and phone number. Plus the inevitable emblem – not head of Greek god, nor flourishing oak tree, nor prancing black stallion but blue swallow in full flight. Why never anything nearer the truth, like a brace of money bags or a vulture picking on a corpse or a shark with a bloodstained mortgage in its teeth? Stupid question, really.

What does puzzle me, though, is why we put up with such pollution of the mind. We go on and on about dodgy food and acid rain and nuclear radiation and other threats to our bodies but we don't bat an eye at abuse of symbols or poison pumped into our minds by advertisers and other con artists, or foul emissions spewed out every day by, for example, so-called 'news' papers and politicians and TV's self-appointed public opinionaters. What's the point of a living body without a living mind to go with it? *Nichts*. All the evidence I need is here.

The driver, studiously ignoring me, was carrying the sign to the corner of the house.

'Has Mister Norris OK'd this?' I asked.

'And who might you be, squire?'

'The toll keeper.'

Sizing up the stonework for a place to fix the pole, he said, 'I'm impressed.'

He leaned the hoarding against the house, returned to the back of his Rover from where he was taking a claw hammer and a handful of round-head spike nails when he caught sight, as I did from following the line of his surprised gawp, of Adam, who must have come outside while our backs were turned, quietly taken possession of the hoarding, and was now casually bearing it, raised like a banner, towards the bridge.

Speechless, the agent's agent watched as Adam, reaching the middle of the bridge, lifted the hoarding over the parapet, hoyed it into the river, ran to the other side, watched it float through and swirl away downstream, after which, without casting a glance in our direction, he walked calmly back to the house and disappeared inside.

Only then did the agent's agent find his voice.

'Who the hell was that?'

'Him? Just my assistant.'

'Your *assistant*!'

'Now you're impressed.'

'What the shit does he think he's playing at?'

'Pooh-sticks.'

'Eh?'

'Do return when you have obtained written permission to molest the building,' I said with all the hauteur I could assume, and stalked into the house, quietly closing the door behind me.

Adam was standing in the middle of the living room, clenched fist raised and pulling victory faces. We wanted to burst out but stifled ourselves in order to hear what went on outside for, there being no curtains, we didn't want to spoil the effect by being seen looking out. Not that there was long to wait before a cruel slamming of car doors, over-revved engine and squealing tyres told us all we needed to know.

A futile gesture but spine-tinglingly satisfying. Naturally, fluffy lip was back by noon, flapping an officious piece of paper in our faces and braying his FOR SALE sign to the wall with all the crucifying passion of a minion with a score to settle. Another episode in the comedy of rage.

❖ 7 ❖

After three weeks of painting and decorating I began to feel ill. Irritated lungs, runny nose and eyes, heavy aching head, dizziness sometimes, queasy stomach, wanting to puke. This went on for a day or two, me thinking I was coming down with the flu, when one night I woke up and made it to the back door just in time. Soaked in fever sweat, freezing in the night frost and dark December air, I threw up till there was nothing left to throw and retching was itself a pain. When it was over I stumbled back inside, washed, drank a glass of water, stirred up the slumbering logs on the fire, and hunkered as close to the warmth as I could, shivering, sniffling, and miserable.

Adam didn't move. I resented that for a while, all my only-son reflexes, I suppose, conditioned to expect coddling and consolation. But as the spasm wore off I was pleased he'd stayed where he was. This was the first time since I came to the bridge that I'd been physically ill. It had never occurred to me that I would be. Now it had happened I felt suddenly vulnerable and was glad there was someone else in the house, but I certainly didn't want him fussing over me, and suggesting remedies.

Once I was warm again and the spasm was properly over, I felt so washed out and weary all I wanted was to crawl back into bed. Which I did, and slept so soundly that I didn't wake next morning till I heard Tess's voice saying my name. She was standing by my bed dressed in her biking leathers, Adam at her side.

'Hello. Are you all right?'

'What time is it?'

'Eight thirty. Is anything wrong?'

'Just a bit queasy.'

'You don't look too terrific.'

Adam said, 'He was spewing half the night.'

'I'll get up.'

Tess said, 'You might be better in bed. Was it something you ate?'

Adam said, 'We both had the same.'

He was, as ever, the epitome of health, being one of those people who look tanned even in the dead of winter.

'I'm all right.'

They looked at me like mourners surveying a corpse.

'Shove off. I want to get dressed.'

'If you're sure,' Tess said.

'I'm sure, I'm sure. Go!'

They went, closing the door behind them. There was mumbling from outside before Tess's bike started and drove off, not over the bridge, as it should have done if she were on her way to school, but towards the village. So I wasn't surprised when Bob Norris turned up twenty minutes later in his van, Tess puttering along behind. By then I was sitting by the fire, feeling like Lazarus, nibbling half-heartedly on a piece of dry bread, which was the only food I could face.

'Traitor,' I muttered at Tess when she and her father came in with that apprehensive look people wear when visiting the uncertain sick. Adam, who had been outside taking tolls, tagged along behind.

'What's this?' Bob Norris said in his foreman's bantering style, which he hadn't been using much lately. 'Skiving, is it? Day off? General strike? Go slow? What?'

'Inquisition followed by public burning, by the looks,' I said trying to respond in kind, but it sounded more like accusation than joke. While I sat quiet I seemed fairly normal; as soon as I spoke, or worse, moved, I knew I wasn't.

'Haven't lost your appetite, I see.'

'Favourite breakfast, dry bread.'

'Stomach is it? Bad chest, snotty nose, dizzy head?'

'Flu, I expect. Nothing to bother about.'

'Sick in the night though.'

I glared at Tess.

'Painter's colic,' Bob Norris went on. 'Breathing those fumes for too long. Not enough fresh air. Not enough ventilation. Windows shut at night to keep out the cold.'

'I'll take a walk.'

'You'll do nothing of the sort. You'll come home with me in the van. The wife'll see to you. You need some time out of here and a day or two recuperating before things get worse.' He turned to Adam, who was leaning in the doorway. 'Can you cope without him?'

'Sure.'

Tess said, 'I could stay and help. We're not doing much at school.'

Her father gave her a wry glance. 'You've done your bit for today, girl. Best get going, you're late already.'

'Girl indeed!' Tess stretched up, pecked a kiss on his unshaven cheek and said, 'I do not bite my thumb at you, sir, but I bite my thumb, sir.'

'Eh?'

And bending down, pecked a kiss on my cheek too. 'O, flesh, flesh, how art thou fishified!' I was too addled to remember what she was quoting. 'Get well soon, dear Jan.' And she clumped away in her biking boots. 'See you, Adam. 'Bye all.'

Mrs Norris fed me bread and milk, a potion for sickly children I'd only ever read about in books, hustled me into the spare bedroom, and left me luxuriating between fresh-smelling pink flannelette sheets, a radio playing quietly, curtains drawn against the light, and firm instructions that I must sleep. A brisk good-humoured spoiling quite different from my mother's all-consuming full-time attention.

For the rest of that day I drifted pleasantly, cosily, in and out of sleep. In the waking times my mind played with memories of the past year and thoughts about my time at the bridge and about Mother and Dad and everything Dad had told me in his letter, and about Gill and me and my confusion about what I really wanted, and about Adam and Tess and the strangeness of everything, the unlikeliness of all life, the unrealness of its reality. For it wasn't only because I was mildly ill that other people and life in general seemed such a puzzle, so surprising and beyond understanding, so *unknowable*, and yet so fascinating. So beautiful and yet so ugly too. In a less fevered way, that is how it was for me always and still is: the surprise and fascination, the otherness, the not-me of it all.

Lying there in the Norrises' spare bedroom, gazing dozily at the wallpaper covered in big-patterned dark green vine leaves entwined with huge bunches of ripe red grapes, and at the family knick-knacks neatly grouped on every flat surface, and at the furniture – heavy dark-wood dressing table and matching wardrobe, cane bedside table, wooden milking stool, ancient Windsor rocking chair with bright red cushion – most of which must have come down from generations before, solid and brightly polished as a freshly opened conker, my own deep confusions about myself became all the more disturbing, and I wished that somehow I could belong to the settled, ages-old certainties that the Norrises lived by. But knew I never could, and maybe only wanted to now in a fit of sentimentality brought on by painter's (melan)colic.

Among the knick-knacks one especially caught my eye, an object so strange, so unlike any of the others, that I had to get out of bed to pick it up. The size of a small mug, it was crudely hand-made of mud-red clay with a stubby almost straight handle across the top so that the thing was like a small pottery bucket. But for carrying what? Raised from the surface of the mug, to each side of the handle, was a plump face, one solemn and stern and clean-shaven with pursed lips, the other moustached and goatee-bearded and smiling mischievously.

The faces were framed by ringlets of hair falling like twined snakes behind the ears – large ears on the stern man – and were circled by a crown, as if both faces belonged to one head.

I knew as soon as I picked it up that this weird antique must have something to do with the god Janus. And as I caressed its pitted cracked sandy surface, and with a delicious shock found that the pad of my thumb and the tip of my index finger fitted exactly into the hollows where the potter had pressed the ends of the handle into the rim of the vessel, I felt a kind of awe, as if some magnetic power emanated from this ancient piece of crudely shaped clay and took me into its possession. I was suddenly afraid the holy pot might break or even crumble to pieces in my hand, yet did not want to put it down, wanted to keep it with me, hold it to me, hide it on me. I actually had to suppress a strong desire to steal it.

Ever since that moment I have been able to understand the magic power of sacred objects. I cannot explain how the magic works but I no longer scoff at anyone who believes in it.

At midday Bob Norris came to see me, bearing a bowl of Mrs Norris's vegetable soup and a chunk of brown bread. He spotted that I'd placed the Janus on the bedside table where I could look closely at it while I lay in bed.

'Like it?' he said.

'Very much. How old is it?'

'Roman-Egyptian, circa first century BC – about two thousand two hundred years old. Know what it is?'

'Something to do with Janus?'

'One face is Dionysus, the Greek god of wine and fruitfulness and all vegetation. He bestows ecstasy and is also the god of drama. They used to worship him with very sexy goings-on. The other is Satyr, a goat-like man who drank a lot and danced in the procession behind Dionysus and chased the nymphs. Bit of a randy devil.'

'Quite a pair.'

'And they make Janus, the god of gates and doorways and bridges and of beginnings in general because when you go through a door or cross a bridge you enter something new, a different place. That's why the Romans made January the first month of the year. For them he was the god of gods, coming even before Jupiter. He's very very ancient, one of the true gods who was worshipped long before Roman times. They took him over and made him into their own, the way they took over Christianity and turned it into an Imperial religion.'

'Doesn't sound as if you like the Romans much.'

'I don't. Totalitarian fascist bunch of thugs.'

'But what was the mug for? Not for drinking out of, surely? You can't get your nose in.'

'It's not a mug, it was used for carrying a prayer. When you went to the temple, you bought one, probably from a stall outside, along with a small strip of lead. You etched your prayer into the metal, bent the strip in two so that no one else could read it, put the prayer into the pot, then took the pot into the temple and stood it on the altar as a kind of supplication to the god.'

'Looks like a pretty down-market example, this one.'

'Does, doesn't it. Made in two halves, each pressed into a mould then joined together, I should think, wouldn't you? Quickly done. Their equivalent of cheap mass-production probably. You can see the join where the two halves were stuck together, the potter hasn't even bothered to smooth it off, and there's pitting on the surface of the faces where the clay wasn't pressed into the mould firmly enough.'

'And the handle! It looks like the sort of thing we used to roll out with modelling clay in infant school.'

'Have you put your finger inside?'

'Mine fits exactly!'

'It does? My goodness! Mine's too big.'

'Weird sensation.'

'Wonderful.'

'Fingers abolishing time.'

'Aye, and space. One thing's for sure – the man who made this doesn't have a headache any more.'

We smiled and nodded at each other, acknowledging the kinship of understanding.

At four thirty, full of fizz, Tess brought up tea and buttered scones along with news that Adam was slogging away at the house and enjoying it all so much he hadn't stopped to eat anything so she was going back to cook something for them both. They were having a ball, I could tell just from the grin on her face.

I said, 'I'll come.'

'No you won't, Mum won't let you. The place reeks of paint, you'd be ill again straightaway.'

'I'm still coming.'

Tess went to the door and called out, 'Mum, he says he's going back to the bridge.'

Which brought Mrs Norris pounding up the stairs. 'Oh no he isn't. You're staying where you are, young man, you're staying here tonight, so compose yourself to it.'

Tess was ushered away, bedclothes were efficiently tidied, Janus returned to his place among the other knick-knacks, the whole room given a critical survey and the door firmly closed. Leaving me to my unwilling isolation and the torture chamber of my imagination, which for the next few hours was filled with gradually more agonizing fantasies in which Tess and Adam performed with enthusiastic gusto all of the sexiest Dionysian dramas in my then, I must admit, not very extensive repertoire.

I sizzled with desire, sweated with jealousy, prayed to Janus to set me free, groaned with frustration and pique. I was like a lone spectator who, locked in an empty cinema, is forced to watch a film specially made to reduce him to a state of lust-racked blither. And the really ridiculous thing about times like that, the thing I always laugh about later, is that you do it to yourself. You are your own jailer, your own film-maker, your own torturer. The fantasies are your own. It's your own imagination that invents them and your own will that lets it happen and your own mind that puts the show on. You could stop it at once if you wanted to but you don't because it gives you some sort of twisted satisfaction. And it's my belief that there's a side to the human race that loves plodging around in this kind of clart. Sometimes we like to be right up to our necks in it. Sometimes people even drown in their own psychic shit.

A film fantasy can't go on forever but the fantasies inside your head can and then other people call you mad. Maybe my feverish fantasies drove me a little mad that night. In the end I could bear them no longer. I had to know what Tess and Adam really were up to. And in my place, my sanctuary, dammit! I had to be there with them. So I got up, dressed as quietly as I could, mumbled a prayer to Janus to protect me, and stole down the stairs, feeling like a burglar in reverse. The noise of the TV, which the Norrises were watching in their living room, covered any give-away sounds.

Outside, I ran all the way to the bridge. Arrived panting so hard I stopped to recover my breath when I came in sight of the house. My inclination had been to burst in before they had a chance to stop whatever it was they were doing. But while I caught my breath, a deeper, stranger desire took hold of me. I wanted to see them as they were, on their own, without me. As a kid I was always wondering what other people did when I wasn't there. Maybe because I knew I had a secret life of my own which I only ever let show when no one else was around, I supposed that other people were like that too. And I felt a consuming desire to know what those private selves were that parents and relatives and teachers and friends hid from me. So I would sometimes steal around, peeking in at windows or snooping at doors in the hope of discovering those hidden selves revealed.

I had not done this for years, however. Had even forgotten that I used ever to do it. Now, as I recovered my breath, that childhood desire overwhelmed me again. The fun of observing people when they are completely unaware of being watched, the nervous excitement of it – the same excitement that experimental scientists must feel, and Peeping Toms as well, I guess.

I checked that no vehicles were approaching before padding quietly up to the house. The bedroom was dark but the living room was softly lit by low table lamps that hadn't been there before, one each side of the fireplace.

It was not the lamps, however, that immediately caught my eye but Tess and Adam tangled naked on the floor in front of the fire. Hollywood TV soft corn. Much pawing going on and sucking and kissing and licking. More complete in range than in my fantasies. More surprising. More tantalizing. More fleshed out would be true to say. Fantasies depend, like everything else, on information. My experience of life so far hadn't informed me all that well; and obviously I hadn't read the right books. They were doing things to each other with fingers and mouths that were stunning news to me.

For a while I watched with the amazement of an initiate secretly learning the mysteries of his trade. Till another kind of amazement grew beside it: amazement at my own reaction to the scene before me. For deep inside I was watching myself with just as great intensity as I was watching them. Observer observing himself. And what amazed me was that instead of anger or jealousy or resentment or envy or hard-on lust there came over me a calm – or maybe I ought to say a calming – satisfaction. I can only compare it to watching a close friend doing something he's good at and doing it very well. You might wish you could do it well too while knowing that you couldn't. But mainly you feel pleased for him, happy that he's achieved the reward, the recognition, the satisfaction, the pleasure he wanted and deserved.

Naturally I felt a little sad for myself too because this was the moment when I properly knew – when I accepted – that Tess was not, would not be, for me nor me for her. Not in the way she was being for Adam right there before me. I even wondered, as he entered her with a shudder of pleasure, whether she knew I was watching, whether she had expected I would find her doing this now, here in my room in my house, whether even by some trick she had planned it. Her way of forcing me to accept what she had told me about us was true. Ridiculous, of course. Another fantasy.

I had not seen 'sex' happening between two people before. I don't mean pretended sex between actors, nor played at by gropers at parties or in pubiic places, nor the clinical demonstrations in sex-education videos at school, but the all-out sweatlathed juicegreasing bodysquirming limbtangled skingreedy gutmelting mindlost neoviolent reality. So I didn't know by first-hand observation, much less direct experience, about its animalness. The exclusive bodiliness of it. The utterly absorbed uninhibited unselfconsciousness of those involved in it as they writhe self-absorbed, lost to the world around them, lost, in fact, just like the cliché says, in each other.

As I watched I realized that I'd never achieved that state with Gill, never been mind-less, never been totally unselfconsciously absorbed, but had always been thinking about it, always been aware of what was going on, always observing myself do it, even as I now observed them and observed myself observing them. An observer by nature, that's me. Did this explain my confusion over Gill? But if it did, *what* did it explain?

I also saw why there is so much talk about sex, why there are so many scenes about it in books and plays and films. Why it causes so much trouble, too. And why those who get it and those who don't make such a fuss. And why there's so much pretending about it – people pretending that they get it when they don't, or pretending that they perform exotic contortions when actually they are as straight as a pencil. And why people who are born with sexy good looks get things easily.

Not that I'm any exception. Adam breaks into my bedroom, scaring the wits out of me, but as soon as I see him stripped, with his foxy good looks and lithe neatly built body and his exceptional dick, I let him stay and sponge off me instead of kicking him out. Not just because the sight of him turned me on but because I'm human, and everybody's like that. I didn't think about it at the time. Animal biology made the decision for me. As I reckon it does countless times a day between people everywhere. The fact is we're all succoured by sex, and some of us are finally suckered by it too.

So I'm standing there for ten, maybe fifteen minutes, watching them, and watching myself watching them, and with a hard-on by then to be honest, making no effort by now to hide myself, when my bridge-keeper's third ear alerts me to the sound of a vehicle I know approaching along the road from the village. Bob Norris's van.

He's bound to stop, even if he's on his way to somewhere else. Bound to see his daughter *in flagrante delicto* with a footloose horny yob he doesn't trust enough to keep the bridge never mind screw his daughter, and me, who he counts responsible, standing outside doing a convincing impersonation of a dirty old man.

I suppose I could – ought to? – have rushed inside, yelling a warning, and hustled the coupled pair out of the back door before Bob arrived. But I doubt if there'd have been time, for at that moment the final act wasn't far from its climax, her on the floor under him, legs over his shoulders, locked together and going like the clappers, in such a state of pleasure that had I burst in they would probably have been beyond recall anyway.

No, that's just an excuse. The truth is more shaming. I was curious to know what would happen when Bob arrived.

Not that any of this was thought out. The second I heard Bob's van approaching, I slipped across the road and vaulted over the bridge onto the bank just where it dropped steeply down to the river. Hidden there I could squint between the urn-shaped balusters.

The van drew up. Bob got out. Tried the house door. Locked. Stepped, without knocking, to the lighted window of the living room, raising his hand to rap on the glass, but, seeing in, never did, his hand arrested in a clenched-fist salute.

I could only see his back silhouetted against the window. For a moment he was a statue spelled by what he saw. Then, as if punched in the stomach, he slumped forward and turned away. I heard a groan as he paused a brief moment then came stumbling across the road directly towards me, reached the parapet, the edge of which he grasped, arms spread for support, right above me, where he struggled to control what were not groans, after all, but angry grieving sobs.

95

I had not seen a grown man weep before. Not like this – so unrestrained, so racked. A second first in basic emotions within moments of each other: I had wanted life stripped to the essentials and I was getting it. And again I was observing myself as I observed the other. The sight of Bob Norris possessed by such naked tears came as a shock, entangling my embarrassment with a sense of double betrayal. I cowered in my inadequate hiding place, head down, terrified that Bob would see me – yet, oh, if only he would see me! – and torn as well by an impulse somehow – but how? – to comfort him. Besides, his sobbing made me want to weep too, for suddenly I saw the scene in the house not with my own eyes but with his, and felt a confusing mix of shame, regret, anger, and worst of all of loss.

Just as I had never seen a grown man weeping, I do not think I had ever really known till that moment what compassion felt like. A third first.

Eventually Bob gained control of himself. Snuffled back his tears. Swore. Spat over the parapet, a gob that landed like a rebuke on my bowed head. Breathed in and out deeply a few times. Returned to his van. But did not start the engine. Instead, letting off the brake, allowed the slight incline to carry the vehicle backwards down the road until a safe enough distance away to drive off without causing alarm in the house.

As soon as his tail lights were out of sight I climbed from my hiding place and set off after him, dregs of guilt stifling an impulse to steal a last glimpse through the toll-house window.

Walking through the village fifteen minutes later I spotted Bob's van parked outside The Plough. Knowing he wasn't a pub man, and even at home not much of a boozer, 'drowning his sorrows' came to mind.

He was sitting on a stool, slumped on his elbows against the bar nursing a large whisky, obviously not his first.

'Saw your van,' I said, half-perching on a stool beside him.

He gave me a sideways look through reddened eyes. 'Had enough of mouldering in bed?' And downed his whisky in one go.

'Something like that.'

'Want a drink?'

He ordered a glass of cider and another large Scotch.

When they had arrived he said, 'The wife was telling me about your mother.' He downed half his drink. 'Sounds badly, poor woman.'

I said nothing, unwilling to talk about that subject.

He turned away, sat square to the bar, not looking at me, thinking, and after a moment said, 'Hard job, being a parent.'

Attempting relief with a smile, I said, 'Wouldn't know.'

'No.' He downed the second half. 'Just as well. If we knew the worst beforehand, maybe we'd never take it on.'

'Is it that bad?'

He ordered another large Scotch.

'If you ever have any –' his words were slurring a little, 'don't have daughters.'

'Didn't know you could choose.'

He huffed ruefully. 'Too true.' Another half glass went down.

I said, chancing my arm, 'Tess doesn't seem so bad.'

'Tess!' he said, swivelling to me, 'Tess! What d'you call her that for? Not her name. Katharine. Her name's Katharine. You know that. Katey, if you like. Not Kathy, though, don't like Kathy. But *Tess*! Dear God!'

'Sorry. Private joke.'

'Wonderful girl. Always was. Right from birth. Beautiful little thing. Nice-tempered. Lovely. Always loved her. Moment I saw her at the hospital.'

'Well then?'

'Another,' he said to the barman.

'Are you sure, Bob?' the barman said. 'Not like you.'

'One more. That'll be it.'

'One more. But leave your van. Walk home, OK?'

He waited till the replenished glass was in front of him before looking at me with that close, slightly unfocused watery gaze of the not-quite-drunk intent on making a point too difficult to get words around. 'What you think then? Of our . . . Tess?'

'What do I think of her?'

'What do you think of her?'

'I like her.'

'Come on, you can do better than that. How much?'

'Dunno. A lot.'

'Fancy her?'

'Well –'

'Go on. Don't be shy. Man to man.'

'Yes, but –'

'But? Can't be buts about fancying.'

'She's a friend, that's all.'

'Never done it. That what you mean?'

'With her? No!'

He slurped from his glass.

'Listen. Tell you something. It hurts. Know that, do you? Hurts like hell. Know what I'm talking about? Children – daughters – specially daughters – most specially . . . Tess. Katey . . . Lovely beautiful Katharine. Daddy's girl. What her mother calls her. Daddy's girl.' He chuckled. 'But they grow up, see? Love them. Want the best for them. Worry.' He shot a glance at me. 'Get jealous. Know that? Know what I'm talking about? Bet never thought that, eh? Fathers get jealous. Eh? Thought that? . . . I get jealous. Put it that way. Understand?'

Gripping the bar to steady himself, he slid uncertainly to his feet. Sweat glazed his face.

'Let's go. Too bloody hot here.'

He staggered. I caught his arm and guided him to the door. Outside, the cold December night slapped us. He braced himself against me, took two deep breaths, pulled his arm from my grip, and set off uncertainly towards his van. I skipped ahead, placing myself between him and the door.

'Mr Norris, I don't think you should drive. Let's walk home.'

He stood scowling at me, swaying slightly. 'Tess! Thought about her name careful, wife and me. Important – names. Yes? Important. You know – mean things. Don't they? . . . Tell something else. Sometimes I feel – sometimes I want . . . Better not. Can't hurt then. Member that.'

'I will, Mr Norris, I will, but I think we ought to walk home now.'

I didn't wake until after nine next morning. By the time I'd pacified Mrs Norris for going out the night before and returning with her husband drunk (a calamity she somehow seemed to blame on me) and argued her into letting me go back to the bridge it was ten thirty. When I arrived Adam was lolling by the blazing fire, supping coffee and looking smug, the room bright with fresh paint. Tess, it turned out, had been busy with Adam all day yesterday while I lay brooding between her mother's flannelette sheets. She had skipped school and she and Adam had finished off glossing the woodwork and then titivated the entire place – living room, bedroom, kitchen area, even the basement lavatorywoodstore.

No longer was the house like the tidy squat Adam first took it to be. Now it was a newly decorated home. Not an especially well-off home, but still, a place where people lived. On the mantelpiece and windowsills winter berries and sprigs of evergreen sprouted from make-shift vases – bottles, old jugs. Stoneware cider flagons had been converted into table lamps to match the one I'd made for a bedside light, only these were topped with wickerwork shades like Chinese hats instead of naked bulbs. Tess had even managed to find an old rust-red rug for the floor. My books had been divided into collections of similar kinds, each collection shelved on its own: poetry on a newly fitted shelf in the living-room alcove to one side of the fireplace, nonfiction books on a shelf on the other side, fiction on the mantelpiece in the bedroom. Posters Sellotaped to the walls (Hockney's 'Bigger Splash', Tom Phillips's 'Samuel Beckett', Jimmy Dean walking in the rain at night). The television set stood on a crudely cobbled table. Even the lumpy old armchair looked revived, a bright red cushion nestling in its seat.

'Like it?' Adam asked.

'You mean, Tess was here all day?'

'Wanted to make the place nice for you. I made the table for the telly though.'

'Where did all the stuff come from?'

'Dunno. Very resourceful is Tess. Knows a lot.' He chuckled, double-meaning. 'All finished. No more painting.'

'Terrific,' I said flatly. Was the place mine any longer?

'Aren't you pleased?'

'Delirious. Had a good time, then?'

'Great.'

'I'm glad. Worked hard, eh?'

'Want some coffee? There's some letters by the telly.'

Letters

❖ 1 ❖

... unless you say no I'll come on the Friday and leave on the Monday ...

❖ 2 ❖

... NO NO NO NO NO NO NO NO NO NO NO NO NO ...

❖ 3 ❖

... a friend of his. My dad is his boss. I expect he's told you that he's decorating the toll house because the owner is thinking of selling it (which we're all against, I'm thinking of starting a Save The Toll House protest group). At first he was working on his own – well, I do help a bit when I can – but for the last couple of weeks another boy has been helping and they reckon they'll be finished by the end of next week, which is great because it means they'll be all done just in time for Christmas.

I thought it might be a good idea if we had a surprise party on Friday 13th (nothing like tempting fate!) to celebrate the end of the decorating. And I wondered if you'd like to come. He's talked about you a lot, that's how I know about you. I sneaked your address from a letter I saw lying on his table. I hope you don't mind, but it was the only way of finding out where you live without him knowing.

It would be great if you could come, the best surprise of all. It would do him good after everything he's been through and working so hard, and anyway I'm dying to meet you ...

Surprise Party

❖ 1 ❖

Maybe the trouble is thinking of days as clock time, regular mechanical measure, when, maybe, time isn't like that at all. We just like to pretend it is because then we feel in control of it. When probably there is nothing to control. What we're doing is confusing different kinds of words. You can measure length. You can't really measure time. How do you measure the past or the future? And the present doesn't have any length, being simply Now. If we try to measure 'now' we find it's always gone, has become part of the past. We shouldn't use measuring words about it, then we wouldn't get so confused about what Time is.

Besides, it seems to me that everything we know of in the universe, everything from clocks to supernovas, every*thing* is both a physical object *and* a shape of energy. Nothing exists, nothing happens without energy. Energy *is* things; things *are* energy. Life is energy. People are energy made flesh. Maybe Time is a form of energy as well?

Is that true? If it is, then it is also true that energy can be compressed into concentrated, powerful units (50 watt bulbs, 100 watt, 2000 watt: energy packaged as light). We know this. We experience it every day around us. So why not the same for human beings and for Time? Surely our lives – our lives as we live them during one day, and our lives as we live them during another day – are also packets of energy? And on some days we somehow concentrate more energy into the day and get more done in the same period of clock time than we did another day when our energy was on low wattage.

So time is not really like clockwork at all, but is a variable resulting from the interaction between energy and thought expressed as event. Energy + Thought = TimeEvent.

Which explains why sometimes we talk of *filling time* (meaning: being easy on ourselves by living our lives at low wattage). And of *making time* (meaning: not that we make more of it in quantity, but that we make more of it in quality – living life with as high wattage as we can). And of there being *not enough time* to do all we want to do (meaning: our ambitions for our lives can't be satisfied and all our flooding energy can't be used up). And of *killing time* (meaning: we wilfully squander the present moment). And of *passing time*, and *wasting time*, and *saving time*.

When I was a baby my mother hung a plaque above my bed, a sliver of varnished wood with these words literally burned into it:

Think big and your deed will grow,
Think small and you'll fall behind,
Think that you can and you will,
It's all in your state of mind.

When I was fourteen I took the plaque down and secretly burned it because I thought it embarrassingly corny. I mean, who wants to bring friends to his room and have them see that kind of kiddy kitsch hanging over the bed? Anyway, it was asking for ribald jokes. But the trouble with clichés is that they stick. I haven't forgotten it because in its trite and twitchy way it is also true. Even time, and how much we can do in a set time, depends as much on our state of mind as it does on anything else. Because of my time at the toll bridge, and because of my time with Adam I know I want to be a user of time, not a filler of it, a maker of time not a killer of it, a compressor of energy not a so-whatter. Adam did not teach me this, but I learned it from being with him at the bridge.

But this part of the story is about a twenty-four-hour stretch into which we all crammed enough watts, gave each other enough surprises, and suffered enough shocks to last a lifetime.

Do we ever know our friends? Do we ever know ourselves?

❖ 2 ❖

Earlier that afternoon, Adam said, 'Don't half fancy a movie.'

'Go!' Tess said. 'Both of you. I'll guard the bridge. Go on! Don't dither! Shop on the way back. Go!'

A stratagem, of course. Betrayal. Returning that evening the house is sardined, pulsing.

'Surprise, surprise!'

Wild cheers.

'What the hell's going on?'

Shopping bag grabbed from my hand.

'Who are all these people?'

Replaced by slopping glass.

More wild cheers.

Tess, beside me, blows one of those referee's searing whistles.

'Listen, everybody,' she yells.

Hushings. Exaggerated party laughter.

'This is a surprise party for Jan, my friend.'

'Who certainly looks surprised.' (Isn't he one of the university cohort we saw that day with Adam at the Pike?)

Laughter.

'With a bigger surprise still to come,' Tess goes on.

'Ooo – naughty, naughty!'

Cheers. Obscene fingers and fists.

'Also, this is the first meeting of PATHS.'

'Hear, hear!'

'Which, for Jan's benefit, as he doesn't know yet, means Protest Against the Toll House Sale.'

'Bravo!'

'Encore!'

'He doesn't know yet because we've just decided it while he was out.'

'Right on!'

'Let's hear it for the toll house. Hip, hip . . .'

'Hooray.'

'Henry.'

Laughter.

'What we're going to do for a start is collect names on a petition to stop the sale.'

'Right on!'

'Where do I put my cross?'

'We'll decide other things later. Now, everybody enjoy yourselves.'

Someone – Adam – sets taped rock rolling. The sardines writhe.

The noise is blinding. Anger withers my mouth. I gulp from the drink. Tastes multicultural.

'What is this?'

'House warming. Come on, let your hair down.'

Tess makes me dance with her. Or what passes for dancing in a sardine tin. Mass squirming.

'Who are they all?' I have to shout, mouth to ear.

'Friends from school,' she replies, her lips tickling my lobes. 'A few from the village. One or two of the girls from Tesco's. Don't know the others. You know how it is. Word gets round.'

'Could've warned me.'

'Wouldn't have been a surprise then, would it, idiot!' The house throbs. If I go outside, will I see the river rippling in harmony, the bridge undulating in rhythm? My mind gives up. There's no competing with a noise that pulsates your teeth.

❖ 3 ❖

Before long Adam has cast himself as a one-man repertory theatre: MC, sergeant major, DJ, mein host, pack leader, party clown, games master. That is, he becomes one of those people who get a kick out of powertooling everybody else. Embryo dictator.

He insists we play some games.

Game One. The Balloon Burst, otherwise known as the Pelvic Bang.

The boy holds a blown-up balloon in front of his crotch. Or stuffs it up his shirt or sweater, as preferred. The girl has to burst the balloon by thrusting her pelvis at it, front on. Close encounters of the pudic kind. Which end in giggles and, on the occasions when the balloon goes off, in exaggerated shrieks. Some cheat by using finger nails or other penetrants.

I opt out, not needing to pretend needing a leak.

On my way back I'm groped at the bottom of the steps by a cruising figure dressed entirely in black.

'Sorry, not my line,' I mutter.

'Could give you a nice surprise. It is a surprise party after all, and you're the party boy.'

'Thanks for the offer.'

'Don't know what you're missing.'

'No, well, another time maybe.'

'Name the day. I do house calls.'

'Don't call me, I'll call you.'

'You've no heart.'

'Nothing against you or anything.'

'Forget it, chuck. Not my lucky night is all.'

He pecks me on the cheek, the rough male kiss of blankets, allows his hands to linger before saying, 'No hard feelings!' and fades away.

It's all happening. You can't say I lack for excitement or that I don't see life stuck out here in the middle of nowhere. Would I have had better luck on the grand tour?

Back inside, Adam is starting yet another game, the remaining participants behaving like nine-year-olds going on seven. Those who have dropped out are mostly draped around the edges of the floor engaged in whatever other party games have taken their fancy. Playing at experimental physiology being the popular choice.

Tess grabs my hand. 'Come on, you can partner me for this one.'

Game two. The Ping-pong Ball.

The boy stands. The girl kneels down in front of him, puts a table-tennis ball inside one of the boy's trouser legs and works it up with her fingers from the outside until she reaches the crotch over which she manoeuvres the ball and then lets it fall down the other trouser leg. The winner does it the fastest. Naturally, everybody goes as slow as she can.

Like mere pastime stories, this game creates a lot of excited antici-pation at the beginning, has an extended middle with plenty of sexy high drama that climaxes in sometimes unexpected thrills, after which it ends with a quick denouement.

This evening there are predictable actions, reactions and dubious dialogue, especially during the crotch scenes.

Tess and I went third. She is busy crossing my crotch and making a meal of it to considerable encouragement and applause, coming at me from front and back at the same time, when Gill appears in the front row of the stalls, sober and ominous and travel-weary.

I don't see her straightaway because I have my eyes screwed shut. I am thinking of a butcher's slaughterhouse, as a matter of fact, in an effort to control my privates by taking my mind off what is happening to them. So Tess at last finishes with my crotch and the ping-pong ball is dribbling down my other leg when I open my eyes with relief only to find Gill glaring at me. Even then I don't react immediately. My first thought is that she is an hallucination brought on by the multicult punch while having my bat and balls played with by someone other than myself for the first time since Gill and I were last together months ago. Only when it dawns on me that she is not gazing at me with the sloe-eyed Mona Lisa smile her face usually assumed during such activities, do I accept that she really is there, touchable flesh, spillable blood, and distinctly unhappy.

Outside in the road, where I hustled Gill, Tess following as it dawns on her who this is, I said:

'What the hell are you doing here?'

'I was invited.'

'Invited?'

'Me,' Tess butted in, 'I invited her.'

'You? What for?'

'Seemed like a good idea at the time.'

'When?'

'What?'

'Didn't think,' Gill said, stunned, 'it would be such a big party.'

'Wasn't meant to be,' Tess said, 'just a bit of fun.'

'So I saw.' Gill looked at me then Tess then me again.

'Nothing like that,' Tess said.

'Could have fooled me.'

'Come on, you know what parties are like.'

'Look,' I said. 'What are you doing here? What are you two up to?'

'Us two up to!' Gill said. 'Don't you mean you two?'

'I told you,' Tess said, 'it isn't like that. Just a game.'

'You planned this just to humiliate me.'

'What the hell are you going on about?' I said.

'Shut up, you,' Tess said. 'This is between me and her.'

'I've never seen you like this.'

'I've never seen you like that.'

'Look, Gill –' Tess said.

Heavy metal started pumping out of the house.

'– I thought it would help him to see you –'

'Help me?'

'– I thought you wanted to see him.'

'How would you know what I want?'

'Your letters were –'

'You've read my letters?'

'Oh, *merde!*'

'You showed her my letters!'

'Look, piss off, will you, I didn't ask you to come here.'

'Thank you! Thank you very much! It's only me you're talking to – your girlfriend.' Looking at Tess. 'At least I thought I was!'

'Typical male,' Tess said.

'Eh –?'

'Yes,' Gill echoed, 'typical male. In the wrong so turn violent. At least you could say sorry.'

'Hang on a minute, I wasn't the one who started this.'

'All everybody else's fault, I suppose,' Gill said.

My head is exploding.

'If you'd answered Gill's letters –'

'Instead of ignoring them –'

'I tried.'

'Excuses.'

'Excuses.'

'Oh for Christ's sake! Get lost, will you! Both of you. Just leave me alone.'

'You said that before. And what do I find?' Gill shouted – the music is *very* loud by now. 'But all right, if that's the way you want it. Two can play that game.'

She turned and stalked into the house.

'Now you've done it!' Tess said. 'Couldn't you just have been nice to her, nothing strenuous, nothing too extreme, just ordinary everyday glad to see you stuff, I mean she is your bloody girlfriend after all ... oh, Christ! ... *Merde!*' and after uttering a few home truths in my direction she sloped off into the house.

I felt deeply furious and miserable and wanted to hit them both, hard. The old Adam. Or Cain, more accurately: mark of. Loud echoes of the old Glum enemy rumbled in my guts.

I couldn't believe all this was happening. Stared at the house. The FOR SALE sign crucified to the wall was defaced with luminous spray paint into PATHS FOR ALE. Heavy metal pulsed from the house. Sex-teased squeals and hyena laughter punctured the beat.

They'd completely taken it over, polluted it, the place where I was recovering, stripping myself down, remaking myself, had been invaded, desecrated, defiled, raped.

Suddenly I hated them.
Yes, Gill, Adam, Tess as well.
All of them.
Paradigm of humanity.
I hated their noise,
their occupation of my space,
hated their sprawl and splurge and clutter and mess.
The splat of their lives.

Hated most of all the pretended individuality of their slavish conformity.

They were not me, nothing I wanted or wanted to be, everything I did not want. Defined by negatives. There was no way I was going back inside while any of them were still there. Trespassers. But there was no way I could get shot of them either, not in the state they were in by now. Worse still, the state I was in myself.

I stood there trembling with impotent rage.

What to do?

Where to go?

Nothing.

Nowhere.

Not with people.

To hell with people.

Nowhere where they'd find me.

I crossed the road and leaned on the bridge and glared downstream, my mind a match for the pummelling noise behind me and the surging swirl beneath my feet.

Just then a thin moon splintered from a bank of clouds, its mist-smeared light revealing the shrouded shape of a wintering cabin cruiser snugly tethered to the bank a couple of fields away downstream.

Because he wasn't there, Jan doesn't know what happened next so I'll tell it, but I'd better say at the start that I'm not a writer, not like Jan is, he really loves it, anyone would have to, to work all day then come home and write most of the evenings, not to mention weekends. I have to prise him from his room if I want him to go out, and God knows when he gets to bed most nights. I'm bad enough, being addicted to watching videos in bed, I can still be at it, eyes glued at two in the morning, but if I go to the bathroom to try and break the spell he's still there scribbling away. I think he's only ever really truly happy when he's writing, it's the only time when he's in focus – when he's doing what he says he lives for.

I envy him, because there's nothing that's like that for me. Well, sex of course, but that's different, that's because I'm human, it's nothing extra, nothing special. What makes me happiest, as a matter of fact, is just life. I mean eating and sleeping and having sex and lying in the sun and playing tennis, and reading a really gripping book curled up on my bed, and being with friends, and wearing just the right clothes, and looking, just looking, at other people doing ordinary things, 'watching the passing' my grandmother used to call it. I completely lack ambition, I suppose, I'm just happy to be here and to enjoy what comes along.

Some of my friends ask why I let Jan stay with me, he can't be much fun they say, but they don't see the best of him because he's so private. Writing Adam's story has something to do with his hiddenness. I think it's a story about himself, maybe a declaration. I'm not sure. But what I am sure of is that he needs me to be here, or rather he needs to be here with me. Not that I do much for him. I don't do his laundry, for instance, and he feeds himself (and me as well) most of the time, and being an inveterate tidier he tends to do most of the house cleaning. In fact, he doesn't make any demands, I wish he would sometimes because it's nice to be asked to do things for a friend, but he never does, I have to suss out what he wants and then offer or just get on and do it. I've talked to him about it, of course, we talk about *everything*, which is another reason why I like him so much (love him, I suppose), and he goes on about imposing on people, hating to feel that someone is doing something for him only because they have to, or worse, because they've been manipulated into doing it, emotionally blackmailed.

[– Aren't you supposed to be telling what happened after I left the party?
  – I'm going to, be quiet, please.
  – And you're the one who says she doesn't like writing!
  – It's just the way it's coming out.
  – You never could tell a story.
  – Rubbish, there's more than one way to tell a story.]

The first day I saw him, standing in the toll-house living room, he looked like the ghost of a ghost. Bony-thin to the point of wispy, blenched, miserable, those big, gripping, hard, grey-green eyes red-rimmed and bleary and staring at me with a mixture of fright and defiance. So first it was the eyes that got me and then later, as he picked through the stuff I'd brought and the eyes were busy elsewhere, it was the hands – long-fingered, thin-boned, talking hands. (I have a thing about hands, I love them, I think they're one of the most beautiful parts of the body, but I can't stand people with ugly hands, especially short stubby fingers and fat palms.)

I thought he was just weary after a bad night and nervous in a new place. But I soon realized he was ill. I don't think he remembers how bad he was. He'd go for a whole day without eating and say he wasn't hungry. Then in the middle of the night he'd scoff all he could find and next day he'd sit around staring at the blank walls refusing to say anything.

He'd also do weird things like spend ages standing on the bridge staring down at the river. I even found him there one day in the rain soaked to the skin. There was a kind of dottiness about his behaviour that sometimes made me want to shake him hard and tell him to snap out of it. Mum said he was like somebody grieving, but who for or what for?

One way and another, what with Dad keeping him steadily busy and Mum coddling him a bit and me being with him, after a month or so he was sleeping and eating properly, and looked much better, less wispy, more *there*. And he always read a lot, even when The Glums came over him again, crushing him down, which happened every few days. He could be awful then, saying bitter destructive things if you made him talk to try and lift him out of The Pit. I soon learned not to try and cheer him up but just to sit with him, letting him read or stare into space. Being there was all the help he needed, I think, but he never said so, though afterwards, when he was properly recovered, he did.

I suppose that's when our friendship really began, which has always seemed kind of odd to me – that a friendship should begin with the bad times and not with the good ones. While he sat there suffering, it was then we felt we recognized each other, knew each other, without explaining or talking about it, and knew that whatever happened we would always be a pair. Complementary. Life companions. Regardless of who else in the future we loved or lived with or kept as friends. We're still like that, and though it always looks to other people as if it's Jan who needs me, I need him too, only what he does for me doesn't show so much. He sustains me in the way I need just as much as I sustain him in the way he needs, and we both know it, so what does it matter what other people think?

By the time Adam turned up Jan was much better. The wraithiness had vanished, he'd filled out nicely, his skin was clear, his eyes not crazed any more. His hands, roughened from the work he'd done, were even more beautiful. He'd persuaded me to chop his hair very short because he said it would be easier to keep right that way, and though it was ragged it suited him, adding a slightly dishevelled severity to his lean looks. Mum said he reminded her of a novice monk, and it is true, he is a bit monkish. And innocent unworldly too – he doesn't quite understand what makes the world go round, though he likes to think he does.

That business with the estate agent, for instance. What got up his nose as much as anything is that B-and-G was so obviously a turd, and what's worse a not very clever turd, and Jan can't understand why people were taken in by him. Jan can't see that people admire the B-and-Gs because the B-and-Gs of the world are clever in a way Jan isn't – they're clever with cunning and self-confidence and at knowing how to manipulate people's whims and fancies. They appeal to people's weaknesses. They know that most people are impressed by flash cars and designer clothes and exotic holidays and the extravagant signs of money and power.

Neither does he understand the way sex works, doesn't see that the B-and-Gs play that game too. Most people's brains aren't in their heads, they're in their crotches. So the B-and-Gs aren't oddities, they're typical. Jan is the oddity, that's the fact, and he gets upset and angry because he doesn't want the world to be the way it is and can't understand that most people don't mind, they actually like it the way it is. People revel in their weaknesses, it seems to me, and admire those who become successful by exploiting weaknesses. Their own and other people's.

Jan wants people to live up to something better than they are. Mostly, they never will so he's bound to suffer for the rest of his life. He's like someone who lacks a protective layer of skin. Every brush against the world hurts. Life will never be what he wants it to be, he'll never quite understand why, other people will always think him a little odd, so he'll never quite be accepted. And, if you want to know, I think his depressions started when this began to dawn on him. Which is why, in my opinion, he came to the toll bridge, to be on his own while he sorted it out. And he was running away too, of course, which was obvious to everybody except himself.

Jan ran to the toll bridge and Adam ran into him there. Two runaways colliding, and the story gets more complicated to tell now because I come into it, like a third particle colliding with the other two.

Yes, it's true, I did have a thing about Adam. From first sight I fancied him. His earthiness, his utterly relaxed, unbothered attitude to life. He wasn't very tall but was supple and beautifully built. I mean, he just oozed sex. But from the very first sight of him I felt that inside him there was a vulnerable, almost frightened boy. Don't know how I knew this. Intuition, I suppose. And perhaps something in his eyes. Didn't think about it. But the mix was irresistible.

Something else made the situation even more sensational, something Jan didn't know because he couldn't see it, being part of it. I mean the two of them together.

Like sea against cliffs, hills against sky, each heightened the quality of the other. Emphasized the other's being and beauty. And each was beautiful, I don't know how to describe it, when you see it you know it, and it has as much to do with personality as it has to do with body.

Anyhow, I admit I let myself be carried away. There I was with these two males, one who made me think and talk like I'd never thought and talked before, and one who I fancied like crazy. And both of them needed me. How could I resist? Why should I? That day Jan was sick from painter's colic arrived like a gift and I grabbed it.

Adam was playful and full of jokes and bursting with energy. I was lusty and insatiable and I didn't care. I never now smell new paint in a room without remembering that day, feeling it in my skin, in my flesh, in my nerves and on my tongue again, and the rough texture of the blanket spread on the bare boards of the floor and the tang of woodsmoke in my nose and the tingle of heat from the fire as we lay beside it and the slip of sweat between us and its salt taste and the sound of the river outside and our blood surging inside as though both might engulf us at any moment and sweep us away, and best and most remembered, the feel and touch of his hands and his kissing and biting and the excruciating pleasure of it.

And then the bittersweet after-taste of melancholy, with Adam beside me dead to the world though I longed for him to hold me and give me his eyes and his mind as he had given me his body and not to drift away and drown in sleep.

In a while I covered him with a blanket and stole away home along the river bank through the empty dark, glad to be alone, glad to be myself in the dank winter night.

But I learned something from what happened later: Never to be taken but ever give. Never to be one but ever two. Never to be possessed by another but ever possess myself.

Jan didn't tell me till long afterwards about Dad seeing us. Thank God for that. Dad's never mentioned it but I realize now that it was about then that his attitude to me changed. For one thing, he became less physically affectionate. Before, he'd always been a hugger, liked to sit with his arm around me while watching telly. After, he became more distant, wasn't so spontaneous in showing his feelings. At the time I put it down to the strain he was under at work, but the real cause must have been seeing me with Adam that night.

The next day was the surprise party and that can't have helped either. Dad has always said I have a wicked streak. 'My little devil,' he used to call me when I was small. When I got older, in my teens and not so cute any more, it irritated him, but by then it was too late, the mould had set. Parents should be careful which traits they coddle in their children. Cute can easily turn into crass. No one can ever escape

113

all her-history. (A Jan-type joke and a truth he finds it hard to live with.)

Not that having a surprise party and inviting Gill was only devil-ment. I really did think Jan needed to see her if he was to make up his mind about her. There were all sorts of things that made me think this.

For example, there were a lot more letters from her than he's mentioned. For a few weeks one came every day. At the beginning he read them all. But they upset him. He's said nothing about that. I got to know about it because one day after he'd been at the bridge about three weeks I arrived on foot after my bike had conked out, so he didn't hear me coming. I saw him through the living-room window, sitting at the table with a letter in his hands, tears streaming down his face. I rushed in of course and comforted him and eventually got out of him that the letters kept him feeling tied to everything he was trying to cut free of – his parents, his home, the school, the town. And what he felt were the demands Gill made – her wanting him so much, her clinging to him, which he said felt like being suffocated.

Anyhow, after that he stopped reading the letters. Now and then he'd try one just to see if he felt any different about them, but he never did. Instead he pinned them, mostly unopened, to the back of the living-room door where they accumulated, always with the name and address right way up, Gill's neat round schoolgirlish handwriting repeating Jan's name and address again and again as if for a school punishment. Then one day I decided the joke had gone far enough and started taking them down. Jan flew into a rage, yelling at me to stop meddling and treating him like a kid, I wasn't his mother, etc. etc. Very vicious and emotionally violent.

After that we didn't speak for two days.

But I've side-tracked. Back to the day of the party.

That morning I felt terrible. As soon as I woke it came over me what I'd done. For the rest of the day during school I reassessed my values in life, as only the self-condemned know how. I didn't exactly pray that if God didn't strike me down with everything from herpes to Aids I'd never do anything so foolish again, but nearly. Then, after school there was shopping for the party and the business of getting Jan out of the house and making everything ready, which took my mind off my worries. In fact, typical me, I went to the other extreme and over-compensated by throwing myself body and soul into the party.

Which party, I admit, went over the top, as usual once word

gets round, especially in an area like ours with a university in range. By the time Gill turned up the house resembled a scene in Caligula's palace during one of his more ingenious periods.

At any rate, Gill flipped into a kind of catatonic shock. After all those weeks of writing all those letters and not getting a kind word never mind a letter in return, and all the time being patient and understanding and making allowances, she arrives to find him apparently having his balls massaged by a black-haired hussy in the middle of a crowd of zonked spectators lolling about in various states of *déshabillé* and at various stages preparatory to coition, if not already at it.

[– Laying it on a bit, aren't you?
– Enjoying it.
– Wasn't quite that colourful, though, was it?
– Moderately hectic. Anyway, that's how it's come out, so however it was *then*, that's how it is *now*.
– So much for history.
– History is only accepted fiction.
– Hey-up! That's not you!
– You mean, you don't think I'm clever enough.
– Come on, be honest.
– Caught you out for once! Read it somewhere. Can't remember.
– So much for memory.
– While memory holds a seat
  In this distracted globe, remember thee!
  Yea, from the table of my memory
  I'll wipe away all trivial fond records.
– Oo, climb every mountain, chuck!]

The row outside the house sets my nerves jangling and jogs my worries and brings me back to my senses. This isn't my day, I think, wishing I'd never suggested the wretched party in the first place. Blame Jan, I tell myself, it's his fault for dithering. (When in doubt, transfer the guilt.)

I follow Gill inside after exchanging a few more ill-chosen words with Jan. But can't find her. The party has reached the slow-(e)motion phase already. Heaven knows what's been going the rounds. Adam isn't there either.

I begin not to care, nudge myself a space on the living-room floor

115

near the fire beside a friend from school who is sitting alone staring at the glowing embers (no one has enough wits left to put a fresh log on) while morosely brooding. She immediately starts to tell me about the loss of her boyfriend and bursts into tears and says she'd better slope off home because she doesn't want people seeing her like this, which she does, leaving *moi* on my *sola* again, not a happy girl, my turn to stare regretfully at the embers.

What happened next happened very quickly and at the time was very confused, anyway confusing.

After the row outside Gill had stomped back into the house, intending to grab her bag which she had dropped on the floor of the living room, and set off for home, or anywhere – she just wanted to get away. But her bag wasn't there (somebody had shoved it into a corner). That's when she saw her letters pinned up on the living-room door, and she flipped.

She ran out through the back door, where the outside light showed her the steps down to the lawn. Dashing down them, she slipped on their frosty surface and grazed her knee (she didn't even feel it at the time, we found out later). She then blundered onto the path that led her along the river bank and under the bridge.

There she stopped, breathless from distress and sensing she had come the wrong way and should go back. But she didn't want to go anywhere near the house again in case she met Jan or me. 'I felt I'd be sick if I did,' she told me later, 'I was so weary and angry at what had happened.'

So she paused while she caught her breath and tried to decide what to do. But after a while, as she stood there in the dank cold with the arch of the bridge curving low over her head like the roof of a dungeon, and echoing the full-spated river swirling at her feet 'as if,' she said, 'it wanted to sweep me away,' she felt so abandoned, humiliated, and churned up with rage that she burst into tears. 'How could they!' she kept spluttering. 'How *dare* they!' No one had ever treated her like that before. 'It was the first time I'd ever really felt betrayed.'

By this time she was in such a state that she wasn't aware of anyone approaching until she heard a male voice right behind her asking, 'Are you Gill?', which so startled her that she screamed, swung round, slipped on the muddy path, and fell, slithering into the river up to her waist before she was grabbed and lifted upright, instinctively grasping at her rescuer, who clung onto her, holding her tightly against him.

Relief turned to panic. She didn't know who this man was. Now she was trapped in his arms. He kept saying, 'It's OK, it's all right, it's only me, Adam, it's OK.' But she didn't know any Adam and it wasn't OK. She struggled against him, screaming loudly again. 'It's all right,' Adam shouted as she struggled and kicked.

'I'd always wondered what I'd do,' Gill said later, 'if someone tried to attack me, you know how you do, but when it starts happening, you just panic so much, you can't think, you just don't want to get hurt and you're scared of doing anything that might make him more violent.'

Her screams must have panicked Adam. At any rate, Gill said, he suddenly let go of one of her arms to squash a hand over her mouth while shouting, 'Shut it, will you! Shut it!' And that, she said, is when anger took over from everything else. She had an arm free so she grabbed him by the hair and yanked his head back as hard as she could. At the same time, bracing herself against the wall, she brought her right knee up into his groin as hard as she could.

The result was that Adam let go and did a kind of whiplash – back and then forward – as the pain in his groin doubled him up. Gill dodged to one side. Adam's head smashed into the wall and he fell to the ground, where he lay curled up, squirming and moaning, with his hands clasping his crotch.

Gill didn't stay to watch after that but fled back towards the house, desperate for help. She and I collided with each other at the top of the back steps.

'God, what's happened?' I said, taking her inside.

'A man attacked me,' she managed to get out. 'A man. Under the bridge. It was awful.'

She started shaking so violently she could hardly speak at all. The others crowded round, asking questions.

'Look, shut up,' I said to them. 'She needs some calm.'

'Shouldn't we see if he's still there?' someone said.

'Some of the boys should go.'

'Get the police,' someone said.

'God, no – the police in here! Have some sense!'

Gill was completely distraught.

'I'll make her a hot drink,' someone said.

*

117

The search party returned, unable to find anyone. They'd looked under the bridge, along the river path, around the house, on the bridge itself, and had even made a sortie to the other side just in case. But no one, except for people deserting the party double-quick. Jan wasn't anywhere to be found, either. Nor Adam. Several of my friends offered to stay in case the guy was a psycho and might try again, but I'd had enough of everything to be honest, and just wanted to be on my own and sort things out with Gill and Jan (who I thought was probably sulking nearby and would come back once everybody had gone).

So I made people clear off and went round picking up the mess while Gill huddled by the fire looking shattered. Jan's little alarm clock said twelve forty-five. Less than an hour since Gill's arrival! I'd thought it must be ages later.

When I'd done as much clearing up as I could bear, I sat with Gill by the fire. I'd been putting off this moment.

We stared at each other, strangers and not strangers, having to make a fresh start. I knew what had to be done but being me it took a big struggle inside myself before I could force myself to say, 'Sorry – sorry, sorry, sorry – this is all my fault.'

Gill looked away and shrugged.

There was a long silence before she said, 'I wish I knew what was going on.'

She was near to tears again.

'Look,' I said. 'Let's start at the beginning – what else have we got to do?' And I tried to tell her what had happened since Jan arrived at the bridge. She hardly interrupted at all, just a question here and there, until Adam came into the story, when, for the first time, she suddenly startled.

'Adam?!' she said.

'The boy who's helping Jan. I mentioned him in my letter.'

'Not his name. You didn't mention his name.'

'I didn't? Thought I had. Why, though? What's the matter?'

'The man who attacked me. I remember now. He said his name was Adam. "It's only me," he said, "Adam – it's OK".'

I stared at her. 'Christ! – are you sure?'

'Certain. I'd forgotten till you said his name.' She shivered. 'It was so awful,' she added bleakly, no tears, just cold fear.

'But it couldn't have been – Just a bit taller than me. Well built. Black hair –'

'I couldn't see! How could I see, it was so dark and we were under the bridge, and I was so upset and so scared –'

'Sorry, yes, sorry, 'course, wasn't thinking –'

Which wasn't true at all, just one of those things we say at times like that. I was thinking hard. I was thinking that if it were Adam, where was he now? Why hadn't he come back? Or was it obvious why he hadn't? If he'd been trying to help, and Gill had misunderstood, not knowing him when she thought she did, and he'd hurt his head and had his goolies crushed, wouldn't the natural thing be to come back inside and get help? Unless he hadn't been trying to help at all. But I didn't want to think about that. The night before came flooding back, exactly the night before: twenty-four hours ago in front of this same fire on this same floor in this same house with someone who might be – That didn't bear thinking about either.

Perhaps there'd been another Adam at the party? But if there were and he was the attacker, why would he say 'it's only me'? Only one Adam would have said that – our Adam. *Our* Adam! Dear God!

And if it were 'our' Adam and he had attacked Gill, what did that mean about 'our' Adam? And might he even be a psycho and be hiding somewhere nearby, waiting his chance to come back to try again – I started to feel scared myself.

Where the hell was Jan? Why didn't he come back?

It was nearly one thirty. Mum and Dad knew we were having a party – though they didn't know it was the kind it had turned into or Dad would have been down sharpish and put a stop to it. They'd have gone to bed, but I knew Dad would be lying awake, waiting for me. And I desperately wanted to go home now. Wanted to feel safe and in my own room and out of all this mess. But I couldn't leave Gill on her own. Apart from the toll-bridge psycho, there was the prospect of her having to face her beloved again: she wouldn't want to do that on her own. And as I'd brought all this about, I did feel it was my fault, my responsibility, and I couldn't just leave her to it.

The only thing I could think of was to get Gill and myself out of there. In the morning things might look different. So I said,

'Look, Gill, we can't stay here all night. I mean, we're both knocked out, and I doubt if you'd feel comfortable trying to sleep here. I've a motorbike. D'you think you could stand to ride pillion, just for ten minutes? I could take you home. My parents won't mind, they're OK, they're used to me having friends overnight.

We could get some sleep and think about what to do in the morning.'

We looked each other straight in the eyes for a moment, neither of us needing to say anything more. And then the natural thing seemed to be to take her hands in mine. She gripped me tight, and nodded, and we hugged each other and had to swallow the tears.

Gill's jeans were still damp, but she pulled them on. I found her bag and tamped the fire down, switched off all but one of the lights, and we left, locking the door behind us and hiding the key in the usual place so Jan could get in, and drove off, me hoping there were no late-night bobbies cruising round the village on the hunt for teenage L-plate delinquents. L for life as well as driving, I thought.

Coming To

Inside, the boat was perishing cold. Trimmed for winter lay-up, no food, very little of anything pinchable left behind and what there was stowed away and locked. Had to force the cabin door. Guiltily. But desperation overrides everyday honesty. There was a Gaz lamp, found when feeling my way round the cabin in the glim of moonlight filtering through the little head-high windows. Matches in a drawer by the galley stove. I used the lamp for long enough to find a blanket in an unlocked locker under one of the bunks and lie down fully clothed, then doused it, fearing detection or attracting a curious boozer from the bridge. Party noises drifted to me, brittle on the frosty air, among them at one moment not long after I'd lain down a girl's screams that didn't sound like party pretence or genuine delight, but I paid no attention, not wanting to know.

Everything a violation. The Glums threatened.

Maybe because of the drink, maybe because of the colic, or of Peeping Tom the night before, or of having had so little to eat all day, or the combination of cold damp in the cabin and warm damp in the wrap of the blanket – whatever it was, and against the odds, I somehow contrived to fall asleep. For how long I couldn't tell when I was woken by the boat lurching as someone clambered aboard. Adrenalin pumped. I sat up and listened.

Hands fumbled with the fasteners that secured the cockpit awning.

I called out, 'Who is it?'

The fumbling stopped.

Silence.

'Hello?'

Nothing.

I pressed my face to a window but, the moon now hidden again, could see nothing except the darker darkness of the river bank. But as

I peered into the dark an object suddenly fell onto the narrow walkway of deck that ran at window level immediately outside. It took a moment for me to realize that the object was a human head. And only after I'd scrambled off the bunk and lit the lamp and held it close to the window did I see that it was covered in blood, which was oozing from a gash in the forehead, that the eyes were closed with the sucked-in dead look of the unconscious, and that the head was Adam's.

What is it about the sight of unconsciousness that makes you desperate? Is it because unconsciousness is halfway to death, and your natural impulse is to save the victim from going all the way? Or maybe that instinct I so much hate in humanity – the instinct to try and keep everybody else in the same state as you're in yourself, even when you know your own state is dangerous or hasn't much to recommend it – as when druggies tice others to shoot up, just to take an obvious example. Deadly conformity, dire conservatism. I'm what's called alive, so you must stay alive as well, even if your life is rotten and worse is likely to beset you, because life is always believed to be better than any kind of death (though how does anyone know, as no one has come back to tell us what it's like?). So taking your own life goes by offensive names – suicide, self-slaughter, sin, crime, self-destruction – and people are pitied who attempt it, as are those who by accident are associated with anyone who succeeds in doing it. What fools these mortals be.

And being no different my mortal self, I'd unlatched the window before I'd thought about it, and was reaching a hand through to touch Adam's face, as if by laying on my hand I would bring him back to consciousness and know he was really there, unquestionably alive.

He groaned at my touch, which was reassuring.

'Adam,' I cried, 'Adam – what's happened? Adam? Adam! Are you OK? Are you all right?'

He groaned again, stirred, turning his face away.

A new imperative possessed me at once. To get him inside, out of the cold.

'Wait! Don't move! I'm coming.'

Blood on my hand. And then standing at his feet on the side deck, holding the lamp over him. How difficult to lift him from that awkward space and down into the cabin. Help from the house? No lights. No noise. What time? Two thirty by my wristwatch. Could it be over already, an all-night glug like that? But anyway, there and back – He needed help now. Freezing. Blood.

He stirred again, trying to struggle to his feet, all his athletic animal ease gone. Awkward stiff angles, yet floppy, a puppet with its strings cut. He wouldn't make it. Might tumble overboard. He slumped to the deck again. I scrambled across the cabin roof to the side deck at his head, stood the lamp on the roof so as to free both my hands, and, taking him by the shoulders, lifted him into a sitting position, his head lolling against my shoulder, his cheek pressing against my cheek, the oily wetness of cold blood lubricating our skins.

❖ 2 ❖

Why am I doing this? I asked myself again and again. Only because I knew him? What if he were a stranger, would I have left him to it? Who could, except some kind of psycho? Another of those human instincts? The law of the irrational. I hate doing something I haven't thought out and decided for myself I want to do. But how often is it truly by thought that we come to do things? I remembered the moment of *déjà-vu* when Adam first came to me. The assurance of the inevitable.

Whatever, there I was stuck with him. Again. There were also moments in the next ten minutes, which is what it took to manhandle him into the cabin and onto a bunk, and retrieve the lamp so that I could see what to do next, that I felt like a one-man Laurel and Hardy (a Laurelandhardy) in the scene where they try to deliver a piano up a long flight of steps. And remembering that saved me from losing heart or even my temper; only it also reduced me to laughter at the thought of how bizarre was my present predicament – another fine mess you've gotten us into – that I had to sit for a while till I recovered myself. I think I was near hysterical from exhaustion after the last forty-eight hours.

When I finally got Adam inside and could give him a close inspection I saw just how bad he was. His skin was putty-coloured and clammy, as if he were sweating chilled water. His breathing was shallow and quick. I tried his pulse, because people always seemed to do that when dealing with sickness; it seemed weak and fast, not a steady confident throb but more like a racing echo of a pulse. The gash in his forehead was neither long nor deep but blood oozed from it in alarming quantity quite out of proportion to its size, and was smudged all over his face so that he looked as if he'd been badly battered. Of course he was covered in muck. And he smelt awful. He'd vomited onto his clothes which were smeared with a rancid porridge of mud and blood and sweat and puke that filled the air in the confined space of the cabin with such a sour stench that I gagged and had to retreat outside till I could catch my breath and prepare myself for the onslaught again.

This was one of the times when I wondered why I was doing what I was doing. And this time, I then thought, I'm not going to be defeated, it's only a putrid pong, after all, not a case of chemical warfare.

Back inside, I watched him closely for a few minutes, trying to assess the state he was in. He seemed to be drifting somewhere between unconscious and semi-conscious – groaning, moving a little but erratically, and not much aware of what was happening, as far as I could tell. When he wasn't trying to move, his body was a floppy dead weight. I said his name into his ear two or three times but got no reaction.

I guessed that somehow or other he'd taken a bang on the head and was suffering from concussion, not that I knew what concussion actually meant, only that anybody suffering from it had to rest and take it easy for a while. I knew from times when I'd banged my own head that it could make me feel sick, so I supposed a very bad knock might actually make you vomit. Also, Adam had been drinking the multicult punch pretty freely so that wouldn't have helped matters either. Maybe he was suffering from a hangover as much as from anything else. But what if he was really ill from something I didn't know about, like a heart attack or . . . or what? That was the problem. If I didn't know about it, I wouldn't recognize it! I suddenly felt utterly ignorant about everything to do with the body. Why didn't I know more, why hadn't anybody told me?

What I knew for sure was that I couldn't leave him lying there in that filthy condition. Somehow I had to clean him up and make him more comfortable. But how? There was no water on board so it would have to be river water. Somewhere, though, there ought to be a First Aid kit; at least that might provide a bandage and some sort of antiseptic for his wound.

Finding a First Aid box in a locker by the cabin door raised my spirits no end. And in a locker by the transom was a plastic bucket. So I opened the First Aid kit and put it on the table in the cabin, and then half-filled the bucket.

At which point, ready to start, it suddenly came over me in a wave of weakening fastidiousness that I'd never cleaned up anybody before. I didn't at all relish the idea of messing with another person's gunged-up body.

I stared at Adam, seeing him in a different light. Not as 'Adam', but as a physical being made up of legs and feet and arms and various parts – fingers, toes – and organs with holes in them, and private nooks and crannies I'd never even seen before, let alone handled and washed and dried and closely inspected.

I began to shake and for a moment wondered if after all the best thing wouldn't be to fetch help. If there was no one in a fit state at the house, then I could run to the phone box in the village and call an ambulance. How long would that take? Half an hour? An hour? Would he be safe alone for that long? What if he came to enough to get up, and then stumbled into the river? And if I called an ambulance, think of the fuss there'd be afterwards. The hospital would want to know how he got into such a mess. The police. Bob Norris. Questions about the party. Trouble for Tess. Mayhem for me. I was supposed to be in charge. They'd hold me responsible, dammit! Maybe if I cleaned him up and brought him round, I could find out what had happened and if he really was in a bad way I could do something about getting him to hospital then.

Nothing else for it, whether I liked it or not, but to swallow my revulsion and clean him up and tend his wound as best I could. So where to start? With his face and head and the wound? Staunch the flow of blood? The First Aid kit included a packet of cotton wool. With a wad dipped in water I dabbed at the outer edges of his face, gingerly at first but with growing what-the-hell, I'll-never-finish-it-like-this confidence, wiping away the blood and muck. The First Aid kit also included a small bottle of antiseptic. I used some of that on a wad of cotton wool to clean round the edge of the cut, which really was quite small in fact. Then, with wincing delicacy, as if it might hurt me too, gently sponged the wound itself, at which Adam did stir and groan and flinch and try to push my hand away so at least I knew he was feeling something.

The antiseptic had the added advantage of scenting the air with something that smelt clean and healthy. But by then I'd grown used to the stink and was feeling quite proud of myself. I'd have fainted just at the thought of doing this only a few days before.

What next? Bind the wound. I readied the bandage, made a pad of cotton wool which I placed over the cut, then wrapped the bandage round his head a few times till there seemed to be enough to keep the dressing in place. To do that I had to keep lifting Adam's head. How heavy an unconscious head is, like a leaden stone! Alas, poor Yorick!

125

Heads I win, tails you lose. With his head tucked underneath his arm he walked the bloody tower. If you can keep your head when all about you are losing theirs and blaming it on you. Lay your sleeping head, my love, human on my faithless arm.

What stupid things come into your mind at such times. Yet not stupid, if you think about it. Pertinent and true in odd unthought ways. Is anything that comes into your mind ever arbitrary, ever meaningless?

That done, I was going to clean up his hands but realized he'd only mucky them again every time he touched his clothes, and besides, they would carry the muck to his face. Take off at least his outer clothing.

I sat him up and managed by a combination of rolling it up from the waist and easing it over his head to slip his putrid pullover off. My pullover, in fact – the best blue one he took with him when he first disappeared and he'd used ever since so that now it was stretched and sloppy which at least made it easier to get off. Next his boots. Then his pungent jeans. Leaving him in grubby white T-shirt and none too attractive blue Y-fronts. My T-shirt, my Y-fronts.

Covered with the only blanket, that was the best I could do. After which, the confined space looking a mess, my conditioned reflexes took over and I tidied up. The bundle of clothing chucked into a corner of the cockpit. The bucket emptied and stowed away. The First Aid box ready on the table in case of need. The wads of soiled cotton wool stuffed into the empty waste bin under the galley stove. I'd clean up properly when daylight came.

What now? Nothing, except watch and wait.

Very soon Adam seemed no longer to be drifting between unconscious and semi-conscious but to be sleeping. He was more 'there' and also, strangely, more relaxed. Before, he'd been floppy but somehow struggling inside himself; now he wasn't floppy any more but together and at ease. His breathing was better, his skin less waxy, less pale and clammy. I tried his pulse: the beat was stronger and steady. I don't think I'd realized before that relaxation is a form of action, of *being*; that when you're relaxing you're *doing something* just as much as when you're walking or eating or reading or running the marathon. It's a particular use of energy.

❖ 3 ❖

Adam was also pleasantly warm under the blanket, which is more

126

than I could say for myself. The exertion of getting him into the cabin and tending him had kept me warm – in fact I'd been so busy that I hadn't been aware of the cold. Now that he was settled and all I had to do was sit there and keep watch, I quickly cooled till I was shivering and had time to notice how I felt. Which was bone weary and miserable. The muscles in my arms and legs didn't just feel weak, to say which implies they still had some strength, but were in an anti-energy crisis. I was sure that if I stood up my legs would flobble under me like a couple of sausage balloons losing air. And if there'd been anything to drink, which I dearly craved, I couldn't have picked up the glass because my arms would have lolloped around as they do when you've lain on them too long.

Sleep was also something I longed for but couldn't achieve. Sitting up, I'd nod off and startle awake again at once. Lying down, the bitter cold seemed worse and woke me up. And so sitting up and lying down by turns a dreary hour passed.

I didn't get far, wondering what to do next, either. The only thought that occupied my mind with any tenacity was a dreary sequence of variations on the theme of unfairness. Which went something like this:

How in hell has all this happened to me? Just because I've been fool enough to give houseroom to a down-and-out would-be squatter, a half-drowned burglar with a big cock and the smile of a dog on heat? Just because of an accident, a quirk, a happenstance – unplanned, unintended, unwanted, unwilled, unprovoked (after all, I'd only been minding my own business stuck out in the middle of nowhere), uninvited, unannounced, undeserved, unforeseen, unforetold, unforgivable, unimagined, unfair.

Unfair, that's what it is, unfair, unfair, unfair.

Et cetera. On and on.

Unfair is such a playground word. The kids' game complaint. The blub of the impotent. The rail of the naïve against the wily. The howl of the baby-innocent against the street-wise. The battle cry of those who desire that no one in the world shall be better off than they are themselves. The pule of the weak benighted temporary deluded mistaken human race against the unthinkable unplumbed unmoved eternal infinity of the vast unregarding forever. What fools these mortals be.

I sat there, lay there, huddled against the frosted night, and whinged.

I'd come to this place, this wilderness, to escape imposition, to strip myself down in order to gain control of myself and build myself up in my own image, and what had happened? Taken over and buggered up, sod it!

Oh, lusty satisfaction of the sexual curse!
        Curse of the inarticulate.
        Sentence of Cain on the able.
        Rape of the word.
        The body's stiff big finger erected against the mind.

❖ 4 ❖

The Gaz lamp stuttered; fuel running out and no spare can. I took a close look at Adam before the light died. Sound asleep, lying on his back, one bare arm curled loosely round his head, a patch of dried blood staining the bandage that circled his brow. The failing light softened the features of his face, deepened the blackness of his dishevelled hair, lent the patina of stone to the folds of grey blanket that cloaked his body like a shroud – disturbing image of a sculpted memorial to a fallen soldier. Not one of those hero-lies, no no, but a boy cut down before the truth of life had woken him from the sleep of innocence.

Soon the cabin would be as dark as the grave. Already it was cold enough for a tomb and I cold enough to be a ghost. Certainly, I felt like one, standing over Adam, as if waiting to welcome him to the afterlife, a prince of death beside a sleeping beauty.

Smiling to myself at that thought, I bent down and kissed him lightly on the cheek. But he flinched at the touch of my chilly lips, shifted his head away, caught at his breath, drew his exposed arm under the blanket, turned onto his side, and slipped into deep quiet slumber again.

For sure, being no prince of any kind I lacked the magic touch.

At that moment, as if on cue, the light went out with a final flare and an expiring hiss.

❖ 5 ❖

Sailors say the dogwatch is the worst. Four till six in the morning. Sitting in the deep before-dawn dark with only my own thoughts for company, this dogwatch was the hardest time of my time at the bridge. A time of reckoning. Of recognition. A slithery time of fractured memories bobbing up from buried passages of my life, and only intuition for guide – the ancient way of knowledge that bridges old Adam to new.

> *when he woke to consciousness*
> *he wondered if it was really him lying there*
>
> *never one*
> *ever two.*
>
> *every I is a You*
> *every You is an I*
>
> *I think therefore I am*
> *I am therefore I am observed*
>
> *which one is you now?*
> *which one would you prefer?*
> *can't I have both?*
> *I've never tried being both at once*
>
> *all one in making*
> *the kiss of two cones*
>
> *constant ambivalence*
> *happy ambiguity*
>
> *wish you were here?*

❖ 6 ❖

The minutes flicked, the hours passed, the smudge of dawn finally arrived. Seven thirty-five. Time to make a move.

We settled down for the night, Gill in the spare room next to me in mine. But after half an hour, when I was warm and cosy and might have drifted off, I heard Gill's door open and the bathroom door close, followed by the pitiful sound of retching.

I went to the bathroom door and said as softly as I could, 'Gill, are you OK?' No answer, just more retching. Mum poked her head out from her room, the very thing I was hoping wouldn't happen. I waved her back inside, whispering, 'I'll look after her,' and luckily she didn't insist.

After a few minutes Gill came out looking sheepish (why do people feel guilty when they've been sick?), I asked her if there was anything that would help, she said that it sounded silly but what she wanted more than anything was a bowl of cornflakes and warm milk, so downstairs we went to the kitchen, which was at least toasty warm from the Aga, where I sat her at the table, heated some milk, and let her make her own cornflake mix, which ended up a soggy stodge that she gobbled up as if she were starving.

After that we sat back and looked at each other. Neither of us said anything for quite a while, the house breathed around us, the coal in the Aga shifted in its belly, the kitchen clock click-clacked.

Now I could look at her properly, not fashed by goings-on at the bridge, and she'd had a wash and tidied herself up, I could see that she was actually rather pretty, sexy even, blonde straight hair, triangular face, wide apart large blue eyes, a straight firm slim nose, long mouth with full lips, good and attractively irregular teeth, chin a little too sharp-pointed perhaps, and a slim figure. Not good hands, though – too plump, thumbs a bit stubby – no match for her boyfriend's.

Out of genuine curiosity and not just for something to say, I asked her how she and Jan got together. 'Piers,' she said, 'I can't think of him as Jan, sorry!' 'Piers,' I said. It always seemed such a naff name to me, Piers Plowman at one end (not Jan at all!) and Piers out-of-the-top-drawer at the other (not Jan either), but nor was he a Pierre or a Peer or a Pedro or a Pietro or a Pyotr or a Cephas or any kind of Peter, which was too stone-age man to suit him, no rock he, and no no no not a Pete or a Pet, none of those, and yet they say what's in a name – everything, it seems to me. People should be careful with their names and the names they give their children. In fact in my opinion there ought to be a custom whereby everyone has a chance to pick the name they want for themselves when they are, say, sixteen or eighteen or whatever age we're supposed to become adult. After all, actors change their names to fit the image they want (Marion Michael Morrison became John Wayne, 'nuff said), writers often have pen names (George Eliot = Mary Ann Evans, George Orwell = Eric Blair), nuns and monks take different names (Sister Mary Joseph could once have been Ms Cheryl Smith, God help her) and of course women are always changing part of their name when they get married and thereby become the nominal possession of their husband and *hi*story, a slave collar that won't be hung round my neck by anyone, let me give notice.

I didn't say any of that to Gill just then of course, and anyway she launched into the story of their romance as if she'd been waiting to be asked.

She'd had the hots for Jan-Piers for a few weeks before she got him to pay her any attention. Something about his eyes and (oddly to my taste) his ears, but mostly it seemed his legs, which she'd been able to view during compulsory games, when he played a bad scrum half at rugby, and to better effect when he was playing tennis, and to best effect of all during swimming sessions in the school baths. She was in the same year as Jan but not in the same class so she couldn't get to him that way. There was gossip about him, isn't there always, which said he didn't have a girlfriend, steady or unsteady, and there were some in whose opinion he was a closet gay. This mix of information and guessery made Gill all the keener. Everybody agreed that Piers was quite bright if not outstandingly so – some said he had been accelerated too early by his pushy dad and that he was now running out of steam – but that he didn't flaunt it and was in general OK if not particularly exciting and sometimes a bit standoffish and secretive. On this assessment Gill decided that the way to this man's heart, probably to his penis as well, and for sure to his legs was via his head. So she started sending him intellectual morsels rather as in a different case she might have sent him love notes. Via the gossip line she researched his current fads, and sent him photocopies of poems, passages of prose, obscure footnotes from obscurer books, postcard pics of the appropriate personages (pin-ups for the mind), etc. etc., all accompanied by little offhand personal messages such as 'I hear you like Dumpty Dum too. Have you come across this? Isn't it great!' (the *appeal confrère*) or 'I can't get the hang of these lines from *XYZ*. A mutual friend says you're the expert around here on this kind of thing. Can you help?' (the *appeal supplicans*). *Mon dieu!* But it cheered me to hear that Jan didn't rise to this ploy, replying only with such putoffs as 'I prefer page 86, it's funnier' or 'Ask Fairbairn [one of the teachers], he'll explain.'

Nothing daunted, Gill decided to take the bull by the horns (what a vivid cliché in this context, Jan would have muttered) and make the approach direct. Having carefully prepared herself for every hoped-for eventuality (i.e. like us all, living for her fantasies) she called at his house one evening about eight, Eng. Lit. set book in hand, and shot a nice line about having an essay crisis, and could Piers please rescue her (the approach *damsel distrait*) and give her a bit of help with lines twenty-five to eighty, Act Three Scene Two.

This time she made an impression even though that evening she got no further than Act Three Scene Two examined in close proximity with the desired as they sat side by side at the dining-room table while desired's mother bobbed in and out every now and then, bearing first some fruit then some coffee and bickies and finally an offer (refused) of ice cream, all actually in aid of keeping an eye on sonnyboy and temptress.

Just before making her grateful what-a-relief thankyous and good-nights, Gill played an inspired unprepared gambit: Would Piers like to accompany her to the play at the Civic Theatre next Thursday, she had a couple of tickets, having intended to take a girlfriend, but the friend couldn't go after all, the ticket was going begging, her dad had paid for both so if Piers would like to . . . well, she'd just love it. Why not? said Mum, by now won over, and Piers fell for it. (Oh Jan-Piers, I'd hoped you were made of sterner stuff!) Of course in truth she didn't have a spare ticket at all, her friend had one of her own, and tomorrow Gill would have to persuade said friend to hand over said ticket as a matter of life or death, which said friend did, what else are friends for, though only after being let in on the reason and after promising a blow by blow (pardon, that one was accidental) account of the evening and to keep said friend informed of advances thereafter, which Gill did until things between her and Piers became serious, after which she naturally kept her mouth shut about the personal details. And she must have done pretty well with him that night (she said it was one of those times when everything goes just right) because only three days later, on the following Sunday afternoon, they were in her bed together while the rest of her family – parents, younger brother and sister – visited relatives for tea, she crying off because she had urgent homework to finish. From the faraway smile on her face when she described this moment in her story I could tell she had enjoyed her homework *très bien*.

I didn't say anything, letting her savour the memory, but she suddenly came to with a jolt, her face clouded, and she looked at me with eyes pained with suspicion and an unasked question.

'No, I haven't,' I said.

'When I saw you at the party –'

'Only a game. Didn't mean a thing.'

She nodded but I could tell she didn't believe me. Why should she? In her place I wouldn't.

'Why didn't he ever write?' she said. 'Or even phone.'

'Not because of anything between him and me.'

'And pinning my letters to the back of the door –'

'Honestly, Gill, I think you ought to ask him about that.'

'Does he still have The Glums?'

'Not lately. He's a lot better than when he first arrived. Pretty normal, in fact, I'd say. Well – his normal anyway!' Gill didn't smile. 'Not that I know what he was like before, so it's hard for me to tell.'

'Has he talked about me much?'

'A bit. Now and then.'

'You mean, he hasn't.'

'To be honest, no, not much. But he hasn't wanted to talk about himself much, either – I mean, his home and everything.'

'So what has he talked about?'

'What he's reading –'

'Might have guessed.'

'Movies, music, his work. People he's talked to while taking tolls. Stuff in the news. What he's thinking – you know how he likes to argue.'

'Do I know!' She managed a trace of a smile. 'Sounds like his old self again. He'd lost that by the time he left home. Wasn't reading anything except what he had to for school, wouldn't go out, wasn't even arguing, at least not about the things that interested him. All he did was row or bitch or groan on and on about being depressed and how stupid he was and how pointless life was. Or he'd pick fights with me over nothing – that was the worst. Wouldn't have been so bad if the times between had been OK, like at the beginning, but they weren't, we weren't even having any sex by the time he left home. And what a change that was! Our first few weeks, he was all over me, couldn't get enough, it was the only thing he seemed to want. I think he was catching up with what he'd missed. From Christmas to Easter we had a pretty good time, with only a patch of The Glums now and then, but during the Easter holidays the depression seemed to take him over and after that he got worse and worse. Funny when I think about it now – we had seven months together before he came here, only two months were the really bad times, but they seem like the longest part.'

'Twenty-eight point five per cent.'

'Sorry?'

'Can't help it, do maths at school. Two months is twenty-eight point five per cent of your seven months together. Not far off being a third. Probably more than a third if you add in the times when he had The Glums before he got really bad. And worst at the end. It must have been pretty awful, trying to cope with him and to help and getting nowhere.'

'I kept trying to remind him of the good times in my letters, hoping it would help, because it's always easier to remember the rotten times than it is to remember the good times, isn't it, all the details, I mean, don't you think?'

'That's why I like taking photos. Why most people take photos, in my opinion.'

'To remind them of the good times?'

'Well, people don't take photos of unhappy times, do they, not usually. Some professionals do, but not ordinary people. Nobody wants photos of themselves being ill or being angry or crying or things like that. They want pictures of having fun on holiday or of getting married and having parties and stuff like that. Nobody takes pictures of funerals or of themselves being divorced or having an operation or when they're in the huff. They just don't.'

'And isn't it funny how everybody has to smile, no matter what they feel like, nobody's allowed to look sad, are they. And as soon as people realize they're being taken, they start fixing their hair and tidying themselves up and pose and put on an act!'

'Vanity, vanity, all is vanity, my dad says, but if I try to snap him he slinks away.'

'Got to look your best, my mum says.'

We were laughing now and I saw how likeable Gill could be, what fun, if she were given a chance.

'Do you take a lot of pictures?' she asked.

'Quite a few. I do Practical Photography as an optional at school.'

'Have you taken any of Piers?'

'Would you like to see them?'

'Could I?'

'They're in my room.'

We viewed the pictures slouched on my bed. Fifteen or sixteen, starting with one taken the first week Jan was at the bridge and finishing with one taken a couple of weeks ago. Having gone through them once, Gill asked me to put them in chronological order. They hadn't been taken at regular intervals, and Jan wasn't in the same pose each time – they were snaps really, catching him off guard doing different things, I don't like posed shots – but still, between the first and the last you could see how much he'd changed, how much better he looked, his face had filled out, his hair of course was very different – long and twerpishly tidy when he arrived, short and natural after he cut it. His body seemed more developed, not so skinny-willowy any more. He was a lot sexier, to be honest. In the early pics, whatever he was doing he looked crushed, dead-eyed, hang dog, an unsmiling withdrawn wimp. In the later ones, he was on the *qui vive*, sparkier, the difference between a plant drooping from lack of water and the same plant revived after a good drink.

Gill noticed, stared at the pictures one after the other, inspecting each closely, another plant slaking a thirst, but she said nothing. Two or three of the later pics included Adam and there were some of him on his own that I'd put to one side after sorting out the ones of Jan.

'Who's that?' Gill asked as she went through the pictures for the third time.

'You don't know?'

'No, who?'

'Adam,' I said as offhand as I could, not only because I expected

Gill to react but also because the sight of him frightened me suddenly.

Gill stiffened, peered at the best shot of him, nose almost touching, then sat up cross-legged on the bed, holding the picture between her knees by thumb and first finger.

'Good-looking,' she said, trying to sound calm.

'Too good –'

'Not as tall as I thought, though.'

'And stronger than he looks.'

'Oh?' She glanced at me to make sure she'd guessed right.

'Told you you didn't have to worry about Jan and me.'

'Like that?'

'Once. The night before last.'

I told her everything, trying to be offhand about that too but couldn't help crying a bit by the end of course, it was all still so near the nerve and such a relief to tell someone. My turn to pass on the hurt.

Gill sat and listened, didn't react, didn't interrupt, didn't cry along with me, just sat there, cross-legged, her eyes never leaving me, the picture of Adam held between her knees, till I'd finished the story and had scrambled off the bed for a tissue. Then she said, 'You'll be OK. You know how it is.' Very matter-of-fact. So there's a cold side to her, I thought as I mopped my eyes, and said,

'Till one day it really is what you dread.'

'But he was all right with you? I mean, he wasn't violent or anything.'

'No no. Well, a bit. But –'

'If it was him.'

'There weren't any other Adams around, not that I know of.'

Gill stacked the photos like a pack of cards, the one of Adam and Jan on top, which she sat staring at, face in hands, elbows on knees, broody.

This is no good, I thought. At this rate we'll end up clinically depressed ourselves.

'Let's get some sleep,' I said. 'And tomorrow, I mean this morning, let's go and face those two. They've both got some explaining to do.'

Gill reacted like a startled rabbit. 'I couldn't, I can't.'

'I know how you must feel, but honestly, it's the only thing to do. We'll go together, I'm used to Adam, I know how to handle him, you needn't worry about him, if that's what bothers you. You know what boys are like, they'll pretend nothing's happened if we let them, they'll just go on as if everything's all right. Well, something *has*

136

happened and it *isn't* all right, and we've got to sort it out for our own sakes, never mind theirs.'

'Only . . . I feel so confused, so humiliated.'

'I know. Me too. And we'll go on feeling like that unless we do something about it.'

I don't remember any more of what we said, not accurately enough to write it down. Nothing of any importance I don't think, but we burbled at each other about the usual things, this time seen through the fog of the night's events. If the earlier talk had been about passing on the pain, now it was about calming each other down, jollying each other along, edging ourselves towards doing what we both knew had to be done.

It was four o'clock before Gill's eyes began to close – I was telling her about them putting the toll house up for sale and why we didn't want them to – till finally she dropped off completely, half curled across the diagonal of the bed, head to foot. I slipped a pillow under her head, lay down beside her, covered us with the duvet, and was soon asleep myself.

Morning After

Adam was still dead to the world. But he couldn't stay where he was much longer. He needed what the house offered: fresh water, food, clothes, warmth. How to get him there? Carry him? Too far. Float him in the boat? Current against us. Nothing else for it: tow.

Hauling a boat the size of a four-berth cabin cruiser upriver on your own isn't easy at the best of times. This was not the best of times. Doing it without anyone to steer is murder. The bow keeps nudging into the bank and sticking. After a couple of bodged goes that got me all of ten metres nearer destination in as many minutes, I managed to secure the tiller with just the right amount of turn to edge the boat out and counter the tendency of the tow rope to drag it into the bank. After that things went well if you allow for a few minor impediments along the way, like slipping every few paces on the muddy path and twice being dragged backwards by the pull of the current when my stamina ran out, requiring me to dig in and hold everything at a stop while I caught my breath and untwisted my muscles.

Tug-of-war donkey work for the four hundred metres to the bridge. The world a collision of contraries: The boat wanting to glide away from the bank and slip downstream, me pulling it into the bank and forcing it upriver against the current. The morning air biting from overnight frost, me sweating from the effort but feeling frozen. Dawn of a new day, me unslept from the old, a refugee from the night. Adam flat out and sleeping in the boat, unaware of anything, me puffing and panting and struggling and aware of every straining cell in my body and of the impelling world around.

> *all things counter, original, spare, strange;*
> *whatever is fickle, freckled (who knows how?)*

138

with swift, slow; sweet, sour; adazzle, dim . . .

Gerard Manley Hopkins lifted my spirits, helping me find in the tug
and swing, dig of heels, cut of rope, pain of breath, stretch of muscle,
the Force of dotty Dylan T.'s breath

> *that through the green fuse drives the flower*
> *Drives my green age; that blasts the roots of trees*
> *Is my destroyer,*
> *And I am dumb to tell the crooked rose*
> *My youth is bent by the same wintry fever.*

Helping me know again that

> *The force that drives the water through the rocks*
> *Drives my red blood; that dries the mouthing streams*
> *Turns mine to wax.*

Poetry is useless, it never changes anything? Tugging the boat
upstream, four hundred metres metered by metre. By life lines changed.
It changes me. Useful to have something that enables you to be useful.

❖ 2 ❖

Inside, the house was a tidy mess. My guts said, Go now, never
come back. My mind said, There is only one thing for it, knuckle
down.

Leaving Adam in the boat, tethered where I could keep an eye
from the living-room back window, I set to work.

First, blankets and pillows and a drink of water into the boat for
Adam. Still out. Fixed him up as comfortably as I could, left the glass
of water on the table where he'd see it if he woke, and went back to
the house. I wanted everything ready before taking him inside.

Next, the fire resurrected.

Then, every scrap left from the party stuffed into rubbish bags:

> a shoal of plastic glasses,
> a contagion of empty cans and bottles,
> an epidemic of crunched and squashed, trodden and
>   half-eaten scraps of food,
> a gallimaufry of discarded clothes:

139

a sicked-on sweater,
a crotch-stained pair of women's tights,
a pungent jock-strap,
a once-white sock,
an almost shredded T-shirt,
a pair of brand-new ultra-maxi-brief frilly knickers,
half an A-cup bra,
two used condoms,
a rash of joint and cigarette butts,
two slippery empty bottles of sunflower oil,
various pat-cakes of unrecognizable
    coagulated gunge limpeting on furniture,
    floor, walls, and ceiling,
a black close-toothed blonde-hair-clogged comb,
a necklace of lurid plastic beads,
a muddy right-foot Reebok,
a blood-stained handkerchief with hand-stitched
    marigolds decorating its scalloped edge,
a scrunched packet of weary jelly-babies,
an empty tube of KY,
the joker from a pack of cards.

(That's all I can remember.)

From among these icons of a fun-filled evening, I rescued my books, radio, own clothes (those still in a state worth rescuing), bedclothes, kitchen and toilet gear, etc. After that, sweeping, washing, mopping, dusting, polishing, reorganizing. Returning the place to myself.

Then returning myself to myself. Wash, shave, change of clothes, breakfast.

By nine o'clock tolls were interrupting progress as the Saturday early shoppers went through.

Checks on Adam every fifteen minutes monitored no change. Deep heavy-duty sleep.

All this achieved by keeping my mind in neutral.

Nine thirty, at the table, breakfast just finished, coffee mug in hand as I took five minutes off before making an attempt at getting Adam inside, Tess walked in.

[– Let's tell the next bit together, then we can get in everything we both knew.

140

– You just want an excuse not to have to write anything!

– Hard *fromage!* He's guessed! But it would be better that way, admit it.

– Wouldn't work.

– Yes it will, you just want to give up all that I-ing all the time. You're such a bloody narcissist!

– Rubbish.

– Yes you are. You like nothing better than staring at your navel all the time. And you're possessive.

– Stop bossing. Just for you, I'll give it a go.

– Good. But we keep it simple, none of your male-order stuff like those titles and numbered sections and everything all very ordered and in charge, and literary crossword puzzles and quoting from poets nobody reads and stuff like that. You're not writing a novel, for God's sake. This is going to be right to the point, OK?

– Conditions already! Keep it simple! Dear God, it'll be only words of one syllable next. Afraid of the dictionary, are we? Afraid we might come across a word we don't know? Afraid we might have to think a bit?

– Go!]

Tess and Gill walked to the bridge together. The two girls had arranged beforehand how they would behave. While Gill waited outside, Tess would discover whether Jan and Adam were there.

When Tess came into the living room Jan was facing her across the table, his hands wrapped round a mug of coffee. Image of so many Saturday mornings. Except this morning he looked desperately exhausted.

But as soon as he saw Tess, all Jan's weariness and the anger he felt for what she had done during the last three days evaporated. The very sight of her was enough to revive his spirits.

Stopped in her tracks by the sight of Jan, Tess suddenly felt confused, all her determination draining away, surprised by the strength of her feelings at seeing him again, as if they had been parted for years.

They gazed at each other for a long moment, neither saying anything, both aware of the moment's significance, knowing beyond a doubt for the first time that each was irreplaceable to the other no matter what, each satisfying in the other some essential need, and each unable therefore to do anything but pay the eternal toll of friendship: forgiveness of the other's failings. It was a sweet moment that could have lasted for ever, neither would have minded, a sublime kind of knowledge that was a strange new pleasure.

But the spell was broken by a car approaching the bridge.

'I'll get it,' Tess said and went.

When she returned a mug of coffee was waiting. Tess sat and avoided Jan's eyes by looking round the room.

'Quite a clean-up.'

'Needed it.' Intending to be genial, Jan heard himself sounding accusatory. Tiredness talking. He cleared his throat and braced himself in his seat. 'Back to normal.'

Tess smiled warily. 'Your normal.'

Jan returned her smile. 'My normal.'

Both were baffled. Having thought so much during the night about this meeting – how it would be, what would be said – it was not as either had imagined. Both also felt an intrusive urgency, Jan for Adam, Tess for Gill. But that intense moment of mutual recognition had come between what had been and what was, changing everything, and leaving each at a loss for words, tongue-tied, waiting on the other to bridge the gulf.

Jan spoke first.

'I need some help.'

'Is it – can it wait a minute?'

'What for?'

'Gill. She's outside.'

'Gill! She's still here? What's she want?'

'To talk to you of course.'

'Not now. I need some help with Adam.'

'Adam!'

'He's in a boat, it's a long story, I'll explain later, he's had some kind of accident, his head was bleeding, it's a cut, he was unconscious but he's sleeping now. I'm not sure what to do, he seems OK, but would you have a look at him and see if you think we ought to fetch a doctor?'

'Christ!'

'I also need some help to get him into the house, it's cold out there and there's nothing in the boat – no heating or water or anything.'

'God! But what about Gill?'

'Can't she wait?'

'You don't understand. She was attacked last night, during the party, under the bridge. It might have been Adam.'

'Adam! Is she sure? I mean, she didn't know him.'

'He said his name.'

'Jesus!'

'Exactly!'

'Can't have been! What did he do? Was she hurt?'

'Not physically. She doesn't know what he was up to. She's not sure. She was confused. It was dark and she was so upset already.'

They stared at each other, appalled.

'What now?' Jan said.

'I'd better get Gill. We can't leave her hanging about out there. Anyway, she's involved. She has a right to know what's happened.'

While Tess went for Gill, Jan visited Adam again, who was still flat out, hardly having moved for the last two hours.

As Jan returned to the living room by the back door Tess and Gill came in by the front. There was an awkward pause as Jan and Gill scowled across the room at each other.

'Hi,' they said in inevitable comic unison.

'I've explained,' Tess said quickly.

'He's still sleeping,' Jan said.

'I'll take a look,' Tess said, and hurried off, glad to escape.

Jan and Gill stood in silence contemplating each other, figures posed in a domestic still life.

When the silence became unbearable Gill said, 'We should talk.'

'Tess won't be long.'

'But we must.'

'Coffee or something?'

'No! Thanks.'

Unable to help herself, Gill closed the living-room door. Her letters were gone. She let out a gasp.

Jan, knowing, said nothing but went to the fire, stirred it with a foot and laid on another log.

Gill wandered round the room, inspecting it distractedly. Before, she had always poked about among the things in Jan's room and he hadn't minded, had rather liked it, in fact, as he had liked her caressing him while they sat and talked – playing with his hair, fiddling with his ears, stroking his legs. He was one of those for whom physical contact, the language of the fingers, was a needed way of communication. But it was also a privilege of friendship. Handling his possessions was an extension of this tactile pleasure. Now he found Gill's assumption of the privilege irritating. He wanted to tell her to leave things alone as he would have told a stranger. He knew that this was unreasonable: Gill was only continuing their relationship from where they had left off. It was he who had changed.

'Why didn't you answer my letters?' Gill said with the sudden brusqueness of someone forcing herself, through clenched teeth as it were, to speak. Having got it out, she turned to face him.

'What's this about Adam?' Jan said.

'Nothing.'

144

'Nothing!'

'Yes! No, not nothing. I don't want to talk about that, I want to talk about us. You're hurting me, you know that, do you?'

'I don't mean to. It's just the way things are. Don't know what to say.'

'That's a change!'

'Is all this just because I stuck your letters on the door?'

'No, all this is not *just* because you stuck my letters on the door, though that's bad enough. It's not even *just* because you didn't answer them, either. It's about what those things mean. Can't you see that? It's about you and me and about you paying me some *attention*. Don't you know how important that is to people?' Tears welled in her eyes. She brushed them angrily away. 'No one has ever hurt me the way you have. Never! It hurts so much I don't know what to do!'

Tears flowed again. Again she wiped them away. Took deep breaths.

She turned impatiently from him, went to the front window pretending to look out at the bridge. Jan remained unmoving by the fire.

After a while she said, 'Didn't mean to say that. Kept telling myself not to say things like that. It's so *boring* saying things like that!' She gave a little rueful laugh and slapped her thigh in frustration. 'And I was determined not to cry. I don't want to. I'm not trying to use it against you.'

Jan, struggling with his own feelings, managed to say, 'You know me well enough to know I don't think like that.'

She turned to face him again. 'But I don't seem to know you well enough to know why you're hurting me the way you are.'

Jan couldn't look at her. 'I'm not sure I know myself. That's why I'm here, to find out things like that.'

'Can't we at least talk about it? Don't I deserve that? Don't you owe me that much?'

Jan heard himself take in and let out the long slow breath of resignation.

He nodded, unable to speak.

His silence was broken by Tess shouting his name.

For Tess, climbing apprehensively down the two narrow steps that led from the cockpit into the cold clammy gloom of the cabin, entering the boat felt like descending into a tomb.

She clasped her hand over her mouth as she looked down at Adam's unconscious pasty face and the blood-stained bandage wrapped like a

145

sweatband round his head. He was breathing heavily through a gaping mouth, each breath rasping in his throat.

There are moments that change people. No, wrong; try again. There are moments when people change. These moments are not isolated, not separate, not removed from the rest of life. They are not independent atoms of existence that suddenly break into your life for no reason. They are made, are created by the alphabet of your life – the ever-shifting phonemes of existence, which sometimes gather into concentrated patterns of such intensity, such unmistakable clarity and significance, that suddenly you know something about yourself, your own *self*, for the first time. Some hidden part of you enters your consciousness. Recognized, acknowledged, accepted, it becomes part of the you you know.

This is how Jan thought later.

Tess, overcome in the cabin at the sight of Adam, knew only the impact of the moment as the narrowing cone of the past few weeks, past few days, past few hours, past few minutes reached a concentration sharp enough to penetrate her soul.

What phonemes spoke to her as she stood in the waist of the boat?

Regret: limb-weakening, stomach-sickening
Fright: bowel-loosening, nerve-jangling, sweat-making
Pity: tear-inducing
Disgust: fist-clenching, mouth-twisting
Anger: breath-catching, heart-gripping

And, counterpoint to these negatives, a positive that held them in play as the pulsing rhythm of a harmonic holds discords, the beat of the heart driving the flow of blood, she was also possessed by (God, how words fail us now!)

Joy
Gladness
Exhilaration
Zest

As she endured this, Tess felt as if she were split in two: one part of her suffering regret and guilt and sorrow; the other dispassionate, detached, cool, observing the self who suffered and taking pleasure in it.

How can I be like this? she wondered. Am I mad? Or sick? Or am I wicked? Evil?

146

Tess did not know whether she believed in Evil – in an entity, an out-there presence or force. The Devil. Her mother did. But Tess regarded that as a hangover from her mother's Catholic convent-school upbringing. Her father never used the word. She didn't know whether he believed in Evil or not. He always avoided talking of such things. Right and wrong, yes, he talked about that. But never about Evil. She herself had never thought it mattered enough to think about. Yet here she was, using the word about herself! Was it her mother speaking in her?

Tess had sometimes caught herself thinking and saying things that came straight out of her parents' mouths. Just as she sometimes caught herself walking like her mother or using her hands like her father. Or, most disturbing, she'd look in the mirror and suddenly see not her eyes but her father's, not her nose but her mother's, and always her father's wide mouth – his lips, their shape and length and thickness, and the odd little upward curve at the left-hand corner that made her look even when blank-faced as if she were smirking slightly, a feature that sometimes landed her in trouble with touchy teachers. How weird, she thought, to be such a mix-and-match product of your parents. And not only your parents but of all your ancestors back to Adam and Eve!

Eve and evil! Dear God! No, not evil, whether Evil existed or not. A stupid idiotic muttonheaded cretinous moronic crapbrained grade-A fool perhaps, but not evil. And not sick. Just a doltbungler. Not mad. Just a pukefaceturdtwit. And enjoying it!

She went on bludgeoning herself with words till the tears ran; and observed herself crying with pleasure. She was glad that all this could happen to her, she wouldn't deny it, which was not mad nor sick nor evil but life, human life – being alive. Pleasure not at *what* she had done or what she was, but *that* she had done and that she was. The tears were merely an outward and visible sign that she wished for better *than* she had done and than she was.

Perhaps it is in this attitude to herself that Tess differs most from Jan: she glorying in what she is, what life is, happy or sad, and, yes, bad or good, a born optimist; he suspicious of himself, sceptical of life, a born pessimist. Tess feels at home in the world, at home with it; Jan feels a stranger, a visitor only, uncomfortable with the world, alien even, someone waiting, bags packed, ready to leave.

Foraging such thoughts, chastened in her soul, she wiped the tears away, before bending over Adam to give him a critical look.

As her face came close to his, Adam's eyes opened and he saw her.

Tess stepped back, letting out a little gasp. Adam sat up, mouth gaping as if to shout, but no sound came.

'It's all right, it's only me!' Tess spluttered.

Adam's mouth moved as if talking fast but again no sound came. His eyes were wide and wild. He sprang to his feet, the blanket tumbling from him, but sat down again on the edge of the bunk as if felled by a blow, his face wincing with pain. He put a hand to his head, found the bandage, felt it with both hands, panic now adding to the look of pain.

'Don't move!' Tess said. 'You've hurt your head.' And instinctively took a step towards him, but Adam scrambled away along the bunk until he was wedged against the bulkhead, glaring at her like a wounded cornered animal.

Tess retreated to the cabin door, at a loss to know what do, jabbering, 'It's only me, Tess, you've had an accident or something, I'm not sure, but anyway calm down, it's OK, I'm not going to hurt you.' She heard herself laugh in the hysterical way people do when they're frightened. 'Should I get Jan? You'd probably prefer to talk to him.'

She began to back out of the cabin. 'Stay quiet. Put a blanket round you, you're only in your – you'll get cold, it's freezing in here, you probably have concussion or something, I'll just fetch Jan, hang on –'

As soon as she was on the bank she started yelling Jan's name.

Jan came running. Gill followed as far as the steps outside the back door.

'Something's up,' Tess said, meeting Jan halfway across the lawn. She was trembling. 'He woke up and went crazy. I thought he was going to attack me.'

'Bloody hell!'

'It might be just because it's me. You know – he might be scared of what will happen after last night. He might be all right with you, he knows you best –'

In the cockpit Jan bent down to look into the cabin. Adam was hunched up in the far corner of the bunk, a blanket gathered round him.

'Hey, Adam,' Jan said quietly, cheerily, 'it's me. You OK?'

No answer. Adam's eyes, ringed with dark circles, blazed at him.

Jan straightened up, looked at Tess watching from the bank, shrugged at her, bent to look at Adam again.

'How'd you like to come into the house where it's warm?'

No reply. Jan stepped down one step into the cabin, Adam stiffened, Jan stopped.

'Look, it's all right, what're you worried about?'

He took another step.

'I'm on my own.'

Another step brought him to the cabin floor.

Adam was shaking his head and making pushing-away movements with a hand. His mouth was working too but all that came out were gasping breaths.

Jan said quickly, 'I'm coming no further, it's OK, I'll just sit here, all right? Just want to talk to you.'

Adam waited. Jan perched on the edge of the bunk, ready to flit, his eyes never leaving Adam as he tried to weigh up his odd behaviour. By instinct he kept up a flow of soothing placatory talk.

'What's up? Is it your head? Does it hurt? I think you banged it somehow, anyway there's a cut just above your forehead, not a big one, but it was bleeding and I bandaged it, I think it'll be OK, nothing serious, it'll heal in a couple of days, but you might be suffering from a bit of concussion, what d'you think?' He paused. No reply. 'I don't know what happened, probably an accident. D'you remember?' No reply. 'Well, you really were soaking it up last night, you have to admit.' He tried a smile. Nothing in return, only the puzzled frightened watchful stare. 'Probably suffering from a hangover as well.' Still nothing. 'Damn near blotto, I expect.' He returned his face to its concerned serious look. 'You don't remember anything about last night?'

A pause. Then Adam shook his head, just once, but enough. A small triumph.

'No, well, I'm not surprised, to be honest. You'll be fine by tomorrow. Need to sleep it off, I guess. How about coming into the house? It's warm in there. The old fire blazing. I'll make you something to eat if you like. Some breakfast maybe, eh? Then if you want you can go to bed. Sleep better in your own bed. How about it?'

He felt like an over-tolerant dad wheedling a pesky infant.

Adam shifted, easing forward from his position huddled in the

149

corner. His mouth started working but again made no sound. He jabbed a finger at his face followed by a frustrated gesture that signalled, 'I can't, I can't!'

Jan said, appalled, 'You can't talk?'

Adam shook his head, eyes pleading.

'Grief!' Jan heard himself say before he could prevent it. A new panic flushed through him. He'd heard of concussion causing temporary loss of memory but never of it causing loss of voice. What if Adam was really badly hurt? Brain-damaged even?

'Look, Adam,' he said, man-to-man serious now, 'we'd better get a doctor, there might be –'

The effect was alarming. Adam sprang to his feet, wild and hunted again, and frantically waving both hands, *no no no*. Jan jumped up too, thinking he was about to be attacked, his own hands raised as a man at gunpoint. 'Right, OK, no doctor, no doctor –'

The pair of them were square to each other now, an arm's length apart, Adam poised for flight, the blanket thrown aside.

There was a pause. Adam began to shiver. Folded his arms round his chest. But the shivering grew worse till he was shaking all over.

'Come on,' Jan said, picking up the blanket. 'Let's go into the house. You can't stay here.' He held the blanket as one holds a coat for another to put on. 'I don't know what's happened, but we can't do anything about it till you're feeling better. You've got to come inside and get warm or you'll be really ill.'

He waited. Adam stared at him for a moment before abruptly, as if acting on a decision before he could change his mind, he grabbed the blanket out of Jan's hands and clutched it round himself.

Jan nodded and smiled and led the way out.

Adam wrote, *Who are you?*

'Jan,' Jan said. 'Well, Piers really.'

Why Jan?

'It's what Tess calls me.'

Adam raised questioning eyebrows.

'The girl in the boat.'

Why Adam?

'That's what you said your name was.'

They were sitting at the table in the toll house. When they came in from the boat an hour ago Tess and Gill had gone.

Jan had coddled Adam through the process of washing, having his bandage changed, dressing in warm clean clothes (Jan's yet again), going to the lavatory, and eating the usual breakfast, which Adam gobbled up having by then calmed down, though he was still jumpy.

Breakfast over, Jan placed a pad of paper and a ballpoint in front of Adam, sat down beside him and, saying nothing, waited. After considering Jan and the paper hesitantly Adam took up the pen and started writing.

Now Jan said, 'Don't you remember anything?'

Where is this?

Jan told him.

When did I come?

Jan began recounting their history together. When he reached the fight over the necklace he pulled it from under his shirt and held it for Adam to see. From his reaction Jan knew at once that Adam recognized it. About the raven, however, Adam's reaction was quite different. As Jan told about the wound, he took hold of Adam's hand and pushed back the sleeve of his sweater, revealing the scabby marks of the raven's talons on Adam's forearm. At the sight of them

151

Adam braced in astonishment, as if the marks had suddenly appeared by magic. He snatched his hand from Jan's grasp and inspected the wound closely. When he looked up again he was frowning. He thought for a moment then wrote:

Could have pinched necklace. Seen mark.

'Why would I make up a story like that? Why would I say you've been living here if you haven't?'

Adam shrugged.

'You don't believe me?'

Adam shook his head.

After a moment's thought, Jan said, 'Hang on a sec,' and brought from the bedroom two of Tess's photos which he laid side by side on the table. One was of Adam and Jan painting outside the toll house. The other was of Adam taking a toll from a car.

Adam studied them intently.

'You don't remember any of this?'

Adam shook his head.

'Nothing? Nothing at all? Do you remember anything before you came here or where you came from?'

This time there was a pause before Adam looked away.

'But you know who you are?'

Eyes averted, another shake of the head.

'Don't even know your name?'

Another denial.

It was Jan's turn not to believe.

'Look,' he said, undoing the chain, 'you'd better have this back.'

Adam hesitated a moment before taking it.

From the second he heard Tess yelling his name Jan had been, as he put it later, flying by radar. He had no experience, the basis of all thought, to go on, for he had never been faced with anything like this before. But now as he sat watching Adam, stubborn but discomforted beside him, he felt an echo of the irritation he used to feel when Adam first invaded the house, and the same desire as then to chuck him out. He wanted to say, 'Oh, come on, don't give me that! You can remember all right, why are you lying?' But he knew that if he did it would be the end, Adam would go, and though Jan could not fully understand why, he wanted him to stay. To let him go, to send him away, would be a loss to himself and a dereliction.

Kafka's strange story came to his mind and vividly the memory

152

of the three of them talking about it as they toasted themselves by the fire. Now the story seemed oddly appropriate to this moment in his life. He and Adam and Tess: each other's bridges, as Kafka's young man had become a bridge for someone else. But was the story prophecy or nightmare – what would be or what could be?

As Jan thought of this, he remembered too the morning after Adam's first arrival, when, coming back into the house from talking to Tess, he had the weird sensation of *déjà-vu*.

Could these be mere accidents, unconnected coincidences? A deep nerve of intuition prickled in his spine, telling him they were part of a larger pattern that made a kind of sense he had yet to puzzle out. Till he could discern the pattern he would have to accept that irrational intuition, take it on trust.

Never before in his life had Jan consciously taken such a risk. Just the opposite, in fact. Ever since he stopped being a child – a change in his consciousness he dated from an early summer afternoon when he was thirteen and an older friend took him into a garden shed and taught him how to masturbate – Jan had only trusted thought. Feelings, he had decided as his adolescence progressed, were often misleading. They came and went with distressing fickleness and speed: likes became dislikes, strong desires turned into revulsions. They seemed to be uncontrollable and to come from somewhere outside himself. He did not feel responsible for them (feelings about feelings!) yet was required by others – parents, neighbours, teachers, friends – to behave as if he were. Of his thoughts, however, he felt more in charge. Unlike his feelings, his thoughts did not immediately shape his behaviour before he could prevent it. And only when he wanted and was ready need he reveal his thoughts to others. He possessed them rather than being possessed by them.

So in all things Jan had come to prefer the life of the mind. Thinking gave him physical pleasure. He wanted never to stop thinking, not even when he was asleep. He had learned to regard his dreams as raw material for thought – mind teasers, puzzles with special peculiar secret codes of their own, which he enjoyed trying to crack. That's why he liked Kafka's story so much. It was a dream full of possible meanings, some of them contradictory, yet all existing in the one story. Their very complexity and coexistent difference pleased and satisfied him.

And now there was this unaccustomed intuition about Adam, about losing him, about their staying together, about being one another's bridge to something else. Another kind of code. Not a code in a story he had read, but a code in the story of his own life as it was being lived there and then, here and now, moment to moment.

Stirred by this revelation, unable to sit still, he got up from the table, and went to tend the fire, thinking as he did so that Adam must stay, must be humoured, must be looked after until he could tell the secret Jan was sure he was hiding.

Be Janus, Jan said to himself as he laid a fresh log on the glowing embers and swept away the ash that had fallen onto the hearth. He smiled as he thought of Janus as his renewing defining all-containing name. There and then he accepted it. Never again did he willingly call himself Piers. December fourteenth was ever after his own, his chosen birthday, the day he became a janus, called Jan.

The effect upon him at that moment was like a lens bringing an image into focus. He recognized himself clearly for the first time, knew who he was, felt the urge of his own life, the pulse of the will to be.

He turned from the fire to face Adam, who was slumped at the table, dejected, crushed, staring at the photos in a brown study.

'Listen,' Jan said gently, 'aren't you worried about not being able to talk and not remembering anything?'

Coming to, Adam lifted his head, looked weary-eyed at Jan, and nodded.

'Me too. If you aren't back to normal soon, a day or two at most, we'll have to do something about it. See a doctor. Maybe all you've got is concussion and it's only temporary. If it is concussion, I think you're supposed to take it easy. Go to bed, I mean, and try and sleep. I don't know what else to suggest. What do you think?'

Adam, listening anxiously, didn't move.

Jan went on, 'There'll be people here soon. Tess. A girl called Gill who's a friend of mine. They'll want to talk to me. And my boss, Tess's father, could come in any time. They know you, they've seen you before, they know you're living here for a bit. If you're in bed, I'll say you're not feeling too great after the party. They'll believe me and leave you alone. And tomorrow being Sunday there won't be much doing, no tolls, you could get up then, see how you feel. What about it? . . . You'll be safe. I'll be here to look after you . . . Promise . . . OK?'

There was a silence while Adam studied Jan's face, weighing up whether he could trust this person he said he did not know. Then with the resignation of one who realizes he has no option, he eased himself up from his chair, holding onto the table for support, obviously groggy, a wince of pain creasing his face as he stood up straight, and now a frightened, confused, pleading look in his eyes.

Jan went to him, put a supporting arm round his waist, and led him to the bedroom.

In town, where they had gone to be out of the way, Tess and Gill mooched from shop to shop saying little.

It was while they were poking aimlessly about in Marks and Spencer's, more to keep warm than anything, that Gill suddenly stopped in her tracks and said, 'I can't stay. I'm going home. It's stupid to stay.'

Tess said, 'But don't you want to see him, don't you want to talk to him?'

'No, it's no use, I've got to go.'

Outside, Gill stopped, confused. 'Which way to the station?'

'You want to go this minute?'

'Yes. Is that the way?'

'No, this.' They set off at a brisk pace. 'But why? What about your things?'

'Don't matter. Got my ticket and some money with me.'

They were almost running.

At the station Tess said, 'What shall I do about your stuff?'

Gill shrugged. 'Leave it with Piers. There's nothing I need. Just overnight things. He can post them or bring them when he comes home. And thanks for last night. You've been great. And look – don't feel bad about inviting me to the party. You were only trying to do the right thing. I'm grateful. No – I am. If you hadn't done it, I'd have gone on and on not knowing, thinking about him all the time, worrying – you know how it is. I've been a fool. I shouldn't have let it drag on. Shouldn't have thought it was all up to him. It wasn't, it was up to me. Everything is, in the end, isn't it, up to yourself? I shouldn't have put up with it and shouldn't have kept on letting him know how much I wanted him. I should have kept quiet. If he'd wanted me, he'd have done something about it, wouldn't he? If people really want something, they go for it, don't they? And, you know, I was thinking this morning on the bus, when people know you want

155

something from them very much, they don't let you have it. So maybe the worst thing you can do is let someone know how much you want them. And especially how much you want them to love you. Perhaps it puts them off. D'you think so?'

Tess sighed. 'Don't know. Could be.'

As they stopped to say goodbye, each searched the other's face before spontaneously they hugged and held on with genuine emotion.

It was Gill who let go first and, turning away, walked onto the platform without looking back.

By the time Tess arrived back at the bridge about midday Jan too was in an emotional slump. She found him sprawled full length in the armchair, his feet in the hearth, his face collapsed, eyes drooping. Adam was asleep in the bedroom.

Tess herself felt much better. Gill's departure meant a considerable complication was out of the way.

Jan had been gloomily considering the prospect of a heart-to-heart with Gill. He couldn't think what he wanted to say and was still suffering bouts of resentment that she was there at all. So when Tess arrived on her own and told him that Gill had gone back home he perked up and chuckled with relief.

Suddenly they were both desperately hungry, and while Jan told Tess what had happened during the night she made Welsh rabbit, double helpings of which they consumed with gusto, both feeling the meal was a celebration, a recovery of their own treasured private rituals, though neither said so.

When Jan had finished his story, Tess told hers: the attack on Gill, their overnight talks, the events of the morning. That done, the meal finished, a quietness settled on them. They sat back, the unadmitted euphoria having evaporated, leaving in its place the awkward unresolved problem of Adam, whose slumbering presence seemed to hang heavily around them.

Their mood was changed again by Jan hiccupping. 'Ate too fast,' he said, standing up and clearing the dirty plates into the sink. He began washing up and tidying away the mess Tess had made. (She was [is] a disorderly cook, never putting anything she used [uses] away and managing to spread her jumbled leavings over all available surfaces. Jan regarded[s] this as bad work[wo]manship; Tess regarded[s] his tidiness as obsessively fussy, a sign of a dangerously neurotic closet-authoritarian personality.)

Later, having looked in on Adam (sleeping still) and at the boat, they sat by the fire and discussed what to do next.

The easiest decision was that the boat must be cleaned up and returned to its mooring before anyone noticed it had gone. They agreed that Jan would clean it while Tess took tolls and kept an eye on Adam. Then they'd shift it downstream together under cover of dusk.

The problem of Adam was not so easy to deal with. They agreed it was unlikely he was any worse than badly concussed. But Tess wanted to call a doctor, saying they shouldn't chance it, and being anyway secretly keen to get Adam off their hands. Jan refused, they started arguing, Jan became stubborn, irrational, almost belligerent, and they ended up having a row.

'Why?' Tess demanded. 'First you didn't want him anywhere near the place, now you won't let him go, even when he might be very sick.'

'You can talk! You're the one who wanted him to stay, and now you want to get rid of him. I wonder why! And he's not very sick. Not *physically* sick.'

'How do you know?'

'I just do, that's all.'

'*Doctor* Jan now is it?'

'Oh, shut it!'

'I won't. I can't see why you're going on like this. Why are you protecting him? What is there between you two?'

'Don't want to talk about it.'

'No, I'll bet you don't! I'm fetching Dad. See what he thinks.'

Tess sprang up and made for the front door. But Jan was there before her, arms spread.

'No!'

'Yes!'

'Wait!'

'Get out of the way.'

They were nose to nose.

'I promised him.'

'Don't care.'

'For me, then, just for me.'

'Why?'

'Because — we've got to give him a chance to explain. Oh, I don't

157

know – I keep thinking . . . It's as if he were me. No, not me. I mean – the other me. Christ; I don't know! It's too hard to explain.'

'But you do know? You can make some sense of what's going on, can you?'

'Not in a way I can say it. Not yet. And I told you – there's something terrible he's afraid of. I don't know what it is but I've never seen anybody so scared. Till I know, I have to help him. I don't know why. I'm responsible . . . Anyway, he's ill, for God's sake, you can see that for yourself.'

'So you admit it, after all, he is ill! And if he's ill, you're not being very responsible keeping him here, are you?'

'Tomorrow. Wait till tomorrow. If he isn't any better then, we'll tell your dad and get a doctor. Promise.'

'Another promise.'

'Yes.'

'One cancels the other out, so what are they worth?'

Jan took a deep breath, dropped his arms, stared at Tess and said in a quiet placatory tone, 'Don't.'

'Don't what?'

'Make it a game. Let's be honest, you and me. That's what makes us possible. It's what I care about, the best thing we have together.'

'So?'

'I want him here . . . I need him here . . . Don't ask why yet.'

Tess took that in before giving a scornful self-protective hoot. But she turned away and went back to her seat by the fire.

Afraid that their noise might have woken Adam, Jan quietly opened the bedroom door and peeped in. Adam was lying on his side, back to the door. Impossible to see if he was awake, but he was very still so Jan closed the door and went back to Tess.

After that they took care of the practical jobs: cleaning up the boat, returning it to its moorings, cashing up the week's toll money so that Tess could take it home and give it to her father in the hope that this might forestall a visit tomorrow.

Tess went off home at teatime, returning later with an extract about concussion jotted down from her mother's home doctoring book.

Identification: Pale clammy skin, shallow breathing, fast weak pulse; may vomit or pass water. Disturbance of consciousness may be so slight as to be momentary dizziness or so severe that unconsciousness continues for weeks.

Treatment: Quiet, dark room, head low until consciousness returns, then raised on two pillows. No stimulants. In severe cases, bed for two weeks at least.

After effects: Usually none, except that memory is absent, and sometimes greater memory loss. Headache may persist, and occasion irritability, and lack of concentration, for some weeks.

This so matched Adam's condition that they were reassured. And Jan was quite cocky that, partly by accident, he'd administered the right treatment. They agreed Adam was suffering from a moderately bad concussion and that if they went on treating it properly there should be no serious after effects. Only the loss of voice continued to worry them but they decided it was probably safe to do nothing about it till next day.

In the afternoon they had talked of spending the evening together huddled by the fire. Snow had begun to fall, big white feathery flakes that sidled lazily down from a leaden sky. But when the time came to settle themselves they both felt so drained, so weary, that the prospect of sitting by the fire talking to each other had lost its attraction. They wanted to be together, wanted to repair the damage, wanted comfort from each other, wanted to be encouraged and reassured, wanted in fact to be coddled, but neither yet possessed the knowing confidence, in themselves or in each other, to say so. And anyway, mistaking tiredness for signs of irritation – he had never seen her so exhausted before – Jan suspected Tess was fed up with him for leaving the party and, worse, for opposing her over Adam. Tess, for her part, mistook Jan's silences for sullen resentment at what she had done in the house and at her springing Gill on him, when all his silences actually meant was that he was too beat to talk.

So nothing of their real desires was uttered. Instead Tess said, 'I'm dog tired,' and Jan said, 'Me too,' and Tess added, 'Perhaps I'll just slope off home and flop out early,' and Jan sighed and said, 'Sure. See you tomorrow about twelve, OK? Give me time to work on Adam a bit,' and Tess trudged off, torn between relief and disappointment and feeling deeply discomfited inside herself at the way the day was ending.

Jan, when she had gone, sat staring into the fire. When he eventually came to, he damped the fire down for the night, used the loo, cleaned his teeth, locked the doors, put out the lights and undressed in the dark before slipping quietly into the bedroom. There he had left a candle burning for Adam should he wake and wonder where he was. He was still lying curled up on his side, but facing the door now. Jan bent over him to check he was all right and saw frightened wide-awake eyes gazing back at him, unblinking, large – hypnotic at that moment in their effect.

What then happened seemed, even at the time, like an inevitable natural culmination of all that had gone before. Suddenly sitting up, Adam flung his arms round Jan, clinging like a child frightened by a nightmare. Jan's immediate impulse was to push him away, but before he could recover from his surprise enough to do this, a deeper instinct took control and he was hugging Adam as resolutely as Adam was clinging to him, one hand stroking the feverish skin of Adam's back, the other holding Adam's head firmly against his own, and he was murmuring a kind of litany, 'It's all right, it's OK, I'm here, I'm with you, you're safe, we're alone, there's no one else, don't worry, it's all right.'

They remained like this for a long time, until the tension in Adam's body was soothed away and he relaxed the urgent fierceness of his embrace. But still he held on, and when at last Jan tried to ease his position Adam gripped tightly again to prevent him letting go. Not that Jan wanted to. The satisfaction he felt was so complete and, he acknowledged to himself, so long desired, that he wanted it never to end.

After a while he became aware of the icy cold of the room chilling the exposed parts of their bodies. Reaching out with a hand, he fumbled for the duvet which he pulled over them as he and Adam shuffled down into the bed, rearranging the mesh of legs and arms till they lay comfortably wrapped together.

Soon afterwards Adam began breathing the heavy rhythms of deep settled sleep, and Jan heard through his bones the slow primeval pulse of Adam's heart. For a few more minutes he revelled in the press of Adam's body against his own, the warm moist fusion of skin on skin, the touch of his fingers caressing the firm contours of Adam's limbs, and he thought: Now I am myself, will never want more for myself than this. Then he too drifted into his first dreamless, peaceful, sur-rendered, reviving sleep since the start of his headaches and the onset of The Glums.

Jan was woken by the cawing of the raven. For a moment he drifted in that blissful limbo before consciousness fully returns. Then the raven croaked again and everything came instantly back. He was suddenly aware of being alone, and not in his own bed either, but Adam's, and of the duvet irritatingly tangled, and of the dim grey miserly early morning light, and the chilly, slightly fetid, damp-fingered air in the room, but also of a warm glow inside himself as from embers hidden at the heart of a night-banked fire.

Anxious about Adam, he struggled to his feet, groaning at the stiffness of his body, the ache in his muscles, and pulled his clothes on fast, gritting his teeth against their icy shock. He thought fleetingly of his centrally heated room at home (home?) and was pleased with himself for not regretting it even at that moment. He wanted to be where he was, was glad of it. Of course he knew this surety was for Adam; and knew in his bones it could not last long and that its end might be painful. But in the longing of the moment he didn't care. Nor did he yet know the reality of such a pain, never having suffered it before. Knowledge of consequences, after all, depends on at least a little experience of them. Sensing the possibility isn't enough, which is why it is so hard to learn anything that matters without living at least a sliver of it.

Adam was standing stock-still in the middle of the road gazing up at the toll-house roof where, Jan knew, the raven must be perched. He was holding out his right arm and making clucking noises with his tongue and saying, as he might to a child, 'Come on, come on down, *cluck cluck cluck*, come on then.'

Thank God, Jan thought, he's talking!

But there was something pathetic about the sight. And when Jan appeared the raven took off, flapping away over the bridge.

Adam turned on the spot, arm still raised, following the bird's flight. Dressed only in his (Jan's) tattered sweater and distressed jeans, no socks or shoes, he paid no attention to Jan but went on staring after the raven, even when it dipped out of sight behind a parcel of trees a field away on the other side of the river. The previous day's snow had vanished. The trees were bare black bones.

Jan waited a moment before saying as lightly as he could, 'Talking to the birds!'

There was a long pause before Adam said, 'It wouldn't come.'

'No . . . Maybe, you didn't speak the right language.'

'Maybe,' Adam said, an edge of mimicry in his voice, 'and maybe it never happened.'

'It happened. And your voice has come back. That's the main thing. Come inside. You'll freeze to death out here.'

'Good,' Adam said, but turned and went into the house. Leaving Adam to brood, less anxious about him now he was talking again, Jan revived the fire, prepared breakfast, which he made more substantial than usual, boiling the last of the eggs because he thought Adam would be hungry and anyway needed nourishment. While he was busy Adam stalked about, the restlesss, angry, desperate, defeated, slow, irritating tread of a caged animal.

They ate, Adam wolfing his food, hardly noticing, saying nothing, eyes avoiding Jan, who, eating very little in small bites, struggled to keep more than his thoughts to himself, for what he wanted most was to reach across the table and take Adam's hands in his own. But intuition – his newly trusted guide – warned him that Adam would shy away from such intimacy.

He thought: I've never been faced with anything like this before – somebody of my own age who is so unhappy. But I recognize the look. I've felt like that. He's badly hurt and I can help. What matters is that I treat him decently. As far as I'm concerned – me myself and what he does to me, what he means to me – I need to work that out on my own for myself and honestly face the truth of it.

Wondering what to do, he remembered Tess sitting with him when he was in the pit of The Glums those few weeks ago that seemed at this moment like so many months ago. Her sitting with him, knowing that all she could do and what he most needed was that she be there with him – enough just by being there, physically *there* and not fussing, not harassing him with busy helpfulness, but simply waiting with him till

162

he was ready for more and then providing the energy, the willpower, the impetus he needed to live eagerly again.

How wise she had been, how truly loving, how truly a friend. And why? Why had she given herself to him in that way? Had she been utterly unselfish? Was there such a state as utter selflessness? He doubted it.

What he did know was that he was not so unselfish in wanting to help Adam. There was, if nothing else, a physical reward. Till last night he had never known the power of physicality. Not cock-pleasure, but satisfaction of the body. Flesh and bone on flesh and bone. And the gut-felt, beyond-thought need of it. His argument with Adam about gifts came to mind.

He cleared away the breakfast things, brought a book, allowed himself to move his chair to Adam's side of the table so that he was in reach should Adam want him, and there settled down to read with whatever patience he could muster. I am Janus, he thought, guarding the bridge, biding my time. Dually watchful. Of the other, of myself. Of outer, of inner. Of my him, of my her. Constant ambivalence, happy ambiguity.

Ten, fifteen minutes went by.

Then Adam said in a sudden rush, 'Last night . . .'

'Yes?'

'I'm not gay.'

'No.'

'Don't mind, just, I'm not.'

'Didn't think you were.'

'Didn't want you jumping to wrong ideas, that's all. Didn't want to disappoint you.' He attempted a smile.

'I wasn't. It's OK.'

'Don't know why I did it. Never done nothing like that before.'

'What's wrong with having a cuddle?'

'Well – it just happened, that's all.'

'You've had a rough time. Wanted some comfort. I was the only one around. What's wrong with that?'

'Didn't seem too surprised.'

'Maybe I needed a cuddle as well.'

Adam said nothing.

Jan said, 'And I'm here if you want any more.'

*

They sat in silence again. The fire crackling, an occasional vehicle crossing the bridge, the constant muffled surge of the river, never as loud inside the house during the day as it seemed during the night. Listening with pin-drop extra sharpness, Jan realized how much he had come to love the river and its ever-present noise, its slip and slide, its shifty moods, its always-the-same never-the-sameness, the hidden mystery of its opaque uncertain depths, its changing colours, the vein of it flowing through the countryside, and he remembered the holiday he and his father spent along this very reach, when he was twelve, the last wonderful week of his childhood, when each evening after their day's boating, his father read aloud from *The Wind in the Willows*, the book that had been the favourite of *his* childhood, and still Jan vividly recalled the passage that came at the end of their first exciting day, when Mole asks Rat whether he really lives by the river and Rat replies, *By it and with it and on it and in it. It's brother and sister to me, and aunts, and company, and food and drink, and (naturally) washing. It's my world and I don't want any other. What it hasn't got is not worth having, and what it doesn't know is not worth knowing. Lord! the times we've had together! Whether in winter or summer, spring or autumn, it's always got its fun and its excitements,* and he had thought how glorious that was, and in his father's face was the look of a boy the age of Jan himself, and for a strange moment he felt as if he and his father were the same age, boys together sharing this riverborne holiday without any adults to harbour them, and the next day they rowed their dinghy and Jan caught a crab just as Mole does in the episode his father read out that evening, while they giggled till tears ran and hugged each other and said what a day they'd had, and next day, his father, still in his boyhood mood, tied a rope to a tree overhanging the river and showed Jan how to play Tarzan just as Adam had his first morning at the bridge and Jan had said he had never played it for fear of what he might have to admit if he said yes and told all.

'Tell me again what you told me yesterday,' Adam said.

'About you being here?'

'Yes.'

Jan retold the story, more shaped this time after yesterday's rehearsal.

'Don't remember any of that,' Adam said afterwards, 'none of it. Doesn't even sound like me.'

'Want to see the photos again?'

'If you like.'

He pored over them, pursing his lips and shaking his head.

'I've never decorated nowhere, don't know a song like the one you say I camped up.'

'How'd you know if you don't remember anything even from before you came here?'

Adam eyed him warily. 'Just do, that's all.'

'Have you remembered something?'

Adam lowered his head to the photos and withdrew into silence.

Unable to sit still any longer Jan left Adam to his brooding and set about the housekeeping chores. Made the beds, tidied the bedroom, washed up the breakfast things, fetched wood for the fire, swept up ashes from the hearth. It was then he remembered Gill's bag left by Tess behind the armchair. He took it into the bedroom, intending to stow it there till he was ready to return it.

But in the bedroom curiosity got the better of him. And more: a desire to handle Gill's belongings, to touch things that had intimately touched her.

As he unzipped the bag and spread it open the familiar smell of Gill's body breathed out, a mix of talcum powder, her soap (Cusson's Imperial Leather), her favourite perfume ('Penelope' by Lauren, which she wore because Jan had given her a small bottle as a birthday present), and the faint musky tang of her sweat. His nose twitched and his mouth watered, and he felt an echo of her hand caressing him between the thighs, which made him feel suddenly very lonely.

He eased the crotch of his jeans and began unpacking. Conscious of his illicit behaviour, he treated each item with delicate fingertip care, laying them out neatly on the bed.

Aubergine jumper.

Breton-sailor-style T-shirt, one of his that Gill had 'borrowed' because she wanted something of his to wear.

Two large sloppy T-shirts, one white with Shakespeare's head on the front in black (bought on a visit they'd made together to Stratford) and a plain red one.

Pair of washed-out pale blue cuff-frayed jeans.

Three pairs of flimsy pink cotton panties.

Flimsy halter bra to match (memories of the pleasure of removing it).

Two pairs of socks: one pair pink; one pair white-and-red stripes.

Traveller's electric hair drier trailing the twisted snake of its umbilical cord.

Orange and yellow polka-dotted hand towel.

Mauve toilet bag with pattern of blue and yellow Matisse flowers containing:

> pink small-handled toothbrush,
> small tube of peppermint 'Sensodyne' toothpaste,
> Body Shop lipstick, mascara, lip balm, face
>   powder, powder brush, little case of make-up like a child's
>   paint box, eye-shadow pencil,
> small bottle of Johnson's Baby Oil,
> roll-on odourless deodorant,
> small bottle of Balsam shampoo,
> packet of six 'Extra-safe, Extra-sensitive,
>   Featherlite' condoms – 'gossamer thin for that intimate
>   touch'.

He held the packet of condoms in the palm of his hand, thinking of the message it bore of a time that might have been and Gill must have hoped would be; and remembering their times together before. Collision of past and present, of sight and smell and touch.

He sat on the edge of the bed surveying Gill's possessions, acutely aware as never before of the difference, the *otherness* of the female from the male: different other smell and texture, difference of *weight*, difference – he searched for a word, for a phrase that named the deepest, most different difference and found: *density of being*.

He fingered Gill's things, his imagination busy. Images of images, he thought now – now in this my now, now in your now, me now not me then. Marks on paper. Bridge between subject and object. Outside over there from inside under here. Janus in this hand, these eyes, this mouth, this head.

Everything was there, what was true of him and why. All there in Gill's possessions neatly laid on the bed and Adam next door and Tess soon to be on her way to them. All there at the bridge. But bridges freeze before roads. So cross with care. But cross you must. And the time when he must cross, he sensed, had come.

He was about to repack the bag when he saw there was something else inside. At first he thought it was a picture postcard. But no: it was a photograph Tess had taken of himself and Adam, arms round each other and laughing. Had Tess given it to her? She had told him

166

about Gill looking at her pictures but had said nothing about giving one to Gill. Had Gill taken it without Tess knowing? Stolen it? Why had she wanted it anyway?

Suddenly, as if a blockage had been cleared, a membrane breached, there rose from the pit of his belly a sickening sense of remorse at his treatment of Gill. He suddenly saw all the past few months from her vantage, saw how he and everything at the house must have looked to her. He could not believe that he had been so unthinking, so unfeeling, so unknowing. Battering himself with self-reproach, breaking into a sweat, too weak to stand, he could not bear the sensation of being imprisoned in himself, unable to escape his self-accusations. Again and again he sighed and thumped his thighs with his fists and rubbed his hands back and forth, back and forth.

He suffered like this for some while before the bout subsided. When at last it did he felt a refreshing sense of relief – the relief of knowing at last something you have not even recognized before. And knowing what to do about it.

He stood and stretched himself, reaching for the ceiling with his fingertips, like a man after a long sleep. Then he carefully repacked Gill's bag, carefully stowed it under his bed, and returned to the living room to attend to Adam.

Time to dress the wound. There had been no more bleeding; the cotton-wool pad had left the skin chicken-skin wrinkled and white. Jan sponged the area with a damp disinfected cloth. Adam flinched as he dabbed at the cut.

'You'll live,' Jan said, 'but best leave it uncovered. Probably heal quicker if the air can get at it. What about the headache?'

'Gone.'

Adam turned away and inspected his wound in the shaving mirror above the sink then, without another word, began making two mugs of coffee. Maybe now he would start talking.

But he didn't. Instead he sat in the armchair and gazed unseeing at the blank TV screen, as shut-in and unwelcoming as before.

When he'd finished his coffee Jan said, trying another strategy, 'Feel like a walk? I phone home on a Sunday morning.'

Adam shook his head.

Maybe some time on his own would be good for him.

Jan stood up. 'You'll be OK?'

167

Adam nodded.

'Not be long. Half an hour or so.'

As he reached the door Adam said, 'Jan –'

Jan turned.

'Thanks.'

'No problem.'

'I mean for everything.'

Nonplussed by this unAdam-like declaration, Jan could only smile and nod.

Snow began falling again as he left the bridge, thick feathery flakes slowly descending as in the aftermath of an astronomic pillow fight. On the phone, he had the usual conversation with his mother: everything was fine, his father had been doing this and that, Mrs Fletcher had had a nasty attack of angina but her son was doing wonderfully in his new computer software job, they hadn't seen Gill yet this weekend but perhaps she'd call later, had this week's parcel (a fruit cake) arrived safely? (yes), had he decided about school next term? (yes, he was staying in his job), she was longing to see him at Christmas, etc. His father followed, talking for five minutes about the garden and painting the inside of the tool shed, telling a lawyer joke heard in court, and working in a coded message – 'Your mother's been in good fettle', meaning she was getting along well after the recent crisis.

Duty done, he took a deep breath before punching Gill's number, the call he really wanted to make. On the way there he had composed a short speech on the lines of how sorry he was about the weekend and everything else, that he hadn't meant to hurt her, that he'd be writing a letter trying to explain and would talk to her at Christmas, but he was ringing to find out that she had got home safely and was all right.

Gill's mother answered. 'Oh, it's you, Piers.'

'Hello, Mrs Redmond. Could I speak to Gill, please.'

There was a muffled pause before Mrs Redmond said, 'Yes, well now, Gill's not here, I'm afraid, well, no, she is here –'

'Could I –'

'– but the fact is, Piers, she'd rather not speak to you today –'

'But if –'

'– and to be honest, we're rather cross with you, her father and I, for the way you've treated her –'

'Would you please ask –'

'She arrived home in a terrible state. I don't know quite what went on between you, she wouldn't tell us, but one thing I do know she's very upset –'

'I'll explain if –'

'So we think it would be best if you left her alone and didn't try and contact her for a while –'

'But –'

'She'll get in touch when she feels up to it –'

'Couldn't I –'

'And frankly, Piers, I'm surprised you've called now after being so silent all the time you've been away, which wasn't very friendly, you must admit, especially when you consider how much Gill did for you before you went away, how much we all did. So I'll say goodbye for the present.'

The dialling tone burred in his ear. He slammed the receiver down and cursed. And remained where he was for some minutes, blank of mind, until Tess's voice brought him to his senses again.

'Making your Sunday call?'

He nodded and they set off together towards the bridge, hunched against the snow, hands in pockets, heads down.

'You all right?' Tess asked as they stomped along. 'Seem a bit down.'

'Tried Gill.'

'But she didn't want to talk.'

'Right.'

'I know, I phoned her as well.'

'She talked to you?'

'Sure.'

'Bloody hell! So why won't she talk to me?'

'Oh, come on! Why didn't you answer her letters?'

'Just wanted to know she got home OK and tell her I'd be writing this week.'

'Promises, promises.'

'I will, I've been thinking.'

'Try doing.'

'Been doing as well, looking after Adam.'

'And how's he this morning?'

'Talking.'

'Thank God! So what's the story?'

'Still can't remember.'

169

'D'you believe him?'

'About the time he's been here. But I've a feeling he can remember before.'

The snow was brisker now, blown by a gusty breeze the flakes having turned to spelks of ice stung the face.

Jan said, 'The raven came back. He tried charming it, but it wasn't having any, which set things back a bit.'

Tess stopped abruptly.

Jan had taken eight or nine paces before he realized she was not beside him.

'What's up?' he called.

She shrugged, head down, huddled into herself.

He went back. 'Something wrong?'

'Can't face it.'

'Face what?'

'Him.'

The unTess-like pitifulness of her voice anguished him. They were on the outskirts of the village, nowhere to get out of the snow. But a few metres ahead was a bus shelter. Jan put an arm round Tess's shoulder and guided her into it. Doing so, he felt a decisiveness that was new; Tess too, and in the calm part of herself she thought: He's changed, grown. More certain of himself. How much I like him.

In the shelter Jan turned Tess to him and held her loosely, his arms round her neck.

'Come on, this isn't my Tess.'

She tried to smile but was close to tears.

'What's up?'

'Everything.'

'What's everything?'

'The last few days, Adam, Gill, me – everything.'

Jan said nothing. Brushed wet hair from her eyes.

Tess sniffled, wiped her nose on the back of her hand. 'Hardly slept since Wednesday.'

Snow swirled round their feet. They nestled closer, Tess resting her brow on Jan's chest, his chin on her head.

'And I'll have to see the doctor,' she mumbled.

Jan tried to take a step back to look her in the face but she prevented him.

'What's matter? Are you ill?'

'He'll give me a heavy lecture, I expect. You'll laugh.'

'Why? What about?'

'Taking stupid risks, not being responsible.'

'What sort of risks?'

'Wasn't going to tell you, but –' She sniffled and raised her head and wiped her nose again and could look him in the eyes now. 'Thursday night, while you were at my place –' She paused, the words clogging in her throat.

Jan said, 'I know.'

'He told you?'

'No.'

'Guessed?'

'Saw.'

Now it was Tess who tried to step back and Jan who held her still. He told her of his jealousy and his lust and about stealing out of the house and running to the bridge and peeking into the living room and watching her and Adam at it in front of the fire, and how happy he'd been for them. But he left Bob out of the story.

Tess squinted at him, tears staunched by an astringent douche of embarrassment.

'You never!'

He nodded, grinning.

'Pervert!'

'Sexpot!'

'Voyeur!'

'Crrritic!'

They cuddled against the cold and hung on for a while before Tess said,

'I will, though, have to see the doc I mean, and I'm worried sick.'

'You'll be OK.'

'How can you say that! How can you know! I was stupid. I've always told myself I'd never be that stupid, but I was, and now I'll have to have awful embarrassing tests and wait till the results come through, and even then, if I'm HIV, nobody can tell for months, longer – years –!' She was crying now.

'Hey, hey! Steady!'

'It's all right for you to say that! Steady! What does *steady* mean? Doesn't change anything, does it!' She stamped her foot in desperation.

'I know, I know, but I don't know what else to say. I don't blame you or anything. And I'm not going to desert you whatever happens . . . I'm here . . . OK?'

'I'm sorry, I'm sorry, I know, I'm being hysterical, but I *feel* hysterical, dammit!'

'Now listen, you! Don't you desert me now. You go twitchy, who've I got to keep me right?'

'I need to be kept right sometimes as well, you know.'

'Now she tells me! And I've always thought of you as confident, knowing who you are, what you want.'

'Well, I'm not!'

'You're not! Dear God, another shock! Well, it's enough for me that I believe you are, so don't go letting me down.'

He wiped her tears away and they clung to each other again, weaving gently back and forth, till Tess said,

'Hello, friend.'

'Hi, pal.'

'I'm feeling the cold a bit.'

'Me too. Want to go?'

'Dunno whether I can face it.'

'I'm hardly the one to say so, but maybe that's the very thing you should do.'

'On the falling off a horse principle?'

'Something like that.'

'You know, when it comes down to it, you're a terrible moralist.'

'There you go, insulting me again.'

'Well, somebody has to tell you the truth about yourself.'

'And what else are friends for?'

'Something like that.'

Tess released herself, glowered at the snowbound scene around them. The breeze had dropped, the snow had eased. She said, 'Come on then. Mount up.'

'Joy at last.'

She laughed and turned to go, but before setting off, her back to him, said in a small voice, 'Jan, seriously – do I matter that much?'

Jan took a deep breath. 'Nobody more.'

Tess left a pause before saying, 'Why?'

'When I understand that myself, you'll be the first to know.'

She turned to face him again, smiling. 'I was right to call you Janus.'

'I know.'

'Now you do, then you didn't.'

'Maybe that's the reason.'

As we came round the bend into the straight stretch of road leading to the bridge, Tess said, 'Do you see what I see?'

An unmistakable figure in the middle of the bridge by the downstream parapet.

'Now what's he up to?'

There was something about his posture that made the pit of the belly lurch.

'He's fiddling with something round his ankles.'

'Doing up his laces?'

It was hard to be sure through the curtain of snow.

Before we could see clearly, Adam stood up straight, leaned on the parapet, peered down into the river as if checking he was in the right place, shuffled round, hitched his bottom up onto the parapet, swung his legs up and then pushed himself to his feet.

By this time we were close enough to see clearly.

'Rope!' Tess exclaimed. 'Round his ankles!'

'Christ, no!'

We started to run. A car appeared, driving slowly over the bridge from the other side.

'Adam!' Jan shouted. 'Adam! No!'

Adam's head snapped round in our direction. He yelled, 'Go away!' and shuffled, trying to twist himself towards the river. The car, almost to him now, blew its horn. Adam swung in its direction, his hobbled feet slipped and he fell backward just as the car went by, hitting its roof, bouncing off, and falling to the road. The car swerved, braked, and, its wheels locking, skidded across the bridge, turning back to front as it went and ending up with an almost delicate bump against the corner of the house.

We reached Adam seconds later. He lay on his side, growling and groaning and cursing and holding his leg at the knee.

As we bent down to take hold of him a man's voice shouted from the car, 'Don't touch him! Lie still!'

We both straightened up like children yelled at in school. The car was a black Ford Granada. We could see the driver through the windscreen, the wiper still going: short-cropped silver-grey hair, large round florid face; he was using a car phone.

But Adam went on howling in pain and anger. He tried to get up but instantly collapsed with an excruciating scream that shook us out of our schoolkid obedience. Jan pulled off his anorak, rolled it into a bundle and placed it under Adam's head before holding him by the

173

shoulders, all the time saying, 'Steady, steady, take it easy, you mustn't move, looks like you've broken your leg.' Adam's face was pallid, a sickly yellow against the snow, except for the wound on his brow which shone a hot raw red.

While Jan tended Adam, Tess was examining the rope tied round his ankles, tracking its length over the parapet and down and looping back up again before it reached the water, the other end tied to the neck of one of the urn-shaped balusters. Her heart thumped with horror, for she realized what it meant; had sensed what Adam was doing from the moment she saw him.

'We've got to fetch help,' she said and set off, only to be stopped by the man getting out of his car, holding out an arm and saying, 'Hang on, where are you going?'

'For help.'

'Done. Phoned for an ambulance and the police. You'll be needed as a witness.'

Tess didn't like the sound of him: officious, overbearing. She said, 'And I should fetch my dad.'

'Why, what's he got to do with it?'

'He's in charge of the bridge.'

The man hesitated, giving her a suspicious look before saying, 'On the phone?'

Tess nodded.

'Use mine. You shouldn't leave before the police get here.'

Tess got into the car. The driver walked over to Adam and surveyed the scene with a detachment that made Jan wonder whether he had any feelings.

'What the hell was he up to?' the man said, but seeing the rope added, 'Oh, yes, like that, is it.'

'We can't leave him here,' Jan said, 'he'll freeze to death.'

The man crouched down and inspected Adam's leg, feeling it as if prodding a marrow for ripeness. Adam let out a yelp. 'Fractured, I'd say.'

'The ambulance could take ages. Has to come from the hospital in town, and with this weather –'

The man straightened up. 'Doesn't matter. Could be injuries to his back, his head, anything. Dangerous to shift him. And you know how bloody touchy the insurance is these days.'

Adam went suddenly silent. He stared at the man with wild panicked eyes.

Jan felt trapped, all the old home-school constrictions clamped over him again. He wanted to pick Adam up and run.

'At least we should try and keep him warm,' he said, hearing the desperation in his voice. 'I'll get some blankets.'

'Where from?'

It struck Jan that the man didn't know who he and Adam were. 'The toll house. We live here.'

His eyes swam. He glanced down at Adam, beautiful lost desperate frightened Adam-that-was-not-Adam, in whose eyes glaring back at him he read the same understanding: that this was the beginning of an end. He bent down, kissed him on the forehead, said quietly, 'I'll be back. I'm going for some blankets.'

[– The rest of that day was horrible.

– One of the worst of my life. *The* worst.

– Do we have to write it all?

– Do I, you mean. The police, the ambulance, your father, that bull-headed Granada lout, all of them wanting to know who Adam was and what had happened and how and why and the lout yammering on about his precious car and his insurance and how innocent he was and how obvious it was what Adam had been 'up to', and Adam being taken away and them not letting us go with him. It was awful.

– So do we have to write it all? Just thinking about it makes me feel sick.

– The thing I shan't ever forget, even if I forget all the rest of it, is them lifting Adam into the ambulance, strapped down, and him pleading for me to help him, and not being able to do *anything*, not a thing, and the doors closing and the ambulance driving off across the bridge and disappearing through the snow like a sarcophagus on wheels. I dream about it.

– I know, I know.

– And do you know that 'sarcophagus' comes from a Greek word meaning 'stone that devours flesh'?

– No, I didn't know that and I think I wish you hadn't mentioned it.

– Appropriate though, don't you think? Poetic. Remember how spelled he was by the stones in the Kafka story?

– I told you this part would get you all upset.

– Upset! What's wrong with being upset? Should I just dam it all up, keep it in, wear a good old English stiff upper lip?

– Don't.]

Of course, as soon as they discovered we didn't know who Adam really was, consternation collided with the vent. What on earth did we think we were doing? Didn't we know what a risk we'd taken? What if he were a violent nutcase? Didn't Jan realize how irresponsible he'd been? Et cetera, *ad infinitum*. They demanded the whole story. We gave them an edited version with the ultra-private bits left out.

The mills of officialdom ground small. Telecommunications bleeped all day. One of Tess's photos of Adam was sent for matching against mugshots in the missing persons / wanted files. A policeman with a Dutch-uncle manner and a cool smile hinted about the possibility of charges against us for aiding and abetting and being accessories after the fact should Adam turn out to be 'a naughty sort of laddie'. Statements were culled and written and signed.

Could I [Jan] see Adam?

Breath sucked between clamped teeth: No, no, not till everything was properly sorted out.

How was he?

In good hands, a bad break but he'd mend.

Had he said anything?

Nothing to report on that one, 'old son'.

At least they agreed there was no need to contact Jan's parents 'unless and until anything untoward comes to light'.

All this at the toll house: a couple of policemen, Bob Norris, Tess and Jan, the Granada driver having been dealt with first and sent on his way.

A bizarre moment in the middle of the questioning: They decided to break for coffee. Because they were in Jan's place, he was asked to make it. Mind-split from shock, observing himself performing the chore. The bobbies and Bob Norris warming their backsides at the fire as if they'd just dropped in for a friendly visit, discussing the weather and the prospects for the local soccer team. Jan glanced at Tess who was sitting forlornly at the table. She got up and joined him.

'I'm going on ten,' she murmured. 'What about you?'

'Old enough to be sent to bed without any supper.'

'That's what comes of being caught wanking in public.'

'How crude.'

'In training for life in the slammer.'

'Is there anything we can do?'

'Weep?'

'Not in front of the children.'

'I'm sorry, Jan.'

'If I'd been here – if I hadn't left him –'

'It's not your fault, don't blame yourself.'

One of the policemen returned to the table saying, 'Now, you two, how about that coffee?'

And the questioning began again and went on till they'd had enough or got what they wanted and went, leaving us 'in your tender care, Mr Norris. You'll see they behave themselves, won't you, and that they remain in the locality in case we need to question them further.'

Throughout the ordeal Bob Norris bridged the gap between us and everybody else. Jan's admiration and liking for him deepened. Not that Bob wasn't upset, furious even, but typical of him, in front of us at least, he was calm, amenable, unruffled.

After the police left he held his own interrogation, guessing there was more to the story than we had let on. We told him about the party, about Gill, about Adam being unconscious all night, about his desperation after he came to, and we explained what we had planned to do. Bob pursed his lips now and then, shook his head, huffed, smiled at our various panics, but took everything in without comment. As for us, we were glad to talk to someone older who we could trust. We both felt a great weight lifted from us and – though we would not have admitted it – relief that it was over.

Tess and Jan spent the rest of that Sunday huddled together by the fire, and went over everything again and again. They snacked but ate little. Two or three times they walked through the still falling snow to the village phone and called the hospital, always to be told that Adam was 'comfortable but not allowed visitors'.

They parted reluctantly late that evening, Tess not wanting to face the family's questions, Jan not wanting to be alone. But they had no choice and they ended the day in an empty exhausted silence before Tess plodded off, her feet crunching and squeaking on the crisp snow while Jan watched the beam of her flashlight to the bend in the road, from where she shone it back at him and blinked it off/on, off/on in a final farewell.

177

Monday. Snow thick on the ground, reflecting the dawn light up into the bedroom and filling the room with an unfamiliar glow.

Jan was up early, unable to lie still. The river was oiled metal edged with frayed lace. Bird and animal tracks criss-crossed the white blanket of the garden, surprising in number, a crowd had they all visited at once.

The comfort of daily routines got him through. But he was heartsick for Adam.

In her room at home Tess was also awake, but she stayed where she was, curled up in bed, horrified by what she had seen at the bridge and wishing and wondering and regretting and berating herself. She got up and left for school at the last possible moment. Because of the snow she took the bus, so didn't see Jan that morning. She passed a dreary abstracted day, only half aware of the excitements caused by the snow and taking nothing in during lessons. Her friends, dying to talk about the party, quickly learned not to try. During the dinner hour her period started, relieving her mind of at least one worry.

Bob Norris turned up at the bridge early that afternoon. Jan could tell from his face there was bad news.

'Adam?'

'Haven't phoned this morning. You?'

'No.'

Bob sat at the table, refused coffee, asked how Jan was, talked about the weather, the state of the roads. Then silence.

Jan waited; Bob always took his time. When he was ready he said with strained quietness,

'There's something I have to tell you.'

'Yes?'

'To do with the estate.'

'They've found a buyer for the house.'

'Worse than that.'

'Worse?'

'The whole estate.'

'All of it?'

'The lot – lock, stock and toll bridge.'

'Dear God! When?'

'Last week. Huge multinational. Plan to build their new European headquarters here.'

'But that means . . .' Jan tried to grasp the implications.

'The whole area will be affected. Lot of new building. New jobs as well of course.'

Jan took a deep breath. 'So what happens now?'

'I've instructions to tell you that your job will officially end on the last day of this month. You'll be sent a letter in the next couple of days.'

Jan could think of nothing to say. Like anyone who's been sacked, he felt like chattel, a powerless object to be discarded at will, that his time at the bridge had been wasted.

Bob went on, 'Traditionally, if you'll pardon me for using a rude word, *traditionally* no tolls are taken from Christmas Eve till the second of January. You were going home for that week anyway so you might as well pack up and leave for good on Friday. Sooner, if you like. The extra few days won't matter. And the new manager says he won't object.'

It took a moment for this to sink in. When it did, Jan said, 'The new manager?'

'Arrived this morning.'

'But you're –'

'Redundant.'

'But they can't!'

'They can and they have. All very proper and legal, redundancy settlement and all that. And they've been generous enough to give me three months to find somewhere else to live. Our house belongs to the estate of course.'

'The bastards!'

'Welcome to the real world, son.'

'Is it?'

'You'll see.'

'No. There has to be a better real than that.'

179

'Oh? Let me know when you've found it. In the meantime, the new boss has a job or two for me so I'd better stir me stumps.'

Neither moved. They stared across the table at each other.

'You must be devastated,' Jan said.

'It's not unexpected. I thought something like this might happen as soon as the major brought in the estate agent. And there've been men in Jags and expensive suits up at the house quite a lot lately. So it isn't the shock it might have been. The major's come up trumps as well, I'll give him that. He'll cover us for a new house wherever we decide to live.'

'So he bloody should after the years your family's given him. Cheap at the price!'

Bob smiled. 'Bolshie.'

'Well, it's true. He'll come off all right, I'll bet.'

'Won't be short of a penny, that's for sure. But at least I'll not be as badly hit as a lot of men in my position.'

'What'll you do, though? Retire?'

'Lord, no! Not ready for the geriatric ward yet. The wife says I should use some of the redundancy to set up on my own – jobbing work. She says people are always complaining they can't find reliable men for small jobs – repairs, maintenance, a bit of building and decorating. But I don't know. Running your own business isn't all it's cracked up to be. And anyway, the paperwork would get me down. Don't mind hard work, but writing letters and filling forms and keeping the accounts. No no, not for me.'

They were silent again before Bob said, 'And what about you? What'll you do?'

'Go home, I suppose, what else? Don't want to, not to stay. Made the break, don't want to go back.'

'Take a tip from me. Finish school, get yourself to university. A good education is the best start you can give yourself. That's what I didn't have. Wouldn't be in this predicament now if I'd had an education. And don't give me that sour look.'

Jan managed a smile.

Bob stood up. 'I'd best be off,' he said and made for the door. 'Let's know which day you decide you'll go. The wife says come for dinner before you leave. We've liked having you around. Oh, and by the way,' he added as if an afterthought, 'brought you this.'

He took a small brown-paper parcel from his pocket and put it on the table.

180

'What is it?'

'Memento. Christmas present. Something of that sort. See you later.'

Inside, wrapped in bubble pack and layers of tissue, was the prayer mug with its two-faced Janus.

Tess heard the news from her mother when she came home from school. She arrived at the bridge blazing. Jan had never seen her in such a megaton rage before. It both frightened and exhilarated him.

When her anger had vented itself they turned their minds to thinking what to do next. Jan's main concern was Adam. All day long he had been nagged by worry about him.

'I can't decide what to do myself till I know what's happening to him.'

'You've rung the hospital?'

'This afternoon. Same story: comfortable but no visitors. I rang the police as well. Nothing. They'll let me know, et cetera. Can't reveal any details, the case still under investigation.'

'You want to see him, is that it?'

'Course I do. Want to know how he is and want him to tell me who he is and what's been going on. Don't you?'

'Don't just *want* to know. *Need* to know. That's right, isn't it?'

'Yes.'

'So we'll find out.'

'How?'

'Go to the hospital. There's bound to be a visiting time in the evening.'

'But he isn't allowed visitors.'

'Oh dear oh dear, we didn't know, what a pity, and we've come all this way just to see him, we're close friends of his, he was staying with us when he had his ... accident, couldn't we just wave to him through the window or something? ... What d'you think?'

'Won't work.'

'Wimp!'

'Bully!'

'Defeatist!'

'Who said there'd be no wars if women were in charge?'

'Sexist. We can at least *try*. And it'll be better than hanging round in this condemned cell all night, I'd just go *mad*!'

The reception area was busy.

'Hang on,' Tess said. 'Let's weigh things up before we take the plunge.'

'Must be the strain.'

'What?'

'Makes you talk in clichés.'

'Don't start, *please*!'

They stood against a wall opposite the reception desk, to one side of which was a notice board listing the wards.

'Know which ward he's in?'

'Seven.'

'Fifth floor.'

Some visitors went to the reception desk, others, knowing their way, went straight to the lifts. Almost everyone was carrying hospitalish gifts.

'Ought to have some flowers or something,' Tess said. 'We'd look more convincing.'

'Maybe if I limped they'd think I was a patient.'

'Maybe if I gave you a tweak you'd shut up and follow me.'

They made their way to the lifts and took the next one to the fifth floor.

'Look confident,' Tess said as they approached the ward. 'That's the secret.'

'Not good at acting.'

'Leave the talking to me.'

'You're enjoying this! I'll never understand women.'

'Not women. Me.'

At the nurses' desk they waited behind a family of four – anxious parents, two bored children of about seven – while the ward sister chatted about their relative. A nursing aide was filing papers and eavesdropping; she glanced at Tess and Jan but did not speak.

The family disposed of, Sister turned her professional smile on Tess.

'We're here to see –' Tess began and dried, suddenly realizing she didn't know what to call Adam.

'Adam,' Jan said quickly, anticipating the dilemma and knowing fom his phone calls that this name worked.

But Sister looked from one to the other, puzzled. 'Adam?'

'The boy in C2,' the aide said.

'Oh, him. Poor lad! Yes. You're too late, I'm afraid. They took him away about an hour ago.'

'Took him away?' Jan said.

'Where?' Tess said.

'Who took him?'

Sister was wary. 'Are you family?'

'Yes,' Tess said.

'No,' Jan said. 'No, not exactly. We were with him when he had his accident. He was staying with us.'

'I'm sorry,' Sister said. 'I can't tell you anything. Not allowed. It's a police matter, you see. Nothing I can do.'

Jan said, 'Was it the police who took him?'

'And a doctor. Now, that's all I can tell you. You really will have to ask the police.'

They retreated into the corridor.

Jan said, 'I don't believe this. They can't just cart him off and not tell us. What the hell's going on?'

They made for the lift.

'I'm going to the police station,' Jan said, pressing the button.

As they waited, too bewildered to speak, the nursing aide came hurrying up to them and said, 'Can I have a word with you?'

She led them through swing doors marked EXIT: STAIRS.

'You're Jan and Tess?'

They nodded. The nurse produced an envelope from the side pocket of her uniform. 'He asked me to post this to you. I shouldn't. There'll be trouble if you tell. I was going to bring it, to make sure.'

'We won't,' Jan said.

'No, we won't,' Tess said.

'He was such a nice kid. His name was Aston Davies, by the way.'

'But where've they taken him?' Jan said.

'Norton Psychiatric Unit. It's near Leeds, a special detention unit for disturbed young offenders. Look, I've got to get back.'

She was gone before either of them could even thank her.

They made themselves wait till they were on the bus home before opening the envelope.

As Jan pulled out a folded A4 page Adam's silver chain slithered onto his lap.

Have to be quick, coming for me soon. Wish you had not stopped me, it is my life, I should be let do what I want with it, I am not fit to live. You were good to me though Jan you tried to help me and I want to thank you and the nurse who gives you this who is nice says I should explain if I really mean it. I do not know how to start, so many things to tell and the main thing that happened is not the only thing.

The main thing is I killed another boy. Did not mean to, it just happened. That is what all we murderers say I expect. 14 then, 17 now, was playing with a gang of other boys, seven of us, larking about with a tennis ball, playing a game, I do not remember what but it had winners and losers and the losers had to give a penalty. I lost and would not give the penalty, I was fed up of losing, I was always losing. The boy who was the leader, he was called Tony, he was older, about 16, was always making snide remarks about me and this time I would not pay the penalty, I was fed up of him. But the others said I had to and I said no it was stupid and the others said Tony had to make me pay, it was the rule. He said Come on you have to do it and I said get stuffed, who are you anyway, you are just a loser yourself or why are you playing with us. I was up against a wall, and when I said that Tony started tossing the tennis ball at me aiming so it would just miss and bounce back, but I kept saying no and then he started calling me names and tossed the ball harder and harder and closer and closer and then the ball hit me in the face. It didn't really hurt, I started swearing at him and crying and I picked up a pebble, threw it at him and he said Come on cry baby you aren't hurt, and threw a stone and the other kids started throwing them as well and after that it all got out of hand. They started throwing bigger and bigger stones, anything they could find. I do not remember much about the rest except I chucked the stones harder and harder back at them and they came closer and closer so I

184

ducked to the side where one of the smaller kids was standing and grabbed him and held him in front of me to protect myself, I thought they would stop then, but they didn't, they just kept on, and I don't know what happened then, I must have flipped or something, I was not seeing anything, it was just a red blur, but in the end the boy I grabbed was on the ground and I was beating him in the head with a big rock in both hands which I only know because it is what the other boys said in court.

Will not tell you all the stuff about the doctors, they said I was not to blame, it was a one-off, but could not promise it would not happen again so they put me away and give me treatment which I will not tell you about either, it makes no difference what they say or what they do, they do not have the dreams, they do not have the headaches which I have because of what I did.

I am sorry I killed the boy, I am to blame aren't I or who is? I know that even though I do not understand what happened to me or why it happened and am afraid about it happening again. I was so scared when I come to on the boat the other night, I was afraid I might of done it again you see, and you helped a lot, you really did, you are a good bloke, Jan, I wish I was as well, we could be friends I know that and wish I could stay with you at the bridge where I think I could be happy if it was not for what might happen. But they are taking me back where I ran away from which I do remember but I do not remember any of the time you told me about at the bridge, I was telling you the truth, it was just a story to me, I wish it was me, I think I would have liked to be me if I was Adam, you had a lot of fun.

I want you to keep the chain, I have nothing else to give you and I want you to remember me and to wish you all the very best of luck in the world which you deserve.

185

Daffodils in great swaying clumps all the way up the drive to the main building. I never see daffodils now without remembering that day. They have always been my favourite flower, such brave bright beauty, fresh yellow clown-collared heads nodding to the world on their straight-limbed stalks.

The unit was a complex of buildings clustering round an old Victorian mansion. The approach looked ordinary, nothing like a prison, but beyond the main house were ugly modern functional buildings behind high security fences and walls.

The reception area in the entrance hall had that hard echoey emptiness of public institutions that occupy old family houses. I had to wait for half an hour, sitting in a plastic-covered armchair that was sticky to the touch, before Doctor Pelham arrived: flapping white coat, jeans and Adidas trainers, bony face, grey eyes, fleshy lips, thinning salt-and-pepper hair, balding at the front, wispy long at the back, big heavy hairy hands that were labourer-rough and gripped hard. He wasted no time on pleasantries, just said, 'Hi, you ready for this?'

'Nervous, a bit.'

'Just take what you see, be neutral. If it upsets you, come back here, don't display in front of Aston, OK?'

A visitor's identity pass was clipped to my sweater, I signed some kind of permission form, after which the doctor led me through a maze of corridors, and outside, through a security gate in a high fence, along a path by the side of what looked like living quarters with bars over the windows, through another security gate in a high ancient brick wall, which let us into a large walled area that I guessed must have been the nursery garden in the old days. There were oblongs of ground cultivated as flower beds or vegetable patches with grass paths between. A couple of warders were on duty, watching five or six young men in regulation

186

trousers and jackets who were hoeing, digging, planting. The doctor spoke to them as we went by, the matey professional, everyday cheery stuff about their gardening. One of the men called out, 'A new chicken for the coop, doc?' Pelham laughed and waved and called back, 'Never know your luck, Freddy.'

The far corner of the garden, away from the flowers and vegetables, an area about forty metres square bordered by paths on two sides and the angle of the high brick wall on the other two, had been allowed to grow wild. A tall Norway maple dominated the area, already thickly dressed in spring-green leaves. A rope ladder dangled down through the branches. Under the tree was a makeshift tent made of an old patched tarpaulin draped over rough-cut wooden poles tied down by improvised guy ropes. In its entrance stood a rickety-looking table and chair each cobbled together out of oddments. There was a book on the table on top of what I thought was a magazine. Cluttering round the tent were wooden orange boxes and packing cases and a barrel. Nearby was a pile of wooden palings about three metres long, also rough-cut. From one wall to the other, curving around in front of the tent and tree, marking it off like an enclosure, was a length of rope held up by stakes stuck into the ground at two- or three-metre intervals, with no gap for a way in. The whole place had the look of an adventure playground in the early stages of construction, yet everything was tidy and neat and carefully arranged as if for some serious adult purpose.

The doctor brought me to a stop at the rope barrier facing the entrance to the tent.

'Hello, there,' he called. 'Aston?'

'Hi, doc.' The voice came from high in the tree, Adam's voice but lighter than I remembered, boyish, a child's voice.

'Would you like to come down for a minute?'

'OK.'

Branches shook, the rope ladder danced, bare feet appeared, legs in tattered jeans chopped off just below the knee, a body in a loose garment, half shirt, half jacket, cackhandedly home-made of pieces of thick brown cloth (curtain material?) stitched together with red gardener's twine, and the unmistakable head with its jet black hair long now and rumpled.

He reached the ground and turned to approach us, smiling broadly at the doctor – that wide anguishing grin, white teeth showing, eyes wrinkling. I wanted to run and grab him and hold him to me. Pelham must have sensed this because he took hold of my arm as if ready to restrain me. What held me back, though, was the complete lack of any sign of recognition in Adam's face. And he moved, not as the Adam I knew, but as a child would, a little less coordinated, uninhibitedly unaware of himself, yet a hint of wariness too, not entirely trusting. His face was grubby, his hands and clothes smeared with moss and dirt from the tree. Already, as he came towards us, it was hard for me to see Adam, but instead a boy who had been made to break off from play.

He reached us and stood dutifully waiting to hear what the doctor wanted.

'So how are you today, Aston?'

'OK.'

'The leg holding up?'

'It's OK. Doesn't bother me.'

'No pain or anything?'

'It's all right. Hurts a bit if I jump on it, but it's OK.'

'Well, take it steady for a few more days.'

'OK.'

'This is Jan.'

The eyes turned on me: the other-Adam eyes. 'Hi.'

'Hi.'

'Jan's having a look round.'

'Is he a savage?'

'No, I don't think so. Would you like him to join you?'

I was inspected more closely. 'Was he sent by Providence?'

'Could be.'

Further scrutiny. I stood, smiling back, trying to be calm and unrevealing, though inside my stomach churned.

'Not Friday, though.'

'No?'

Pelham let go of my arm and took a step away, exaggeratedly viewing the enclosure. 'Looks like you're about ready to start your fence.'

'A wall for my habitation.'

'Finished your chair as well.'

'Robinson took five days. I only took two.'

'Great! Well done. Perhaps you'd like to show Jan your books?'

'Life and Strange Surprising Adventures.' He pronounced the words like a rune.

'Would you?'

'Well . . . OK.'

He went to the table and brought them back, handing them over with the anxious pride of a fan offering his most treasured souvenirs to someone who might not be properly respectful. The book was a modern edition of *The Life and Strange Surprising Adventures of Robinson Crusoe of York, Mariner*, with black and white illustrations. The magazine wasn't a magazine after all but a well-thumbed American comic-strip version of *Crusoe* in colour. I flipped through their pages, and, as Crusoe when he first saw Friday's footprint in the sand, stood like one thunder-struck.

'Good, eh?' Adam said.

'Amazing.'

Doctor Pelham took the books and handed them back, saying, 'Need anything?'

'I'll search for it myself.'

'I'll see you later today as usual, then.'

'Can I go now?'

'Sure.'

'So long, doc.'

'So long, Aston.'

I wasn't even given a glance. He turned, ran to the ladder, and climbed into the tree.

'He didn't remember me at all!'

'That's one way of putting it. Another way is to say you haven't entered his life yet.'

'Don't understand.'

'The person you just met is not the Adam you knew, nor is he the seventeen-year-old he is biologically. The person you met is Aston Davies, aged eleven.'

We were sitting on a bench by the wall at the other end of the garden five minutes later.

The doctor said, 'Aston was fourteen when he suffered his trauma. After that he went through a kind of hell of guilt and remorse. It was so bad he twice tried to kill himself. Part of the difficulty for anybody trying to help him is that no one can explain why he acted as he did – why the sudden switch from a childish game to uncontrollable violence that ended in horrific, brutal murder. He doesn't know how bad it was because he was quite literally mindless at the time. He doesn't remember

189

anything about the final moments, and the worst details have always been kept from him for fear of what the knowledge might do to him. But he does dream them. Terrible nightmares, which he believes are some kind of warning of what he might do one day rather than being records of what he once did.

'In August he escaped while on a routine outing. Psychologically speaking, he wasn't really running away from us, he was trying to run away from himself. When he was brought back in December he could vaguely remember making his escape but then nothing till he came to on the boat.'

'So what happened? When he broke into the toll house he wasn't desperate, anything but.'

'We don't know the details, of course, but we do know about his condition. The fugue state isn't very common but it's well documented. The patient goes on the run – becomes a fugitive, if you like, and completely loses his memory of his previous life. He invents a whole new personality, even down to the smallest details. We're not sure how this works. It might be a moment to moment thing, like making up a story as you're telling it. Or it might be that the new personality is made up of wishes and desires and aspects of the patient's personality that have been suppressed or have never found expression. So someone who has always been shy and fearful and meek turns into an open, outgoing, confident person who does all sorts of things that in his other life he never dared try. There are even cases where the patient has spoken a language he's never been taught, and others who have performed skilled tasks, like a medical operation, for which they've never had any training. The people they meet are usually completely convinced that they are who they say they are. One thing they all are, however, is restless. They usually keep moving. Physically or mentally, they're always in flight. In fact, the fugue state is a kind of suicide.'

'So when he broke into the house he wasn't Aston but his other invented person?'

'Right.'

'And when I said I didn't know him from Adam –'

'He accepted that as his name. Built it into his new personality.'

'But did he know what he was doing?'

'We don't think so but we don't really know. No one ever comes out of a fugue state remembering what happened while they were in it so they can't tell us. Just as they forget their previous life when they go into the fugue, they completely forget their fugue life when they return to their normal personality – whatever normal means.'

'That's incredible!'

'What is it we say up here? All the world's queer save thee and me, and even thee's a bit queer!'

'Thank God!'

He laughed.

I said, 'Sometimes there was something that bothered me. In his eyes.'

'The windows of the soul – the great betrayers of falsehood.'

'Was Adam false? Maybe he was the real person and Aston the false one?'

'Could be. Or both are the real him in different versions.'

'That as well, OK. But those times, it was like somebody else was looking at me. I used to call him the other-Adam. What changed him back from Adam to Aston?'

'Banging his head on the wall of the bridge during the struggle with Gill, I should think. Blows to the head often occur in fugue cases, seeming to switch the patient into the fugue or out of it.'

'And when he came to, he could remember his Aston life but not his Adam life?'

'Correct.'

'So why did he lie and say he couldn't remember anything at all?'

'Fear. He was afraid you'd turn him in once you knew about him. But worse than that, he was terrified he might kill someone again. He'd been told, you see, that this was possible. It's one reason why he's kept here.'

'And it was all so awful that he tried to commit suicide by jumping from the bridge?'

'The ultimate fugue.'

'And the rope? That seemed so weird.'

'Not so weird when you think about it. Logical and well planned, in fact. He wanted to make absolutely sure he drowned. Tethered by his feet he wouldn't be able to swim, and, if you work it out, you'll see he wouldn't be able to raise his head above water. Like a fish on a hook, except the hook was in the tail. The current rushing through the narrow arch of the bridge would be too strong for him to twist round or do anything to save himself. And what irony, don't you think, to tie himself by the feet – the very limbs on which one runs away.'

'He must have been utterly desperate. Poor, poor Adam.'

'Poor Aston, you mean. Adam was a happy-go-lucky uninhibited

191

guilt-free sexy young man. He'd never have tried to kill himself. The very opposite of Aston, the inhibited shy guilt-ridden inadequate boy who found it hard to make friends with anyone but especially with people his own age. Adam was everything that Aston wanted to be but couldn't be.'

Across the gardens I could see Aston-Adam working in his enclosure, standing on a crate, hammering a paling into the ground, the beginning of his fortification. Boy at play, young man at work.

I said, 'I don't understand what's happening to him now, though.'

'He came back in deep depression. His leg was in plaster of course. He couldn't be very active and needed quite a bit of nursing just to keep him physically healthy. For a few days he remained like that, a depressed immobile frightened angry patient. But then he began to withdraw completely into himself, would say nothing at all, and started behaving like a child.'

'A kind of regression?'

'Regression suggests something negative, or a going back, as if life were a linear journey, birth point A to death point Z. I don't see it like that.'

'How then?'

'We coexist as our *selves*. We are multiple beings. A mix of actualities and potentialities. One of the many things the so-called mentally ill have taught me is that we so-called healthy people are not very good at exploring our possible selves. Perhaps because we feel reasonably happy with the selves we are living. But perhaps we are the most imprisoned of all because of that. Whereas the mentally ill, being uncomfortable with their actual selves, sometimes explore their potentialities and find selves they like better and try them out.'

'But surely with Adam, I mean Aston, it's another flight, isn't it? He's become what he was once before.'

'Not quite. As a boy of eleven he couldn't have done what he's doing now as well as he's doing it. He's being eleven only as a seventeen-year-old young man can be eleven.'

'But why eleven?'

'Because that was the happiest time of his life, just before the onset of the bad feelings about himself, the feelings of powerlessness, of always being a loser, a failure, of never making it, and always being picked on, that ended with the murder. In that sense, the murder was a mistake he couldn't correct. What do you do when you've made a mistake you can't put right?'

'Start again?'

'But you don't just go back to the point before you got into difficulties, you also use what you've learned from the experience of getting it wrong to help you get it right next time. We do that in everyday life all the time. Aston is doing it rather more dramatically and obviously, that's all.'

'No matter. Try again. Fail again. Fail better.'

'Clever.'

'Beckett.'

'What?'

'Quoting. Irritating habit. Samuel Beckett.'

'Ah yes, well, he's right. The secret of a happy life.'

'And the Crusoe stuff? How did that start?'

'After he became eleven he was cheerful of course, and much more active. Instead of being withdrawn, he was quite a busy handful. He took no notice of his plastered-up leg. Paid it no attention. Just hobbled about regardless. So he'd have a plausible reason for it we told him he'd fallen out of a tree while climbing.'

'What did you tell him was the reason for being locked up?'

'He never asked. Perhaps the deep secret mind of his soul screened the question from his conscious everyday mind because it knew better than to let the question be asked.'

'You mean, we only ask what we need to know?'

'Something like that. Shall I go on?'

'Please.'

'In what we call the family room there are books and magazines. Among them was the comic-strip version of *Crusoe* that you saw. Aston became very attached to it. Acquired it as his own property, read it and read it, time and again. Not only that, he started talking about the story during his therapy sessions. When I realized this was more than a passing fancy, I bought him the copy he showed you of the original novel. He devoured it, every word. Began talking about Robinson, as he always calls Crusoe, all the time, as if he were alive and his best friend. He'd tell the story to anyone who'd listen.'

'So he started to identify with Crusoe.'

'No, no! You're missing the point. He doesn't believe himself to *be* Crusoe – that would be a kind of madness, and Aston isn't mad, not at all. As I say, Crusoe is his friend, a companion, someone he

193

admires and likes, who helps him through life, especially at a difficult time.'

'So why *Crusoe*? Why that book?'

'Now come on, don't leave all the work to me.'

'Well – whatever the reason, you'll let him play it out? Build the fence and live like Crusoe and all that?'

'We'll see, I expect so, if that's what he needs.'

'Even sleep in his tent and everything?'

'I doubt that he'll want to. You're quite right, it is a kind of play. A very serious game. You saw how he behaved. He knows what he's doing, takes it totally seriously, but knows he's playing, knows the boundary between the everyday real and the imaginary real. Both are real and he knows the rules that apply to each.'

'But how long will it go on?'

'Sometimes a phase like this doesn't last more than a few days, sometimes it can go on for years.'

'And how will it end? Will he become his proper age again?'

'I'm waiting to find out. It's like a story with an ending you can't quite predict. It might end the way you think it will from all the clues, or there might be a twist in the tail. Or there might be no conclusive ending at all, it might just stop, in the middle of a sentence even. It's my job to stay with the story and help him if I can while Aston works it out for himself. He'll devise his own ending when he's ready, which means when he's got everything out of the story – out of the act of telling it – that's useful to him. Then, perhaps, he'll move on to another story, try out another imagined real, another version of himself, become yet another Aston. Till eventually he may even become the person the deep secret mind of his soul wants him to be, and then we'll say he's cured, though all we'll mean is that he doesn't need me or anyone like me any more, because this story is enough to keep him going on his own. He'll be content with himself.'

One of the warders came up to us.

'Wanted inside, doc. Darren trouble again.'

'Be right there.' The doctor stood up and held out his hand. 'Got to go, sorry. Duty calls.'

I shook his hand. 'Is it OK for me to come again?'

'If you like. If you need to. And not too often. It won't mean anything to Aston of course. But if it would make you feel better –'

'It would. I mean, if he becomes the Adam who remembers me

194

again, I'd like to be there, if he wants – Well ... you under-stand?'

'I think so. You've also got a story to tell. Everybody has.'

Other great reads ⤸ *from* **Red Fox**

Further Red Fox titles that you might enjoy reading are listed on the following pages. They are available in bookshops or they can be ordered directly from us.

   If you would like to order books, please send this form and the money due to:

ARROW BOOKS, BOOKSERVICE BY POST, PO BOX 29, DOUGLAS, ISLE OF MAN, BRITISH ISLES. Please enclose a cheque or postal order made out to Arrow Books Ltd for the amount due, plus 75p per book for postage and packing to a maximum of £7.50, both for orders within the UK. For customers outside the UK, please allow £1.00 per book.

NAME_____

ADDRESS_____

_____

Please print clearly.

Whilst every effort is made to keep prices low, it is sometimes necessary to increase cover prices at short notice. If you are ordering books by post, to save delay it is advisable to phone to confirm the correct price. The number to ring is THE SALES DEPARTMENT 071 (if outside London) 973 9700.

BESTSELLING FICTION FROM RED FOX

☐	The Present Takers	Aidan Chambers	£2.99
☐	Battle for the Park	Colin Dann	£2.99
☐	Orson Cart Comes Apart	Steve Donald	£1.99
☐	The Last Vampire	Willis Hall	£2.99
☐	Harvey Angell	Diana Hendry	£2.99
☐	Emil and the Detectives	Erich Kästner	£2.99
☐	Krindlekrax	Philip Ridley	£2.99

PRICES AND OTHER DETAILS ARE LIABLE TO CHANGE

ARROW BOOKS, BOOKSERVICE BY POST, PO BOX 29, DOUGLAS, ISLE OF MAN, BRITISH ISLES

NAME ....

ADDRESS ....

....

....

Please enclose a cheque or postal order made out to B.S.B.P. Ltd. for the amount due and allow the following for postage and packing:

U.K. CUSTOMERS: Please allow 75p per book to a maximum of £7.50

B.F.P.O. & EIRE: Please allow 75p per book to a maximum of £7.50

OVERSEAS CUSTOMERS: Please allow £1.00 per book.

While every effort is made to keep prices low it is sometimes necessary to increase cover prices at short notice. Arrow Books reserve the right to show new retail prices on covers which may differ from those previously advertised in the text or elsewhere.

BESTSELLING FICTION FROM RED FOX

☐ Blood	Alan Durant	£3.50
☐ Tina Come Home	Paul Geraghty	£3.50
☐ Del-Del	Victor Kelleher	£3.50
☐ Paul Loves Amy Loves Christo	Josephine Poole	£3.50
☐ If It Weren't for Sebastian	Jean Ure	£3.50
☐ You'll Never Guess the End	Barbara Wersba	£3.50
☐ The Pigman	Paul Zindel	£3.50

PRICES AND OTHER DETAILS ARE LIABLE TO CHANGE

ARROW BOOKS, BOOKSERVICE BY POST, PO BOX 29, DOUGLAS, ISLE OF MAN, BRITISH ISLES

NAME...

ADDRESS...

....

....

Please enclose a cheque or postal order made out to B.S.B.P. Ltd. for the amount due and allow the following for postage and packing:

U.K. CUSTOMERS: Please allow 75p per book to a maximum of £7.50

B.F.P.O. & EIRE: Please allow 75p per book to a maximum of £7.50

OVERSEAS CUSTOMERS: Please allow £1.00 per book.

While every effort is made to keep prices low it is sometimes necessary to increase cover prices at short notice. Arrow Books reserve the right to show new retail prices on covers which may differ from those previously advertised in the text or elsewhere.

Other great reads ← *from* **Red Fox**

Top teenage fiction from Red Fox

PLAY NIMROD FOR HIM   Jean Ure

Christopher and Nick are each other's only friend. Isolated from the rest of the crowd, they live in their own world of writing and music. Enter lively, popular Sal who tempts Christopher away from Nick . . .
ISBN 0 09 985300 0   £2.99

HAMLET, BANANAS AND ALL THAT JAZZ
Alan Durant

Bert, Jim and their mates vow to live dangerously – just as Nietzsche said. So starts a post-GCSEs summer of girls, parties, jazz, drink, fags . . . and tragedy.
ISBN 0 09 997540 8   £3.50

ENOUGH IS TOO MUCH ALREADY
Jan Mark

Maurice, Nina and Nazzer are all re-sitting their O levels but prefer to spend their time musing over hilarious previous encounters with strangers, hamsters, wild parties and Japanese radishes . . .
ISBN 0 09 985310 8   £2.99

BAD PENNY   Allan Frewin Jones

Christmas doesn't look good for Penny this year. She's veggy, feels overweight, *and* The Lizard, her horrible father has just turned up. Worse still, Roy appears – Penny's ex whom she took a year to get over.
ISBN 0 09 985280 2   £2.99

CUTTING LOOSE   Carole Lloyd

Charlie's horoscope says to get back into the swing of things, but it's not easy: her Dad and Gran aren't speaking, she's just found out the truth about her mum, and is having severe confused spells about her lovelife. It's time to cut loose from all binding ties, and decide what she wants and who she really is.
ISBN 0 09 91381 X   £3.50

Other great reads <-*from* **Red Fox**

Teenage thrillers from Red Fox

GOING TO EGYPT   Helen Dunmore

When Dad announces they're going on holiday to Weston, Colette is disappointed – she'd much rather be going to Egypt. But when she meets the boys who ride their horses in the sea at dawn, she realizes that it isn't where you go that counts, it's who you meet while you're there . . .
ISBN 0 09 910901 8   £3.50

BLOOD   Alan Durant

Life turns frighteningly upside down when Robert hears his parents have been shot dead in the family home. The police, the psychiatrists, the questions . . . Robert decides to carry out his own investigations, and pushes his sanity to the brink.
ISBN 0 09 992330 0   £3.50

DEL-DEL   Victor Kelleher

Des, Hannah and their children are a close-knit family – or so it seems. But suddenly, a year after the death of their daughter Laura, Sam the youngest son starts to act very strangely – having been possessed by a terrifyingly evil presence called Del-Del.
ISBN 0 09 918271 8   £3.50

THE GRANITE BEAST   Ann Coburn

After her father's death, Ruth is uprooted from town-life to a close-knit Cornish village and feels lost and alone. But the strange and terrifying dreams she has every night are surely from something more than just unhappiness? Only Ben, another outsider, seems to understand the omen of major disaster . . .
ISBN 0 09 985970 X   £2.99